Sour Grapes & Balmy Knight

Muriel Ellis Pritchett

Black Rose Writing | Texas

First printing/ First Hardcover Printing

This is a work of fiction. Names, characters, businesses, places, events, and incidents are either the products of the author's imagination or used in a fictitious manner. Any resemblance to actual persons, living or dead, or actual events is purely coincidental.

ISBN: 978-1-68433-824-5 (Paperback); 978-1-68433-825-2 (Hardcover)
PUBLISHED BY BLACK ROSE WRITING
www.blackrosewriting.com

Library of Congress Control Number: 2021912071

Printed in the United States of America
Suggested Retail Price (SRP) $19.95 (Paperback); $24.95 (Hardcover)

Sour Grapes & Balmy Knight is printed in Book Antiqua

*As a planet-friendly publisher, Black Rose Writing does its best to eliminate unnecessary waste to reduce paper usage and energy costs, while never compromising the reading experience. As a result, the final word count vs. page count may not meet common expectations.

This book is dedicated to my grandmother,
Elmina Ann Sigman Gazaway.

Acknowledgments

A big thank you to my dear friend and editor Judy Purdy—for the many hours she has spent over the years, carefully reading and editing my manuscripts. I couldn't have made it this far without her support and expertise.

Also, many thanks to the members of my writers' group—Gail Karwoski, Susan Vizurraga, and Debra Harden—who critiqued and improved each chapter of this manuscript.

And finally, many thanks to my patient, skilled, and amazing husband Hal Pritchett—my personal computer guru—who was always there when things went awry with my computer.

Sour Grapes
& Balmy Knight

Chapter One
Sunny Days Are Here Again

Alabama "Balmy" Knight made a beeline with her walker for the front door. A walker she really didn't need. But by using the walker and dressing shabbily in a baggy cardigan over a faded-cotton housedress, she felt like she had the upper hand. That the joke was on her daughter and son-in-law. That this was payback for losing her home, her independence, and her life.

Alabama opened the front door and wrapped her sweater tighter, as a cool, fall breeze swirled fallen leaves around her. At least the sun was shining, she noticed, so the afternoon would be warmer. As Alabama bent over to pick up the *Savannah Morning News* off the porch, she saw the next-door neighbor, Jimmy Nixon, walking his aging dalmatian. She watched the dog do a few circles, squat, and strain, but nothing came out.

"Good morning, Jimmy," Alabama said, straightening up. "How're you today? And how's old Spot? Looks a little constipated to me, son. Take my advice and give him a little bit of mineral oil tonight, and tomorrow he'll be all regulated."

Rapidly buttoning her blouse, Alabama's 45-year-old daughter Sara Webb, materialized at the front door. "Mother, is that necessary?" she fussed. "The entire neighborhood can hear every word."

With the newspaper tucked under her elbow, Alabama turned to face her agitated daughter. She pushed the walker slowly inside and shut the door behind her. "Just trying to be helpful, that's all."

Sara sighed. "That's the problem, Mother, you're always trying." Sara turned and headed back to the bedroom. "I have to finish getting dressed for work. Please try to behave yourself."

"Like wire my mouth shut," Alabama said softly, half mumbling. It seemed like no matter what she said or did, somebody in the family was always offended. But, she had to admit, if Sara hadn't taken her in after the stroke, she could be living in a nursing home. Maybe crammed into a room with one or two frail, sickly old women. Or even sitting in a wheelchair with drool running down her chin. She shuddered at the thought.

Sara stepped back into the living room. "What did you say, Mother?"

Alabama sat down at a small table in the corner of the living room. "Nothing, dear," she answered as sweetly as she could.

Sara shook her head and sighed. "Mother, I just don't know what's gotten into you lately. Sometimes I think you intentionally try to annoy me."

"Not me!" Alabama gasped. "I only want everyone to be happy and loving to each other." And to show me a little respect, she added to herself.

"I'm glad to hear that, Mother."

As Sara disappeared down the hallway, Alabama put on her bifocals, which hung around her neck on a purple shoestring, opened the morning newspaper, and began reading. Suddenly she stopped turning pages and held the paper closer to her face. "My goodness gracious!" she said out loud, looking at a feature article in the Lifestyle section about Harrison Ford and his good deeds. "Is he ever looking damn good!" She kissed the photo of the actor. "Oh, you handsome, sexy devil, you! I have a special place in my scrapbook just for you."

Smiling and humming "Whatever Lola Wants, Lola Gets" to herself, Alabama looked cautiously over her shoulder for any signs of Sara or her son-in-law Richard Webb. Bypassing the walker, she skipped to the end table, opened the drawer, and pulled out scissors, glue, and a jewel-encrusted scrapbook. Clutching her treasures, she carried them back to the table.

Gently touching her lips to the photo of Harrison Ford, Alabama sighed happily. Very carefully, she cut out the photo and feature article about her favorite actor, and glued it into her scrapbook, making sure to smooth out any wrinkles. Then very neatly, she folded up the morning paper and left it on the table for Richard. And just in time, too, as her son-in-law, dressed in suit and tie, walked out of the kitchen with his morning coffee and sat at the table. Alabama immediately pushed her walker to the sofa and sat down to avoid any more than the usual daily confrontation.

"If that's all you're having for breakfast, Sara will fuss," she pointed out, because Sara always insisted everyone eat a hearty breakfast for energy to face the day.

Richard picked up the paper and scanned the front page. "Thanks for your concern, Alabama, but I'm having a business breakfast later."

"New account?" she asked. She did so love to attempt a conversation with Richard while he was trying to read the paper. Alabama knew it utterly irritated him to no end.

"Hopefully."

"Better than that last cereal commercial?" She sang the song lyrics softly.

"Most definitely."

"Better than the constipation commercial?" She switched song tune and lyrics.

"Absolutely."

"Better than . . ."

Richard, who worked for an advertising/PR firm in downtown Savannah, turned his head in her direction. "Alabama, it's the New Wave Theatre account. Now can I finish my paper, please?"

Smiling the victor's smile for getting an entire sentence out of Richard—how she loved to get his goat—Alabama's face quickly changed to a look of hurt. "Well, excuse me for being interested in my son-in-law. I'm just a lonely, old woman hungry for conversation."

Richard put down his paper, sighed, and turned to Alabama. "I'm sorry. How are you this morning?" He turned back to his paper.

Alabama settled back into the sofa. "Not too good, I'm afraid. My arthritis is giving me fits this morning. It's all I can do to pick up the walker and take one step." Richard took a sip of his coffee, turned the page of his newspaper, and continued reading. "Couldn't sleep last night for this terrible pain that starts here in the top of my brain and winds down my neck all the way to my big toe." Richard turned another page and stopped when he saw a big hole in the middle. "And now I've got this ache in my gullet that feels like Mohammed Ali used my innards for his punching bag."

Richard frowned and shook the paper. "Alabama?" he said softly.

"And see this here spot on my arm? Looks just like a cancer picture I saw in the *Reader's Digest* medical guide."

Richard stood up abruptly and spoke louder, "Alabama Knight!"

"But I don't want you and Sara to worry none. Just promise me you won't keep me hooked up to those awful machines once it's all over."

Richard stepped closer to Alabama, shaking his newspaper and shouting, "Alabama Knight! You cut up my newspaper, again!"

"But, Richard, you don't care one iota about Harrison Ford."

Visibly trying to restrain himself, Richard responded, "No, I don't care one iota about Harrison Ford. However, I did want to read the new tax law article on the back of what you cut out."

"Not a problem for me, dear. I'm only interested in articles about handsome, sexy, older actors." Alabama smiled at her frustrated son-in-law. Did she know how to push his buttons or what?

Richard shook the paper, again. "Since I pay for this paper, can't I at least read it before you shred the contents?"

Alabama raised her eyebrows in mock surprise. "Of course, Richard. How inconsiderate of me. Can you please forgive a dotty, old lady?" She fluttered her eyelashes at him.

"Well . . ." Richard looked at his mother-in-law. "Next time, please make sure I've read the paper before you cut it up. Sorry I growled and shouted at you. I'm sure I can find the story on my iPad."

"That's all right, dear. You're forgiven. Just make sure it doesn't happen, again." Score another win for Alabama, she told herself, as she watched Richard leave the living room. She knew he was headed back to the bedroom to complain to Sara. Sure enough, in less than a minute, Alabama could hear Richard's muffled voice. Alabama was thankful she'd remembered to put in her hearing aids. But just to make sure she didn't miss a word, she hit the button behind her right hearing aid and turned up the sound two notches.

From the other side of the door, Alabama could hear the voices of Richard and Sara having a heated discussion about her.

"Your mother . . ." Richard's voice sounded annoyed and frustrated.

"Richard, please, not now . . ." came the voice of Sara.

"I get no respect from anyone in this house. Not from my mother-in-law, not from my children, and definitely not from my wife."

Alabama bent over and covered her mouth with both hands. Richard sounded so pathetic, she almost felt sorry for him.

"Richard, if you don't get a move on, you'll be late for work," Sara said.

As soon as Alabama heard Richard step toward the closed door, she ran to the sofa and sat down, smiling and trying to look innocent. A frowning Richard walked into the living room carrying his brief case. He paused in his tracks, turned toward the bedroom, and shouted, "At least at the office I get treated with respect." Then he walked out the front door, slamming it hard behind him.

Sara walked into the living room and stopped in front of Alabama. "Mother, were you aggravating Richard, again?"

Alabama's eyes widened in surprise. "What on earth are you talking about, dear?" she asked her daughter, but knowing good and well that she was indeed aggravating her son-in-law. After all, it was her new fun activity. An escape from the tedious boredom of her existence. Not to mention that she loved to see Richard lose his cool.

Sara threw her arms in the air in mock surrender. "I give up!"

"Give up on what, Mom?" Sara's 11-year-old son Doug slammed his book bag on the table.

"Nothing important." Sara put her hands on her hips. "Douglas, did you eat breakfast?"

"I'm working on it, Mom." He turned. "See? I'm walking toward the kitchen now."

Sara shook her head. "And NO Pop-Tart!" She turned and shouted, "Alison Webb, stop primping or you'll be late for school!"

As soon as his mother left the living room, Doug returned with Pop-Tarts in hand. He ran over to Alabama and hugged her from behind. "Good morning, Grandma!"

Alabama returned the hug. "Good morning, sweetheart!" How she loved her grandson! She always took his side in every situation, and he always had her back.

"Have a Pop-Tart?" Doug asked.

"What flavor?" Not that it mattered. Alabama would be the first to admit she had a terrible sweet tooth. She and Doug shared a love for carbs. The more carbs, the better. But Alabama did draw the line at sweets that were mostly flavored sugar. She considered that carb overkill.

"Hot Fudge Sundae." He handed one to her.

"With vanilla and fudge icing, and sprinkles?" Alabama asked, accepting the toaster pastry.

"But of course!" Doug hugged Alabama, again, and grabbed his book bag. "See you later, Grandma!"

As soon as the front door closed, Doug's 15-year-old sister Alison sauntered into the living room with her Nirvana book bag. Alabama shook her head at her granddaughter, whose face was heavily made up as usual with black lipstick and eyes lined with kohl. Alabama did not like Alison's black attire or her numerous body piercings or her long, straight, dyed black hair. But Alabama realized that like herself, Alison was only trying to make a point of being defiant and different because it irritated her parents.

From the bedroom, Sara shouted, "Alison, did you eat breakfast?"

A car horn blew outside. Alison threw her book bag over her shoulder. "No time, Mom. Tina's waiting for me."

"If you didn't spend two hours putting on your face, you'd have time to eat," Sara shouted from the bedroom.

"My face has a higher priority than breakfast." Alison walked briskly toward the door.

As Alison passed the sofa, Alabama greeted her with a smile. "Good morning, Alison. What a pretty outfit. Let me take a look at it."

"No time, Grandma! Bye!" She bounced out the door as the car horn sounded, again.

Alabama picked up the television control and hit the ON button. "I swear young people today have no respect for their elders." She turned up the sound extra loud.

"Mother!" Sara shouted from the bedroom. "Please turn it down."

"Hmph!" Alabama mumbled. "Guess that goes for middle-aged folks, too." Then she turned up the TV even louder and continued eating her Pop-Tart.

Sara appeared at the living room door looking frustrated. "Mother, that is absolutely too loud," she yelled over the "Good Morning, America" commentary. "Are you deaf?"

"Absolutely not!" Alabama yelled back.

"Do you have your hearing aids in?"

"Of course."

Sara stomped toward Alabama. "Then why is the sound turned up so loud? It hurts my ears."

"Sounds okay to me," Alabama replied, licking icing off her fingers.

Sara snatched the controller out of Alabama's hand and turned down the sound. "Why don't I make an appointment to have your hearing checked?"

"My hearing's fine, thank you!"

"I'm only showing two houses this morning. I could call Dr. Baker for an afternoon appointment."

Alabama glared at her realtor daughter. "Are you listening to me? Watch my lips. I. Am. Not. Deaf."

"You can be so stubborn and exasperating!" Sara fumed and started to leave.

Oh, but don't I know that, Alabama thought. "Sorry, dear. You aren't sweetness and light yourself," she mumbled.

Sara halted in mid-step. "Excuse me, Mother? What was that?"

Alabama feigned surprise. "I didn't say anything."

"Of course not. Maybe I'm the one who needs her hearing checked." Sara sighed.

The front door opened, and Alison's head appeared. "Mom, before I forget, I won't be home for supper. I have a French Club meeting."

Sara frowned. "But Alison, your meeting doesn't start until 7:30. Is it out of town?"

Alison leaned against the door in frustration. "No, but Tina and I decided to grab a bite at the mall before the meeting."

"Bad idea, Alison. You need to come home and do your homework first."

Alabama cringed. She could see what was coming. A control confrontation between mother and teenage daughter.

"I can do my homework after the meeting," Alison said, her voice louder.

"Alison, you know how I feel about you gallivanting around on a school night."

A car horn sounded from outside. Alabama felt things escalating. "Now, Sara, supper at the mall hardly constitutes gallivanting around." The car horn blew, again.

"Mom," shouted Alison, "Tina is waiting. We'll be late for school."

"Sara, let the child go," Alabama pleaded.

Glaring at Alabama in total annoyance, Sara nodded. "Fine, young lady, but you better be home by 9 o'clock or you're grounded."

"Thanks, Mom," Alison said, and was gone before Sara could say anything else.

Sara marched over to Alabama. "Mother, must you always take sides with the children? I'm their mother, not you! Stop undermining me." Sara looked at the Pop-Tart in Alabama's hand and grabbed it. "How many times must I remind you, we don't eat on the sofa! Go to the kitchen table, if you want to eat." She looked at the half-eaten toaster pastry. "Why do I bother getting up early to cook oatmeal for you. You aren't rushing out the door to work or school. What's your excuse for not eating it?"

"It tastes disgusting!" Alabama made a face and stuck out her tongue.

"You made me eat it when I was little," Sara protested.

"They didn't have Pop-Tarts back then."

"Pop-Tarts are not nutritious, and you shouldn't encourage Douglas to eat them."

Alabama put a sofa pillow over each ear. Sara snatched the pillows away.

"Mother, I'm not fussing at you." Alabama raised both eyebrows. Sara sighed. "All right, maybe just a little." Sara leaned over and gave her mother a hug and kissed her forehead. Alabama smiled and caressed her daughter's arm. "You know I love you, don't you, Mother?"

"I know, honey. I love you, too. I just need a little more respect around here."

Sara straightened up and stepped away from Alabama. "Seems like I heard something similar from somebody else in this family today." Alabama grimaced. "Mother, I'll call and check on you at lunch. If you want to help with supper, boil some eggs and set the table. But don't do anything foolish today."

"I promise not to pull off my clothes and crawl naked down the street," Alabama said.

"Mother, you know what I mean."

"No soup kitchen on the front lawn?"

"I should say not."

"No poor homeless folks camped out in the garage?"

Sara frowned. "You remember how well that went over last time? So definitely not."

"Oh, and I shouldn't give away anything that belongs to Richard, no matter how old or unused?" Alabama asked.

"That is absolutely correct."

Alabama puckered her lips. "Even if there is a naked homeless man standing and shivering on the front porch?"

Sara shook a finger at Alabama. "Mother, you're trying my patience, again."

"I don't mean to, Sara," Alabama said softly. "I just need to know what specific things I shouldn't oughta do."

"I'm leaving, now, Mother." Sara walked to the door and opened it. "Good bye." She closed the door behind her.

Alabama sat silently, not moving for a couple of seconds to make sure Sara was really gone. Then she turned up the TV, pulled out a package of Oreos from underneath the sofa, and began eating them. In a few minutes, loud knocking could be heard on the back door. Alabama clapped her hands and laughed. Jumping to her feet, she picked up her walker and carried it to the kitchen door. Immediately, she put down the walker and peeked through the curtains.

"Jake!" she shouted and opened the door. "Come on in."

Jake—a scruffy-looking man with salt-and-pepper, shoulder-length hair and a nearly all-white beard—grinned at Alabama. Dressed in a red-and-white flannel shirt and holey jeans, he stepped through the door. He was followed by a somewhat younger man, who appeared uncomfortable and ready to run if anyone spoke to him.

Collapsing in a chair at the kitchen table, Jake pulled off a beige, knitted cap and combed his fingers through his hair. "I didn't think your daughter would ever leave. I wish she liked me, so I wouldn't have to sneak around like this."

Alabama pulled out a chair for the younger man, who looked cautiously around the room before finally sitting down. "As long as Sara doesn't know about your visits, Jake, everyone is happier," she said.

"And healthier, too," Jake said, rubbing his arm. "My arm still hurts from that licking she gave me with her broom."

"She thought you were stealing her clothes," Alabama explained.

"I was helping you get them off the line."

Alabama put her hands on her hips. "You were caressing her favorite nightie."

"Gosh dang it," Jake said, "I was enjoying how nice and soft it felt. I was caught up in the moment."

"Don't forget about the incident with the sleeping bag."

"Don't remind me," he said and frowned.

But how could Alabama forget? It happened not long after she first met Jake in the park, where he lived in a cardboard box encircled by thick bushes. The box could not be seen from the sidewalk, unless a passerby walked up close enough to look between the branches and leaves. The only reason Alabama was in the park was because the physical therapist told her if she wanted to graduate from her walker to a cane, she had to start walking. Sara figured out the distance from their house to the park and back was about a mile with no streets to cross. So, every day, if the weather was nice, Alabama pushed that walker to the park and back to build up her strength.

The first day she attempted the walk, she was worn out by the time she reached the park. Silently thanking her daughter for buying the fancy black walker with the hand brakes and padded seat—Doug called it Grandma's Ferrari—Alabama pushed her walker from the sidewalk to a grassy area in the shade of an old oak tree, where she was able to sit on her Ferrari. She was just starting to catch her breath, when a bearded, long-haired man crawled out of nearby bushes. Alabama remembered feeling terrified of the man as he ambled toward her.

"Mister, please don't hurt me. I'm just a fragile, old woman recovering from a stroke. I have no money. Nothing of value to steal." By the time she realized she was sitting on one expensive item that could be pawned for drug money, the man was standing over her.

"I hope I didn't scare you, ma'am. I only want to make sure you're okay. You look like you're about ready to keel over." He pointed to the bushes. "I'm Jake, and I live in those bushes. It's been my home for several months now."

Alabama's racing heart began to slow down when Jake smiled. He didn't have a gun or a baseball bat or a knife in hand. Even though he needed a haircut and a beard trim, his clothes and work boots were clean, and he didn't smell bad. She decided everything would be okay. "Good morning, Jake." She stuck out her hand. "Pleased to meet you. I'm Alabama, and I live down the street."

Jake gently squeezed her hand. She remembered feeling surprised at the softness of his hands. Not rough or callused, but more like the hands of a man temporarily down on his luck. She guessed he was 60-something, since his beard and shoulder-length brown hair were streaked with white. She liked his smile. It made him look trustworthy.

"May I join you, Alabama?" he asked politely.

"Please do. I need to sit a spell before I'll have enough strength to push my walker back to the house."

Jake, nodded and sat cross-legged on the grass in front of her. "You say you had a stroke? How long ago? A bad one?"

"It's been about nine months or so. Unfortunately, it left me in such bad shape, the doctors said I couldn't live by myself. My daughter didn't want me to live in a nursing home, so during the time I was in rehab, my daughter bought a bigger house that would hold her family and me," Alabama said.

"I commend your daughter for doing that," Jake said. "You're lucky you didn't end up in a nursing home."

After that first meeting, Jake was always sitting in the grass waiting for Alabama to arrive and catch her breath. She looked forward to seeing him nearly every day. When Sara, Richard, and the children left for work and school, Alabama could feel the loneliness surround her. Having someone pleasant to talk to, someone to listen to what she had to say, brightened her days.

What bothered Alabama about Jake was that when she asked him personal questions, he brushed most of them aside to ask her questions about herself. She did find out he was born in Georgia. He'd been married once to his college sweetheart, but they'd never had children, and she'd died over twenty years ago of ovarian cancer. Alabama tried her best to find out how he'd ended up homeless in the park, but he'd only say it was a temporary downside in his life.

As Alabama began to feel stronger, he encouraged her to try walking without her walker. Standing next to her, Jake held her elbow while she took her first steps and cheered her progress. Their visits continued until the weather started getting colder at night and remaining chilly during the day until the sun warmed things up. While Alabama wore a warm jacket on those mornings, she noticed Jake sat on the ground wrapped only in a well-worn quilt.

"Is that all you have to keep you warm?" Alabama asked.

"I have a jacket, too, but I'm saving it in case it gets cold," Jake explained. "I wear it for extra warmth under the quilt. It's not too bad. This is Savannah, after all. You know it doesn't get too cold here in the fall."

"That's usually the case, but there's a cold front moving down from Canada. One of them freaky weather things caused by climate change, they say," she pointed out, concerned that he might get sick or die from hypothermia. She remembered hearing on the evening news about homeless people in Atlanta dying of it last winter.

The next morning, Alabama pushed her walker into the garage and looked around. She remembered seeing four sleeping bags on a shelf. Doug told her that the family used to go camping together, until Alison objected to roughing it in the woods with wild animals that could kill and eat her in the middle of the night. Sara wanted to give all of the camping equipment to a local Boy Scout troop, but Richard said no, they might decide to go camping again one day.

Alabama looked over the sleeping bags and chose the one that looked the least worn. Probably Richard's, she guessed. She placed it on the seat of her Ferrari and set out for the park. Jake looked like he was going to cry when Alabama gave him the sleeping bag.

"If you don't need it for warmth at night, you can sleep on top of it like a mattress." That would have been the end of it, until Richard noticed one of the sleeping bags was missing.

"My sleeping bag is gone," Richard said, after a trip to the garage to get a hammer. "Somebody took my sleeping bag."

"I'm sure it will show up sooner or later," Sara said. "We don't go camping any more, Richard. What does it matter?" After Richard stomped out of the room, Sara turned around and looked at Alabama. "Mother, do you know anything about a missing sleeping bag?"

Alabama shrugged. "Maybe."

"Mother! What did you do with Richard's sleeping bag?"

Alabama grunted. "I gave it to some old homeless man living in the park. He was sitting on the ground shivering in the cold."

"That sleeping bag belonged to Richard."

Alabama pulled herself to her feet. "Fine. I'll push my walker down to the park and tell the poor old man I have to take it back."

Sara sighed. "Mother, that's all right. I'll order Richard a new sleeping bag on Amazon. But please don't ever give anything of Richard's away, again."

Alabama sighed softly. As far as Sara was concerned, that had been the first of several strikes against Jake.

"Alabama!" Jake interrupted her thoughts. "Where are my manners? This here's my new friend Clarence. Clarence, this is Alabama, that famous singer and dancer I was telling you about."

Clarence stood up, removed his orange knit cap, spit on his hand, and wiped it off on his pants. Then he hesitantly reached out for Alabama's hand.

"Jake, you embarrass me." Alabama said. "I was never famous." She offered her hand to Clarence. "Nice to meet you, Clarence. Are you new in town?"

"He's been here nearly a week now," Jake answered for him.

"Where're you from, Clarence?"

"He grew up in New York," Jake said.

"New York? That's a long way from Georgia. Lived there once, but I haven't been back since I moved to Georgia over 40 years ago. Spent six happy years up there. Times Square . . . Broadway . . . Fifth Avenue . . . Central Park ..." Alabama paused and looked at Clarence, who was fidgeting with his hands. Sometimes, when she started talking about her good old days performing on stage, she'd get carried away. "Clarence, did you ever perform in a Broadway or an off-Broadway production?"

"No, but his sister did," Jake spoke up for Clarence. "In off-off-Broadway productions."

Alabama's eyes widened at the news. She rarely met someone who knew someone who had performed on stage in New York City. "Musicals?"

"Nah!" Jake said. "Just bit roles in regular plays. She finally quit and became a school teacher in the Bronx."

Alabama glared at Jake and turned back to Clarence. "Why did you move down South?"

"He was tired of sleeping in the snow," Jake said.

Alabama slapped her hand on the table. "For goodness sakes, Jake, can't you let Clarence speak for himself?"

Jake jumped to his feet and yelled, "'Cause he's bashful, that's why!"

"No, I ain't." Clarence locked eyes with Alabama. "I'm hungry. But Jake said if I let him do the talking, you'd fix us up with a big breakfast."

Jake sighed and collapsed in his chair, shaking his head.

Alabama laughed. She pushed back her chair and stood up. "Well, Clarence, you'll be glad to know that I have some buttermilk biscuits warming in the oven and a fresh pot of coffee. Also, there's lots and lots of leftover oatmeal."

Clarence went over to the stove and lifted the lid off the pot. "Oh, no, I ain't gonna eat that brown, lumpy stuff."

"I don't blame you, Clarence. Can't stand it myself. How about some scrambled eggs to go with the biscuits?" Alabama was interrupted by the doorbell. "Now who in the world could that be?" She glanced at the men and put her finger to her lips. "Don't say a word. I'll be right back."

Clutching her walker, Alabama slowly made her way through the kitchen, across the living room to the front door. When she cracked the door, she saw her grandson standing on the porch. "Douglas Webb! What are you doing home? Didn't you go to school?" Alabama opened the door wide enough for Doug to slip through. She was shocked to see that his clothes were dirty and in disarray, his face swollen, and his nose bloody. "Your clothes are all messed up and your face . . . What happened to your face, young man? Have you been fighting?"

"Don't want to talk about it, Grandma." He ran over to the sofa and fell face down into a pillow. "I'm in a lot of trouble, and I didn't even get to homeroom," he said, his voice muffled by the pillow.

Alabama sat down on the sofa and pulled Doug into a hug. The best hug that only a grandmother could give. Doug hugged Alabama ferociously and started to bawl. "If it's that bad, Douglas, you better tell me, so I can spin a good story to your mom."

Jake and Clarence came into the living room with their coffee and plates of buttered biscuits. "Alabama, these are delicious," Jake said. Both men halted at the sofa.

Doug released his death grip on Alabama and sat up. "Grandma, isn't that the man who tried to steal Mom's nightie off the clothesline?"

Jake rolled his eyes skyward and took his coffee and biscuits over to the table, followed by Clarence. "I have you know I don't steal. Anything. Ever." Jake sat down and took a bite of his biscuit.

"You stole Dad's sleeping bag!" Doug said indignantly.

"No, he didn't," Alabama protested. "It was near freezing that night, and I gave it to him to stay warm. Would you want to sleep outside on the ground in cold weather?"

"We only camp in warm weather," Doug said, staring at Jake.

"That's your choice," Jake pointed out. "I camp out year-round."

Doug left the sofa and stood by Jake. "You do? In the park?"

"Yes." Jake sipped his coffee. "With Clarence, here." Clarence slid his chair closer to Jake, as if he would protect him from Doug."

"Do you live in a cardboard box?" Doug asked, wide-eyed.

"A heavy-duty, discarded cardboard box that a fridge came in. It sits in the middle of a thick growth of bushes that protect us from the wind," explained Jake.

Doug smiled. "I bet you don't have to take a bath every night."

Alabama could see where this was going. "And he doesn't have a TV or play computer games, and he's never been to Disney World."

"But he doesn't have to go to school or do homework," Doug pointed out.

"And his grandmother doesn't give him peanut butter cookies when he gets sent home from school for fighting."

Doug sighed and hug his head. "Then you better give them to me now before Mom gets home."

Jake almost turned over his chair getting to his feet. "What? Your mom's coming home?"

Doug nodded. "Afraid so. The principal was calling her when I left."

Jake's face paled. He grabbed Clarence by the collar. "Clarence, if you're through eating, we're going."

Clarence swallowed a bite of biscuit. "But Jake, these are lip-smacking good."

"I don't care. This is a crisis emergency. We're leaving now!" Jake was waiting by the kitchen door before he finished his sentence.

Clarence quickly wrapped his leftover biscuits in a paper napkin and reluctantly followed after Jake, who blew Alabama a kiss. "So long! See you tomorrow."

"Good-bye, boys!" Alabama yelled after them. She was sorry to see Jake leave. She was becoming rather fond of him. If only she knew how to help him. He seemed too smart a man to be living in a cardboard box. He sounded educated, like he might have a college degree. She wondered if he would let her cut his hair and what he would look like without the long beard and mustache?

Alabama turned to her grandson. "Come along, sweetheart. Let's get those peanut butter cookies. Every doomed man deserves one good last meal" She headed to the kitchen, bypassing her walker.

"Grandma, don't forget your walker." Doug pushed the walker to her. "If Mom finds out, it won't be our secret anymore."

"Relax, Douglas. Don't get excited. I'll be right back, but if you don't run wash your face and hands, I get to eat your share of the cookies."

By the time Doug returned with clean face and hands, Alabama was sitting on the sofa with a tray holding two glasses of milk and a plate of cookies.

Doug plopped down next to Alabama. "Grandma, you know we can't eat on the sofa."

"Hogwash!"

Doug hesitated only briefly before grabbing a glass of milk in his right hand and a large peanut-butter cookie in his left. "Grandma, please don't get me into any more trouble than I'm already in."

Alabama took a sip of milk. "Douglas, if your troubles are that bad, then eating on the sofa pales by comparison. Now, do you want to tell me what happened at school this morning?"

"So . . ." he mumbled through a mouthful of cookies. "What're your plans for today?"

Alabama chewed on a cookie thoughtfully. "Probably watching a Cary Grant movie." Watching all the old movies with stars like Humphry Bogart, Audrey Hepburn, Gregory Peck, Doris Day, and Jimmy Stewart helped her get through the boring afternoons.

"Wait, don't tell me. Let me guess. *That Touch of Mink?*"

"Nope."

"Mmm. *North by Northwest?*"

"Nope."

"Oh, I bet it's *Charade?*"

"Nope."

Doug took a sip of milk and closed his eyes. "Then you'll have to give me a hint." He looked at her sideways.

"Cary Grant helps the military on a South Pacific island during World War II. How's that?" Alabama wiped cookie crumbs and milk off her mouth.

"Gee, Grandma, I just wanted a small hint, not half the plot."

Alabama smirked. "Then what's the movie, smarty?"

"That's a no-brainer. *Father Goose.*"

Alabama reached over and ruffled Doug's hair. "That's right! Such a smart grandson. Now stop stalling and tell me what happened at school."

"Forget about the fight." Doug pulled a half-wadded envelope from his backpack and handed it over to Alabama.

"For me?" Alabama accepted the envelope and examined it carefully. "It looks like it's been in a fight, too."

"Nope, no fight. It just got squished being in my backpack so long."

"How long?"

Doug grimaced. "I dunno. A week, maybe?"

Alabama raised an eyebrow. "I can believe that." She ran a finger along the edges of the envelope.

Doug cocked his head. "Grandma, couldn't you read it better if you opened it?"

"When you get as little mail as I do, you have to savor the moment."

"Why don't you get much mail, Grandma?" he asked, watching his grandmother smell the envelope and rub her hand over the front.

"Because everyone I know is either too sick to write or too dead. Say, it's postmarked Los Angeles." Alabama laughed. "It must be from Sunny."

"Sunny? I've heard that name before. She's someone important to you and Mom."

"Sunny Day. My old friend from the time I lived in New York. Your mother's godmother. You must remember her? She visited me after I had my stroke." Alabama carefully inserted a fingernail under the corner of the flap and worked her finger around until the envelope was open. She pulled out a handwritten sheet of pink paper, unfolded it, and smoothed the pages flat.

"You know, I do remember her," Doug said. "Didn't she and her husband fly out for Grandpa Ray's funeral?"

"Yes, they did fly out after Ray died. You were around six," Alabama said. "When you were five, the whole family flew to Los Angeles to visit Disneyland. Surely you remember that? One evening we went out to dinner with Sunny and Jeff to celebrate our 45th wedding anniversaries."

Doug's eyes narrowed. "Because everyone got married on the same day?"

Alabama laughed and squeezed his shoulder. "You do remember?"

"Some stuff. I remember riding around in a golf cart and seeing real actors."

"Yes, that was fun. Sunny and Jeff arranged that. It was a studio backlot, where several movies were being filmed," she said, but she couldn't remember the name of the studio or the name of any movie being filmed or the name of any actors they saw. How aggravating it was not to remember things like names or events. She sighed and picked up Sunny's letter.

Doug reached out and touched Alabama's hand. "Grandma, I remember that Sunny is the real wacko lady who danced and sang with you and Grandpa way back in the old days, right?"

Alabama looked up from the letter. "She's not wacko, Doug. Just different. I call her a free spirit. And it wasn't all that long ago. Only the late '60s and early '70s. The good old days." Alabama turned back to her letter and started to read. "Oh, my goodness! Sunny's flying to Georgia to see her brother, and she's coming to visit me!" Alabama jumped to her feet and whooped.

"You and Grandpa, and Sunny and her husband Jeff, performed on stage together?"

"Yes, that's correct. We started out singing and dancing in the choruses of Broadway musicals like *Camelot* and *Hair*. I loved performing on Broadway and off-Broadway, but what I really loved best was the four of us performing our 'Knights and Days' act in small nightclubs."

Doug frowned and chewed on his lower lip thoughtfully. "Horace Paurowski said you were a pole-dancing stripper."

Alabama jerked herself up straight on the sofa and nearly dropped the tray. "I beg your pardon, Douglas Webb. For your information, I danced and sang quite properly."

"I figured as much," Doug said, looking visibly relieved. "That's why I belted him."

Alabama's jaw dropped. Cookie crumbs fell from her mouth. "What!? Are you telling me the principal sent you home for protecting your grandmother's honor?"

"No, Grandma, he sent me home for bloodying Horace's bottom lip." Doug slapped both his hands over his mouth.

Alabama's eyes widened. She couldn't believe what she was hearing. She couldn't believe that her sweet grandson had actually smacked a student and bloodied his lip to protect her honor. Then suddenly—and she didn't know why—the whole idea struck her as hilarious. Alabama started laughing. She laughed harder and harder, until the tears were rolling down her cheeks. Finally, she wiped them away and leaned back against the sofa exhausted.

After a minute of silence, Doug cocked his head and glanced over at Alabama. "Grandma, if you didn't pull your clothes off in night clubs, what did you do?"

Alabama stood, dropped the tray on the table, and faced Doug. "Well, first there was a loud drum roll. Then the master of ceremonies would march out on stage and announce, "And now, ladies and gentlemen, from the far southern state of Georgia, we bring you Ray and Balmy, and Jeff and Sunny. Let's have a round of applause for the Knights and Days."

Alabama curtsied and Doug applauded. "Then what, Grandma?"

Smiling, Alabama pictured herself performing in Greenwich Village at Café au Go Go and sighed. "Your grandpa would twirl me out onto the stage. Then Jeff would twirl Sunny out, and we would sing and dance the night away." Alabama closed her eyes, wrapped her arms around herself and began to sway to music only she could hear.

Doug nodded. "Why did you leave New York and move back to Georgia if you loved living and performing on stage?"

Alabama returned to the sofa. "Your grandpa became tired of the stage life. It's a hard life, and he wanted to have roots and raise a family."

"What happened to Jeff and Sunny after you and Grandpa moved back to Georgia?"

"Like so many performers before them, they headed to California with big Hollywood dreams." Alabama sighed.

"Did you ever wish you'd gone to Hollywood and made a lot of money, too?" asked Doug.

"Sometimes, I regretted that," Alabama replied. "But if we'd not returned to Georgia, then most likely your mom wouldn't have been born."

Doug frowned. "Then Alison and I wouldn't have been born, either."

"You are right about that. Fortunately, your grandpa was a homebody at heart. He would've moved to Hollywood, too, if I'd insisted, but he would've been miserable. The Hollywood life wasn't what he wanted for us." She sighed, again, remembering how jealous she was at first when Jeff and Sunny started getting roles in movies — first as extras and later in small, supporting roles.

Douglas reached out and placed his hand on Alabama's. "Grandma, haven't you always said it's never too late to do what you really want to do?"

"That's easy to say and do when you're young and healthy," Alabama said. But now she felt it was too late for her to have any dreams about a brighter future. She had nothing but failing memories and regrets. She was an old woman circling the drain. The only real fun she had now was aggravating her son-in-law.

The front door opened and Sara stormed in.

"Why, Sara, what a surprise," Alabama greeted her. "I wasn't expecting you home for lunch."

"Mother, you know why I'm home," her frustrated daughter replied, glaring at Doug. "All right, young man, what were you fighting about this time?"

Doug rolled his eyes. "Horace started it."

"Horace always starts it, but do you always have to finish it?"

"No, Mom, but you don't want the guys to think I'm wimpy, do you?"

Sara stepped over to the sofa and looked down at her son. "Douglas, a real man doesn't bow to peer pressure. Only crude people settle their differences with their fists. Now go to your room, young man. You're grounded for three weeks."

Doug jumped off the sofa and yelled, "Three weeks? But Mom, Gregory's birthday party is in two weeks."

"Then you should have thought about that before you hit Horace in the mouth."

Doug stomped his foot. "But he said ugly things about Grandma in front of my friends."

Sara locked her eyes on Doug's. "If my friend Sherry Bohannon talked ugly about Grandma, do you think I'd hit her in the mouth?"

"Horace is not my friend," Doug said, crossing his arms across his chest. "My friends never talk ugly about Grandma."

Sara opened and closed her mouth, but nothing came out. She shook her head. "Douglas Webb, that's enough! Go to your room."

"But . . ."

"Go!" Sara yelled, pointing toward his bedroom.

Doug stomped out of the living room and down the hall. His bedroom door slammed shut.

Alabama, who had been biting her tongue during the mother-son conversation, couldn't stand it any longer. "Don't you think you're being a little hard on him, Sara? Boys will be boys."

"Yes, Mother, and girls will be girls, but that didn't stop you from punishing me when I misbehaved. Children need to be disciplined or they could grow up to be entitled hooligans."

"I never laid a hand on you," protested Alabama, heading toward the kitchen with the tray.

Sara followed Alabama into the kitchen. "I didn't lay a hand on him. He's only grounded."

Alabama dropped the tray on the counter. "But having him miss the party seems too mean. You could ground him after the party or unground him for the party."

"Like you were so lenient that time I left the library and went to the movies instead of doing research on my history paper?" Sara tapped her foot and raised her eyebrows.

Alabama frowned. "But you made a D on that paper, Sara. You deserved to be grounded."

"Yes, and so does Douglas."

Alabama was starting to feel a little bit exasperated. "Sara, for goodness sakes! He was protecting my honor."

Sara threw her hands in the air. "Yes, Mother, but what he did was bad. Next time someone verbally insults his grandmother, Doug will think twice about punching that person in the face." Sara turned and headed out of the kitchen. "You raised your child your way and, with your permission, I'll raise my children my way."

"I wouldn't dream of you doing it any other way, dear," Alabama called out, as Sara left.

Sara immediately spun around and walked back to Alabama. "Thank you, Mother. I appreciate that." She leaned over and gave Alabama a peck on the cheek. "I love you, Mother. I appreciate your input, but I know what I'm doing."

"I understand that, dear. Times are changing."

"You are so right. At least Richard and I aren't helicopter parents or child abusers who keep their kids shackled and caged." She paused. "By the way, are you feeling all right, Mother? You seem a little quiet today. A little off."

Alabama cocked her head and frowned. "Now that you mention it, I've noticed this queer feeling deep inside my ear every time I swallow and . . ."

"Do you have any life-threatening problems, Mother? I don't have time for nagging little aches. I have enough of those myself."

"Then I guess I must be the perfect picture of health."

"I'm glad to hear that." Sara said.

"Are you going back to the office?" Alabama did have a full afternoon planned—watching her favorite soap, *The Young and the Restless*, and taking a well-deserved nap.

"No, I figured the day is ruined, so I cancelled my afternoon appointments. I have some phone calls to make to prospective buyers. I can do that here at home. If that won't ruin your social life?" Sara said.

"Hmph!" exclaimed Alabama as she shuffled and pushed her walker into the living room. "I swear I didn't realize I raised such an uppity woman. I get no respect around here." Alabama clicked on the TV and turned up the sound very loud.

Sara returned to the living room and turned down the TV. "Mother, please, that hurts my ears. Listen, I'm running to the grocery store. Is there anything you need?"

Alabama slid to the front of her seat. "I think I'll go along for the ride."

"Not this time, Mother. I'll only be gone a few minutes." Sara picked up her purse.

Alabama stood and reached for her walker. "That's all right, I just need to get out of the house for a little bit. It's depressing sitting here looking at these four walls all day long with no one to talk to."

Sara touched Alabama's arm. "Mother, I'm sorry, but I don't have time to fool with you today. The time it takes to put you and your walker in the SUV, I could already be there and back. All you do is slow me up. I'll be right back."

Alabama snorted. "If you and Richard hadn't sold my house behind my back and stolen my car, I could go and come as I please."

"Mother, please don't start that, again. You know as well as I do that after your stroke the doctor said you weren't able to take care of yourself."

"I can take care of myself just fine, thank you." Alabama sat back down on the sofa. She could feel her blood pressure rising just thinking about her life before the stroke. How she missed her home and her independence.

Sara leaned over and squeezed Alabama's hand. "Mother, you know I feel better with you living here with us instead of assisted living or — heaven forbid — a nursing home. This way I don't have to worry about you getting sick or dropping dead all alone."

Alabama glared at her daughter. "But you're never home, Sara. Everyone runs off to work or school, and leaves me here. I can get just as sick or just as dead living here with you. So, what does it matter?"

Sara sighed and tenderly rubbed her mother's hand. "Mother, it matters to me. I don't want anything to happen to you."

"You could make me happy by giving back my car keys and letting me drive myself to the store whenever I want to."

Sara laughed. "Mother, you're hobbling around the house on a walker. You're in no shape to drive anywhere."

"They let folks with no arms and legs drive."

Sara threw her arms in the air. "Mother, I'm not going to stand here and argue with you. I'll be back in a few minutes." Sara grabbed her purse and left.

Alabama threw her walker across the room. "Fine! I didn't want to go with you anyway, so there!"

Chapter Two

Doug ran into the living room. "Grandma! What's going on? Are you okay? Who're you talking to?"

Alabama picked up her walker and grunted. "No one." It wasn't often that she lost her temper, but lately, it was happening more and more often. Next thing you knew, Sara would have her going to anger management classes.

"Were you talking ugly to Mom behind her back, again?" Douglas asked.

"*Moi?*"

Douglas walked over to Alabama and hugged her tightly. "Oh, Grandma, what are we going to do with you?"

Alabama hugged Doug back and kissed him on his forehead. "Bury me eventually."

"Grandma!" Doug stepped back. "Don't talk like that. Dad said you were gonna outlive all of us."

Alabama sat on the sofa and pulled Doug down next to her. "A mother's worst fear is outliving her family." She hugged him and tousled his hair.

"What?" He pushed back from her. "Never mind, don't explain it." He looked down at his hands. "Grandma, I have this problem."

Alabama squeezed his hand. "I should say so. I think if I were you, I'd avoid Horace. You two have some bad juju going on between you."

"No, this is not about Horace. This is a different problem. Coach Mike wants me to try out for the soccer team."

"Let me guess." Alabama chewed on her lower lip thoughtfully. "You'd rather be on the boxing team because you like hitting students in the mouth?"

"Oh, Grandma, can't you be serious?"

Alabama put her arm around Doug and squeezed him to her chest. "I'm sorry. Okay, the coach wants you to try out for the soccer team. What's the problem? You played soccer at the Y for years. Don't you like soccer anymore?"

"Yes, but . . ."

"But what?" Alabama touched Doug's chin and tilted his face up to see his eyes. "Is Horace trying out for the team? Did he tell you not to try out?"

Doug shook his head. "No, nothing like that. I'm not sure I should try out. I don't know if I want to play."

"Why not?"

"This is serious middle school soccer. I'm not sure I'm ready for that." He rubbed his fingers and his hands.

"Afraid you'll get hurt?"

"Afraid I'll get laughed at or yelled at if I do something wrong," he said, fidgeting. "In middle school, they play for blood. What if I let the team down? What if the team lost because of my mistake? I couldn't handle that. Do you understand?"

Alabama nodded her head, opened the table drawer, and pulled out paper and pencil. "Before we get all mushy headed about this, let's look at it logically, fact by fact." She started to write.

"Okay." Doug moved closer to Alabama to see what she was writing.

Alabama showed him the paper. "See here? We write pros on this side of the page and cons on the other. Now give me a reason why you should play soccer."

He grimaced. "I like to play? I enjoy the game?"

"Good." She wrote that down on the "pro" side. "Now why shouldn't you play?"

Doug pulled on his ear. "Horace might make the team, and I might mess up?"

"Okay, that's obviously a con. Give me another pro."

"Dad and Coach Mike would be very happy."

"Good. How about another con?"

"I'd have to put up with girls who go crazy over boys who play sports. Yuk!"

Alabama smiled and touched Doug's face. "Trust me when I say in a few more years, sweetheart, that will be a pro. Okay, another pro."

"I might get my name and picture in the newspaper and become famous."

"And a con?"

"After school practice and Saturday games."

"A pro?"

"If we go to the national championship, I would miss a week of classes. Gee, Grandma, this is a good idea. It's all laid out there where you can see it and think about it."

Alabama handed him the sheet of paper. "Good, now take the list to your room and keep adding until you have enough pros and cons to make a decision."

Doug took the paper and pencil. "Thanks, Grandma, I love you." He gave her a hug and kissed her cheek.

"I love you, too, Doug." Alabama watched her grandson head back to his bedroom. He was one of the few things that made her present life palatable. She felt a tightness in her throat, and her eyes filled with tears.

Chapter Three

Alabama was dabbing her eyes with a handkerchief when the doorbell rang. "Douglas, somebody's at the door."

The doorbell rang, again. Doug called out from his room, "Grandma, somebody's at the door."

"Oh pooh!" exclaimed Alabama, getting up as the doorbell rang a third time. "Hold your taters, I'm a coming." Alabama had only taken two steps with her walker, when Doug dashed into the living room.

He whizzed by Alabama and yelled as he passed her, "I'll get it, Grandma!" Doug skidded to a halt and yanked open the door. His jaw dropped. "Oh wow!" He took two steps back. "Oh wow! Double wow!"

A colorfully dressed older woman sashayed past him into the living room. She wore an ankle-length orange dress splattered with a black-and-white leaf pattern. Draped over her shoulders was an orange knee-length coat with collar. Chandelier earrings with strings of white-and-silver beads dangled down to her shoulders. Her eyes locked on Doug. "Young man, where are your manners? Close your mouth before something flies in." Doug obediently closed his mouth. "Good, boy. Now tell me if this is the Webb household or ..." Her eyes wandered over to Alabama standing frozen with her walker. "Balmy? Is that you?"

Alabama took a step away from her walker. "Sunny?"

Within seconds, both women were hugging each other and crying. Alabama pushed back from her friend. "Let me look at you." She smiled. Just looking at Sunny sent her happiness scale soaring. Sunny's curly gray hair was carefully pinned up on top of her head and topped with three yellow flowers. Alabama could smell their sweet perfume. How she had missed her friend. "You look like a celebrity walking down a Hollywood red carpet." She felt frumpy by comparison. It'd been a long time since she'd cared enough about her appearance to put on nice clothes and attempt to style her hair or wear jewelry or dab on a little bit of lipstick.

Sunny laughed. "Care for my autograph?"

"You crazy old woman! Why would I want your autograph?" Alabama asked with a smirk. They both laughed. "Just seeing your wrinkled old face and being in the same room with you is all I want." Alabama put her arm around Sunny and led her over to Doug, who stood wide-eyed and frozen in the same spot. "Sunny, do you remember my grandson, Doug?"

"How could I forget him? Jeff and I loved touring the family around the studio backlot when you flew out to California." Sunny took the end of a white-and-orange boa that was wrapped around her shoulders and waved it in front of his face. "Hello, Doug." She reached out her hand.

Doug shook her hand hesitantly, focusing on her long black and white nails. "Are those real?"

"I hope so, Doug—I paid over $100 to have them painted."

Still clinging to Sunny's hand, Doug asked, "Isn't it difficult to use a cell phone with nails that long?"

Alabama rushed over and pulled Doug away from Sunny. "I'm sorry, Sunny. He isn't usually this rude."

"Not a problem. He's apparently a curious child," Sunny said.

Not taking his eyes off of Sunny, Doug pulled away from Alabama. "You don't look as old as Grandma says you are."

"Douglas Webb!" Alabama yelled.

Sunny tilted her head. "You find it hard to believe that I'm 105?"

Doug stammered, "No-o. Ye-s-s. Really?"

Sunny chuckled and winked at Doug. "How old did your Grandma say I am?"

Doug licked his lips. "Older than her?"

Sunny rolled her eyes. "Only by a few months."

Doug continued to stare at Sunny. "You look so much younger. And prettier. Did you and Grandma really dance together?"

"Did we ever!" Sunny grabbed Alabama's hand. "Come on, Balmy, let's show your grandson."

Alabama and Sunny curtsied, nodded to each other, and began to sing awkwardly, "We're Balmy and Sunny; we're happy Knight and Day."

Douglas shook his head and looked puzzled. "Why do you call my grandma Balmy? Her name is Alabama."

Sunny laughed and elbowed Alabama. "We tried to shorten her name to 'Bama, but it became Balmy after a producer said he liked the sound of Balmy Knight and Sunny Day."

Doug, both hands pressed against his cheeks, frowned and started backing out of the room. "That's interesting, Sunny Day. Thank you for sharing that. Now if you'll excuse me, I need to get back to my room and study."

Sunny and Alabama did not seem to notice when Doug left the room. Alabama pulled Sunny over to the sofa and sat down. "Sunny, I can't tell you how glad I am you came to see me." The floral smell of Sunny's favorite and expensive Joy perfume teased out memories of their good times together.

"I've been worried about you, Balmy. You stopped writing. What happened?"

Alabama looked down at her hands. "What do I have to write about? I sleep, eat, poop, sleep, watch TV, sleep, and go to bed. You have to be doing something more exciting than that."

Sunny covered Alabama's hands with her own. "What are you talking about? You have a family. You have grandchildren. Now that my Jeff's gone, I have nothing."

"I don't understand." Alabama shook her head. "You have your brother."

Sunny sighed. "Yes, but we were never close. If we see each other once a year, he's good with that."

Alabama leaned toward Sunny. "I know how lonely it is when the love of your life dies. After Ray passed, I would turn toward his recliner to ask him a question – or tell him something I'd heard – only to remember he wasn't there."

Sunny nodded. "The worst part was reaching for Jeff in the middle of the night and finding his half of the bed empty."

"Or setting the table for two," Alabama added.

"I found myself drowning in despair and sinking into a deep depression," Sunny said.

"That's terrible. You've always been so upbeat and happy," Alabama said. "I'm sorry I didn't make it to Jeff's funeral. Especially after you and Jeff flew to Georgia when my Ray died."

"I regret that we couldn't stay in town longer than the one day, but we had to get back to the set," Sunny explained. "Once a movie is in production, you have to keep to the schedule or kiss your acting career good bye."

"The family understood, Sunny. We were surprised that you were able to get away at all." Alabama rubbed her hands together. "I still regret not being able to fly out to comfort you."

Sunny gave Alabama a hug. "I knew why you weren't there, Balmy," Sunny said, waving her hand dismissively. "You were at death's door. I didn't expect you to come."

Alabama wiped away a tear. "I wish I could've. Then you were so sweet after Jeff's funeral to fly out and stay with me at the rehab center."

"How could I not? I knew that Sara and Richard would be working. I didn't want you to be all alone." she said softly. "Besides, it gave me something to think about besides losing Jeff. It was time spent not wallowing in self-pity." Sunny paused and glanced around the living room. "Is this the house you helped Sara and Richard buy?" Alabama nodded. "That was very generous of you to do that."

"Like there was another choice," Alabama explained. "The doctors said I couldn't live alone. Sara didn't want to move me into assisted living or—heaven forbid—a nursing home. Their old house didn't have an in-law suite or even an extra bedroom. So, Sara and Richard bought this house using a 'swing loan,' which was paid back after their old house and my house were both sold."

"It was incredible how it all came together," Sunny said.

Alabama nodded. "Yes, by the time I was released from rehab, Sara and Richard had mostly moved from their old house into this one."

"Four bedrooms and four baths?" Sunny asked.

"Yes, and after my house sold, they were able to completely pay off the mortgage on the new house. Sara and Richard did all of the work emptying both houses," Alabama admitted. "Everything I wanted to keep, they stuffed in their double-car garage. What remained in my house was either sold at a living estate sale or hauled off to Goodwill."

"How is this living arrangement working out?" Sunny asked, just as Sara walked through the front door with an armload of groceries.

"Fairly well on a good day," Sara answered, dropping her groceries on the table and looking at Sunny. "I wondered whose car that was in the driveway. Mother didn't tell me you were coming to visit."

Sunny stood up and hugged Sara. "I did send her a letter."

Alabama grabbed her walker for support and stood up. "Your letter didn't get here until today, Sunny. It had to travel all the way across the United States to get to Savannah, and then it became lost in Doug's backpack."

"How's my beautiful goddaughter?" Sunny asked Sara.

Sara rolled her eyes. "I'm fine, thank you. You're looking glamorous and healthy, as usual."

Sunny smiled. "Yes, my life is going quite well at the moment. I saw your son, Doug. He's growing into a handsome young man. How's Alison doing?"

Sara shook her head. "We're struggling with hormones and adolescence at the moment. Some days her behavior makes me want to strangle her. Other days I want to hug her tight and tell her life will get better, eventually."

Sunny chuckled. "I know it can't be easy for you, having to deal with a teenage girl, take care of your mother, and—" Sunny raised an eyebrow "—maybe starting to feel the approach of menopause yourself? That's enough to stress out anybody."

Alabama rolled her eyes.

"It's not easy, but we're making it work." Sara rubbed her arms and forced a smile. "You certainly look quite spectacular, Sunny. Is that a little something you picked up on Rodeo Drive?"

"Actually," Sunny said, holding out her arms and turning around, "I bought this on Hollywood Boulevard."

Alabama pushed her walker closer to Sunny. "At Frederick's of Hollywood or straight off a hooker?"

Sunny playfully reached over and gave Alabama a shove. "Your tongue certainly hasn't mellowed any with age, Balmy."

"No, but my body sure has malfunctioned." Dang, but she couldn't believe how good Sunny looked for an old woman. Like a million, trillion bucks.

"Mother!" Sara yelled. "Is this how you talk to your best friend who came all the way from Hollywood to see you?" Alabama shrugged. "Sunny, I hope you plan to be in town for a few days. Are you visiting with your brother in Atlanta?"

"Yes, I'm visiting with my brother, but not in Atlanta. When Derik retired from being a plastic surgeon, he moved to Tybee Island. I'm staying with him and his third wife, but just briefly, I'm afraid. I have a flight back to LAX Saturday night."

"Well, I'm glad you're here. Alabama always loves to have you visit." Sara picked up the groceries and headed to the kitchen. "Maybe you can put a smile on her face."

Alabama's eyes narrowed. She saw an opportunity for a pot shot. "What have I got to smile about? I certainly never get out of this house. Folks are too ashamed to be seen with me in public."

"Oh, Mother, let it go," Sara called out from the kitchen and shut the kitchen door.

Sunny followed Alabama back to the sofa. "I hear a lot of frustration in your voice," Sunny said. "Why don't you tell me what life is like in the Webb household on a bad day?"

"Are you asking me to depress you and ruin your day?" Alabama asked, pulling a bag of Reese's Peanut Butter Cups out from beneath the sofa and offering some to her.

Sunny reached into the bag and pulled out three of the miniature cups. "What are friends for?"

Alabama carefully unwrapped one cup and plopped the chocolate into her mouth. Then she licked the chocolate off the brown wrapper and wadded it up in the foil. "They treat me like a child. Always telling me what I can and can't do," she said softly, looking over her shoulder to make sure the kitchen door was closed. "Do you realize that what you and I are doing is forbidden?"

"What? Talking ugly about your family is forbidden?"

"No, eating on the sofa."

Sunny jumped and dropped a piece on the floor. "Then why're we eating on the sofa?"

"Because we aren't supposed to! Don't you get it? This is my way of protesting and getting even."

Sunny frowned. "Pray tell, Balmy, what are you protesting about?"

"Losing my independence, of course."

Sunny quickly collected all of the candy wrapper evidence and carried it to a small trash can in the corner. She shook her head. "My dear Balmy, you do know your family loves you, right? They don't want anything to happen to you. Why else would they take in some crazy old woman who only wants to cause trouble and get even?"

"No, no, no, Sunny. You don't understand. No one in this family wants to hear what I have to say. I get absolutely no respect. Zip. Zero. Nada. Nothing."

"Are they physically abusive to you? Do they starve you? Do they not take care of your needs?"

Alabama spluttered. "No, it's nothing like that. The problem is I need more attention. I want respect. I want them to listen to what I have to say. And I want what I say to matter."

Sunny reached out and touched her forearm. "Are you sticking your nose in matters that don't concern you, Balmy? Are you being bossy or interfering? Or aggravating? Are you openly hostile?"

Alabama paused in thought. Was it possible that she was all of the above? No, she was the victim here. "Sunny, they won't take me anywhere—except to the doctor."

Sunny grimaced and shook her head. "Alabama, sweetie, have you looked in the mirror lately? When was the last time you took a shower or shampooed your hair?"

Alabama raised her right arm, sniffed her armpit, and shrugged. "Doesn't smell that offensive."

"Frankly, to be perfectly honest, if that's your best outfit, I'm not sure I'd want to be seen in public with you either."

Alabama smoothed out her faded cotton dress and wrapped her baggy sweater tightly around her. "Hmph! Whose side are you on? I thought you were my friend."

"I'm on your side, of course, dear friend." Sunny slid over and gave Alabama a hug. "But I'm a little more objective than you could ever be. You need to stop this runaway, pity-party train."

"You don't get it!" Alabama snapped. "Nobody ever sold your house out from under you," she said, lifting her chin. "Nobody ever took away your car keys and your independence."

"That's true, but I had to plan ahead for my old age. I don't have a son or a daughter—or even a brother for that matter—who would invite me to live with them should I have a debilitating stroke. I would have to pay an obscene amount of money to live out my days in assisted living or nursing facility."

"Maybe that's a blessing in disguise," Alabama said.

Sunny grunted. "Is that sour grapes coming out of your mouth, Balmy?"

Alabama decided it was time to change the subject. "Tell me Sunny, are you moving to Tybee to live with your brother?" The thought of having her best friend moving from California to the Georgia coast gave her warm, fuzzy feelings. Savannah's beach town was only minutes from the Webb house.

"No, I'm not moving in with my brother, but I did put my home in Beverly Hills on the market." Sunny took Alabama's hand. "Because I'm moving to Georgia."

"What?" Alabama pulled her hand back. "Seriously? And I'm just now hearing about this from you?"

"Now don't you go get all huffy on me, Alabama Knight," Sunny said. "All of this happened really fast. A few years back, I was watching a documentary on some cable channel about great places to retire. One of the newest retirement communities was a high-rise retirement complex on the Georgia coast."

Alabama ran her fingers through her unkempt hair. "Where?"

"It's called the Villas at Kensington Grove. The building, which sits on the Brunswick River, overlooks St. Simons Island, Jekyll Island, and the Atlantic Ocean. It's close to Savannah, the Golden Isles beaches, and the Port of Jacksonville in Florida, where you can board a cruise ship to the Caribbean."

"Sounds like an area near the Sydney Lanier Bridge."

"Yes, I believe some of the units overlook that bridge and the Brunswick River below," Sunny said.

"You planning to check out the Villas while you're visiting your brother?" Alabama asked, wondering if perhaps Sunny had stopped by to see if she wanted to go with her. The thought perked her up. Surely her best friend would not be embarrassed to be seen with her in public?

"Now don't get upset with me, Balmy, but the time I came to Georgia to visit with you at the rehab center, I spent one whole day at the Villas, touring it from top to bottom."

"Oh?" Alabama sighed. So much for getting out of the house with Sunny and having some fun.

Sunny grabbed Alabama's shoulders and gently shook her. "The Villas is totally awesome!" She squealed. "It's the perfect place to live. So perfect, that before I left the Villas, I filled out an application for a two-bedroom unit."

Alabama felt pangs of jealousy. Maybe a little self-pity. Not that she would want to live in an old folks' home. A large petri dish full of germs. Like a college dormitory for the elderly. Who would want to live there? Now that, Balmy Knight, she admonished herself, is truly sour grapes. "One day there and you decided you wanted to move from California to Georgia?" she asked softly.

"You don't know the half of it, Balmy. At the Villas there are all sorts of organized activities, field trips, plus an indoor, Olympic-size, saltwater pool; exercise and workout rooms; tennis courts . . ."

"Stop it, stop it," said Alabama, who had been sitting on the edge of the sofa. "It couldn't be that perfect?"

"Oh, my goodness, Alabama, it's absolutely perfect. During my one-day visit, I met some awesome women and a couple of good men. At dinner that evening, I talked to three women who went on a one-week Caribbean cruise. Listen to this, Balmy: They found a stowaway on board, helped take down a smuggling ring on the ship, and got kidnapped."

"What? That sounds like the plot for a thriller movie, not a Caribbean cruise."

"I'm serious. You can't make this stuff up. One of the women, Yasuko Crane, met and fell in love with another passenger on the ship named Charlie Chan."

"His name was what?" Alabama threw her arms up. "That sounds crazy. Who would name their son that?"

"His mother, obviously," Sunny said. "Just hush and let me finish." She took a deep breath. "Now where was I? Oh, yes. Charlie moved into the Villas, and now they're getting married. A second woman, Carolina Cunningham, met and fell in love with an undercover agent. He's retiring and moving to the Villas, too. Carolina calls him her Hunky Spy. They're getting married."

"She's marrying a Hunky Spy?"

"Balmy, will you stop interrupting me?"

"Honestly, Sunny, these folks living at the Villas sound like characters in a mystery novel—not retired folks living out their golden years in peace and quiet."

Sunny frowned. "None of them are dead yet, Balmy. They're living exciting lives. Trust me, you'll like them. But you'll really love Eula Mae Davis. She's a hoot and a half. A good old Southern girl who keeps everyone laughing."

"Sunny, all of this sounds too good to be true. You make the Villas sound like the perfect place to live." Unlike here in the Webb household, she thought, where I'm trapped and getting no respect.

"I know. That's exactly what I kept thinking. It was too good to be true. I totally put it out of my mind until a few weeks ago."

"What happened a few weeks ago?" Alabama asked.

Sunny grinned. "The director of the Villas called to say my application had been approved and a two-bedroom unit on the fifth floor was available for me, if I was still interested."

Alabama's eyes widened. "You mean you're really moving to Georgia?" Alabama couldn't believe it. Her best friend would be able to visit her often. They could eat out together and do all sorts of fun things. Or maybe she would be so busy with her new friends and new life at the Villas that she wouldn't have time for her.

"But wait, Balmy, I haven't told you the best news."

"What's that?" But Alabama wasn't sure she really wanted to hear any more about Sunny's perfect new life choice.

Sunny flicked her earrings with her long, lacquered nails. They delivered a high-pitch tinkle. "I called my agent and told her I was interested in working, again."

"Working? What are you talking about?" Had she found another dancer and singer to partner with on stage? A lump formed in her throat. Suddenly, she wished that Sunny hadn't stopped by with her good news.

"Working for the fun of it, of course. I don't need the money. Just a few small TV and film parts to keep life interesting. Apparently, Savannah hosts lots of film projects. Think about the older actresses still working. Judi Dench, Helen Mirren, and Maggie Smith haven't given up the ghost yet."

Alabama was relieved. Sunny wasn't going to sing and dance with anyone else. She simply wanted to perform, again. She held up her finger. "Don't forget about Julie Andrews."

"Yes, exactly! There are plenty of roles for women in their seventies, eighties, and even nineties. My agent says as soon as I move to Georgia, she will sign me up for auditions. I tell you Balmy, being active keeps you youthful and alive."

"Did you just drop by to flaunt your plans and news in my face?"

"Oh, no, Balmy, not at all. Tell me you wouldn't like a limousine to take you to work on a set with your favorite actor, Harrison Ford?"

Alabama gulped. "Harrison Ford?" She knew everything there was to know about Harrison Ford. She had a fat scrapbook full of magazine and newspaper articles about him. The thought of riding in a limo and working side by side with Harrison Ford made her giggle. "That would absolutely make my day. I could die happy after that."

Sunny grabbed both of Alabama's hands. "Then tell me you'd love to come live in the Villas with me."

Chapter Four

Alabama's jaw dropped slightly. She stuck her finger in her right ear and poked her hearing aid. Sometimes it slipped and her hearing went kaput. But it seemed in place. No slippage. Alabama guessed she must have misinterpreted what Sunny said. "I'd love to visit you, but . . ."

Sunny shook her head. "No, not visit, Balmy. I want you to live with me—just like in the old days living at the Y together. Only this time you'd have your own private bed and bath. No walking down the hall to shower." Sunny stood and started to sing one of her favorite songs.

Alabama looked at Sunny in shock as she heard the lyrics from "Consider Yourself." "That's the *Oliver* song we sang on Broadway." Her eyes widened. "What are you saying?"

Sunny sighed and started singing the lyrics, again.

"You want me to consider myself part of your family?" Alabama covered her face with her hands and started to cry. She could not believe what Sunny was saying. It was a dream come true.

A concerned Sunny rushed back to the sofa and pulled Alabama into a big hug. "Oh, Balmy, what did I say? I'm so sorry. Please don't cry."

Alabama wiped her eyes and nose on her sleeve. "It's all right, Sunny."

"Then why are you crying?"

"Because I'm so dang happy."

"I don't understand," Sunny said dumbfounded.

Alabama sniffed and wiped her nose with the back of her hand. She couldn't believe this. "Did I hear you right? You really want me to live with you?"

"Isn't that what I've been saying and singing? I didn't know it would upset you. It's okay if you'd rather stay here with your family. I understand. They love you."

Alabama began to weep, again. "Yes, I know they love me, but I feel like I'm a burden to them. Sara feels obligated to take care of me. I really miss my independence, which makes me angry and drives me crazy."

Sunny nodded. "I've definitely picked up on the angry-crazy thing. So just say 'yes' and move in with me."

"It's not that easy," Alabama said.

"I'm sure it isn't." Sunny stood and held out her hand to Alabama. "Come with me and I'll help you explain it to Sara."

Alabama chewed on her lower lip thoughtfully. "My life is quite complicated at the moment. When do you plan to move into the Villas?"

"Hopefully, in a few weeks."

Alabama gulped. "That soon?"

"Hey, what can I say? When my name popped to the top of the waiting list, I didn't want Flora Ruth Biggers to have died in vain. After all, I've been waiting two years for this, Balmy."

"Holy moly! Two years and you never said a word to me?" Alabama fussed. But then she thought that maybe it was just as well she hadn't known.

"Believe me, it wasn't intentional, Balmy. Two years ago, when I filled out the application, I didn't know what I wanted to do or where I wanted to live for the rest of my life. And let's face it, you were so sick and frail at the time, I wasn't even sure how much longer you'd be around."

Alabama thought about that and nodded. "I understand, Sunny. I wasn't even sure if I would make it out of rehab myself. I thought I'd be a vegetable and a burden on the family for the rest of my life."

"But you didn't crawl in a hole and die, my dear friend. You persevered," Sunny pointed out. "You're now ready for new beginnings."

"Obviously you are, too. You certainly jumped on this."

"I wanted to take a few weeks to think about it, but the director said the waiting list was long. I needed to make a decision soon. Before I left LA, I had a realtor look at the bungalow Jeff and I bought when we moved to California."

"In other words, you already had your mind made up?" Alabama asked.

"Heavens, no. I knew the buy-in for a two-bedroom unit at the Villas would be pricey. I wanted to know how much I could get from selling my home. Jeff and I paid less than $100,000 for it, but I wasn't sure how much it was worth today."

Alabama cringed. She and Ray had paid $52,000 for their Savannah home, but it sold for ten times more than that. "How much did she think it would sell for?"

"You won't believe this, Balmy. She said at least $900,000!"

"What?" Ray had been right, Alabama thought. He once told her what was really important to the cost of a house was "location, location, location."

"It was like the stars were lining up for a move to Georgia," Sunny said. "So, I flew to Atlanta, rented a car, and drove to Brunswick to inspect the unit. Balmy, the Villas at Kensington Grove was as perfect as I remembered. I immediately signed the paperwork and spent the rest of the day buying new furniture for the unit."

Alabama leaned over and pulled the bag of Reese's Peanut Butter Cups out from under the sofa. When she got excited, her chocolate addiction kicked in. "And then what?"

Sunny grabbed a few candies out of the bag. "Then I called the realtor and told her to start showing the house. She also gave me the number of an auctioneer who promised to sell nearly everything I own at a living estate sale."

"Holy moly! This is more excitement than I can handle." Alabama unwrapped a peanut butter cup and popped it into her mouth. "How long will it take to sell your house?"

"Funny thing you should ask that," Sunny said, carefully peeling the foil and brown paper off the chocolate cup. "The realtor called this morning. She's already had three offers on the house." She squeezed Alabama's hand. "Life is short, Balmy. The Villas is the perfect place to live out our golden years. Eula Mae Davis told me it was God's waiting room. Well? Are you with me or not?"

Chapter Five

Two days after Sunny moved into the Villas at Kensington Grove, Alabama invited her over to meet her homeless friends, Jake and Clarence, and play a game of Scrabble. Sara was attending a realtors' workshop and wouldn't be getting home until that evening. There would be no unforeseen interruptions. Or so she thought. Alabama was looking forward to a good morning of fun, plus some serious plotting and planning with Sunny on how she could escape her life in the Webb household and move into the Villas at Kensington Grove.

For the occasion, Alabama wore a nicer outfit—red knit pants and a red and white striped-knit pullover. She had washed her hair, put on a little bit of lipstick, and shocked Sara by asking her to help comb her nearly uncontrollable hair into a bun.

"Don't think I haven't noticed that since Sunny's visit a few weeks ago, you've been showering regularly and dressing better," Sara said, putting a final hairpin into the bun. "You're sleeping better, too, and I was happily surprised when Dr. Baker told us at your last checkup that you're strong enough to get around without your walker."

Alabama picked up the hand mirror and checked out the bun. "Thank you, dear daughter, for your help." She grabbed Sara's hand. "Yes, Sunny has been a good influence on me. And my daily walks to the park have made me stronger and healthier." She stood up and turned around. "I want to look good for Sunny's visit today. What do you think?"

Sara smiled and hugged Alabama. "Mother, you look spry and ten years younger."

Good for me, Alabama thought. Her goal was to hear her daughter say those words. When the time came to talk about moving in with Sunny, she needed to appear to be strong, fit, and healthy.

Even Richard appeared surprised when Alabama entered the living room. "You got a hot date today or something?" Richard asked, his face buried in the morning paper, which was intact for a change.

Alabama had not cut out any articles since the Harrison Ford incident. She was trying hard to behave. It was another important part of her plan for Richard and Sara to see that she was more than capable of taking care of herself, acting responsibly, and making good decisions. "Sunny is coming over for Scrabble and lunch today."

Richard looked at Alabama over the top of his paper. "Oh? Is she all settled in at her new place?"

Alabama sipped on a cup of hot chocolate. "She loves it."

"I've heard that the high-rise retirement community near Brunswick is quite popular," he said, burying his face back into his paper. "Not sure I would want to downsize into a tiny apartment myself. No, I think I'll stay here in this house. They'll have to carry me out of here in a wooden box."

That might work for you, thought Alabama, but she planned on getting out of the Webb house way before she needed any wooden box.

• • •

Jake and Clarence arrived at the Webb house first. More than likely, Alabama thought, they'd been hiding behind the oleander bushes, waiting for Richard to leave for work. Alabama was pleased to see both men wearing clean—if quite worn—faded jeans and shirts. She'd asked Jake earlier in the week if the men could clean up before meeting Sunny. Jake was amenable. He said they could shower at the homeless shelter before coming over. Alabama was glad to see that Jake's hair was gathered at the base of his skull with a scrunchie, and it looked like his beard had been trimmed.

"Why are you staring at me?" Jake asked. "Don't I look decent enough to meet your friend?"

Alabama smiled. "I'm sorry, Jake. You look very nice." So nice, she thought, he almost didn't look like a man who lived in a cardboard box under the bushes. So nice, she wanted to get to know him better.

She couldn't understand why he was so reluctant to talk about himself. "Thank you, Jake, for making the effort. This is important to me."

"I know it is, Alabama." Jake smiled, and his eyes seemed to twinkle. "I will do my best to impress your friend."

"Thank you, Jake. That means more to me than you'll ever know."

•　　•　　•

By the time Sunny knocked on the front door, Jake and Clarence were munching away on buttermilk biscuits, loaded with butter and blueberry preserves. Alabama, who had set up the Scrabble board on the kitchen table and mixed up the wooden tiles, rushed to the front door with a big smile on her face. "Sunny!" she called out happily as her friend stepped into the living room. Today, Sunny was casually dressed in a multi-colored kaftan and wearing wedge sandals, woven bracelets on both wrists, and a eucalyptus seed-pod necklace.

After hugging each other, Alabama led Sunny into the kitchen, where she introduced her to Jake and Clarence. "Fellows, I want you to meet my best friend Sunny Day, who recently moved into the Villas at Kensington Grove. Sunny, this is Jake and his friend Clarence."

Jake stood up, wiped his hands on his jeans, and shook Sunny's hand. "It's my pleasure to meet you. Miz Day."

"Please, just call me Sunny."

"Yes, ma'am, Sunny," Jake said and smiled. "I hear you and Alabama used to dance, sing, and perform on stage back in the old days."

"Were you famous?" asked Clarence, shaking Sunny's hand.

"Hardly," said Sunny with a laugh. "But we had our fans."

Soon Alabama was able to get everyone seated around the Scrabble board and the game began. Clarence had never played before and claimed he didn't know how to spell. "It's all right, Clarence," explained Alabama. "It's just for fun, and all of us will help you find a word."

"I don't know . . ." Clarence said.

Jake nudged him. "Come on now, yesterday you agreed to give it a try."

"Yeah, I know, but I didn't realize you had to think. That will make my head hurt."

"Stop complaining," Jake said. "We're letting you go first. All you have to do is find a few letters and put down a word."

Clarence scratched his head, picked up four tiles, and placed them in the middle of the board: S-T-A-R.

"That's not a bad start," Sunny said. "Which star do you like best? I like them all, especially the North Star."

Clarence smiled goofily. "I like you best, Miz Sunny. You're my own favorite star."

"Thank you kindly, Clarence, but I'm afraid I was never a Hollywood star."

"Weren't you nominated for Best Supporting Actress?" asked Jake, placing letters off of Clarence's R to spell A-R-T-I-S-T-I-C.

"How did you know that?" Sunny asked, looking at Jake strangely. "That was a long, long time ago."

Jake looked down at his tiles and shrugged. "Maybe Alabama told me."

"Maybe so," Alabama said, but she knew she hadn't. So how would a homeless man living in a cardboard box know that about Sunny?

"My husband Jeff was very proud when I was nominated, even if I didn't win." Sunny pointed at Jake's word. "You used all of your tiles, Jake. You get 50 bonus points for that, plus 11 points for your word. 61 points total. Good play!"

"Now wait just a darn minute," Clarence exclaimed. "Why did Jake get more points than I did?"

"Because he used all of his tiles," Alabama explained.

Clarence counted his tiles. "But that's seven tiles. I don't know any words with seven letters. You should give me extra points for that."

Jake tilted his head and cracked his neck. "Clarence, in Scrabble, you don't get bonus points for ignorance."

"I told you I couldn't play this game, Jake." Clarence stuck out a trembling lower lip.

Alabama, afraid that Clarence would burst into tears and quit the game, reached out and touched his forearm. "It's okay, Clarence. Everyone will help you find bigger words."

Clarence sniffed and wiped his eyes. "Okay," he mumbled. "Thanks."

"You know, Sunny, it's never too late," Alabama said, spelling QUAINT for 17 points. "At least that's what my grandson says. If you're going back to work, you might win an Oscar yet."

Sunny chuckled. "Yeah, right. I don't think they give Oscars to actors for commercial work."

"Even if you never get nominated for another award, it doesn't matter," Jake said. "Look at all of your accomplishments over the years. You've done a lot of work on stage, and in TV and films, with big name actors. No matter how old and feeble you get or how poor and down and out you get, you'll always have those memories. Nobody can take them away from you."

Alabama blinked and stared at Jake. "My goodness, Jake, but you are a surprising fountain of information and insight this morning." She realized that she wouldn't be surprised if he had a college degree. He appeared to have good research skills, too. Were there computers at the homeless shelter, she wondered? Did he like to search online for information? Was he looking for a job in the Savannah area?

Jake moved his new tiles around in search of a word to play. "See? And all this time you thought I wasn't listening to you when you talked about Sunny and your memories of your time performing together."

Sunny placed six of her tiles on the board to spell SMOLDERS for 22 points. "Boy, do Balmy and I have some memories."

"That we do," agreed Alabama. "All the way back to grade school."

"And to think my mother wanted me to be a nurse," mused Sunny.

Jake squirmed in his seat. "Not too many folks know this, but I wanted to be a surgeon."

Alabama's eyes widened and her jaw dropped. "What?" Was Jake fixing to share something about himself? This was momentous. She didn't even know his last name. He told her last names weren't important when you were homeless.

"Why didn't you become a surgeon?" Sunny asked.

"I went to see a stage play," Jake said. "Suddenly, the thought of cutting into folks in an operating room didn't seem as appealing as working in a theatre. So, I started unloading crates of fruit and vegetables at the Piggly Wiggly during the day and learned about stage lighting in the evenings. When I wasn't helping to hang lights in the theatre, I was delivering sandwiches and mail for actors and crew."

"Where was this, Jake?" Alabama was interested in hearing more. "Were you in New York when Sunny and I were there?"

"Um—no, I was in Atlanta," Jake said.

Clarence, grimacing and wringing his hands, slowly placed four tiles on the board. "I only know four-tile words," he whined. "How many points is this?"

Alabama, Sunny, and Jake stopped talking and looked down at Clarence's word JACKS, which ran off of the S in Sunny's word and stretched from the Triple Score to the Double Letter Score underneath his K for a total of 79 points—giving him a total of 93 points.

Jake pounded Clarence's back. "That's fantastic, buddy! You're now in the lead."

Clarence covered his face with both hands, danced his feet, and shook his body. Everyone laughed and cheered.

Jake turned his attention back to Sunny. "What happened to you? Why didn't you become a nurse?"

Sunny shoved Alabama. "Balmy happened to me."

"Huh?" asked Clarence.

"Sunny decided she wanted a life on stage," explained Alabama.

Sunny laughed. "The truth is Balmy stole over to my house one night and talked me into running off to New York with her."

"No, no, no," protested Alabama. "The real truth is she didn't want to empty bed pans or give sponge baths."

"No," Sunny disagreed. "You wanted to leave the state after Phillip Oppenheimer asked your father if he could marry you."

"Stop it right there," Alabama said. "Truth be told, Sunny and I loved to dance and sing with a passion. We knew we wouldn't be happy if we didn't go to New York and give it a try."

"Then one day, we met the Knight and Day singing-dancing duo," said Sunny.

"After watching us sing and dance one night at one of the clubs in the Washington Square area, these two cute guys—Ray and Jeff— asked us to join their performing group," said Alabama, putting down QUAY for 21 points.

"We married them, and the rest is history," said Sunny, pouncing on the Triple Word Score with WHAB for 45 points. "We became Sunny Day and Balmy Knight!"

"WHAB?" questioned Jake. "What the heck is a WHAB?"

Sunny rose to her feet. "It's when you combine whipping and dabbing together." Jake frowned, as Sunny did some fancy footwork and sang out, "I'm Sunny!"

Alabama immediately joined her friend. "I'm Balmy!"

"We're here to entertain you!" they chorused loudly. They danced a shuffle-ball chain and gave each other a hug.

"We were inseparable," Sunny said. Nonchalantly, she leaned over Alabama's tiles. "Hah! Balmy has nothing left but impossible-to-use letters. You don't stand a chance now!"

"Hah, yourself!" Alabama blurted. "You sit back down and put your tiles where your mouth is. This game is not over yet!"

Sunny sat down and plunked down all of her tiles to spell CURTAINS, using the Triple Word Score. "That is curtains for you, Balmy Knight. And don't forget the extra 50 points for using all of my tiles."

"I'd like to know where the name Balmy came from. Is there a story here?" Jake asked.

"At one of the clubs, they wanted to shorten my name. 'Bama Knight didn't work, but Balmy Knight and Sunny Day worked perfectly."

"I like the name Balmy," Jake said with a smile. "May I call you Balmy, too?"

"Oh, why not?" Alabama replied.

"Is it my turn now?" asked Clarence.

"Yes, Clarence," said Jake.

"Okay, here I go. Phobia. F-O-B-I-A."

"Wait a cotton-picking minute," Sunny complained. "You can't spell it that way. It's P-H-O-B-I-A, not F-O-B-I-A."

Clarence spluttered. "But I don't have a P."

"I do, Clarence," said Jake. "You want mine?"

"You can't give him your tile," complained Sunny. "That's against the rules."

"What's it to you, Sunny?" Jake asked. "You're beating me by 100 points."

"Hey," Alabama interrupted. "I'm losing, too. What has that got to do with abiding by the rules?"

"Now Balmy, we are abiding by the rules. We're just bending them a might," explained Jake. "What if I swap tiles with Clarence. Give him my P for his S?"

"That would be mighty nice of you, Jake." The two men swapped tiles. Clarence spelled P-H-O-B-I-A on the board.

"Happy now?" Jake asked, spelling A-D-V-E-N-T for 20 points.

With a grand flourish, Alabama dropped her tiles on the board to spell XENOPHOBIA, hitting two Triple Word Score boxes. "Bet your booties, mister. Thanks for the setup."

Sunny shook her head. "Now see what you let her do?"

"Did you make that word up?" Jake asked.

"It is a perfectly good word," Alabama said. Out of the corner of her eye, she saw Clarence slip the Scrabble dictionary onto his lap, discretely open it up, and thumb through the pages.

Clarence looked up from the dictionary. "She's right, Jake. It means fear of strangers."

"Phooey," said Jake. "You sure are getting awfully smart for a high school dropout." Jake's eyes narrowed. He pointed at Clarence. "What's that in your lap?"

Clarence carefully slipped the small dictionary between his thighs. "What's what?"

Jake rolled his eyes.

Sunny took all seven of her tiles and put them back in the bag. "I have nothing but vowels. I'm swapping them for hopefully something better."

"Is it my turn now, Jake?"

"Yes, Clarence, go for it."

"Xenophobia is a nice word, Balmy. Watch this, Jake. First, I will put an 'S' on the end of Balmy's word. Then I will use that 'S' to spell a second word." Clarence carefully put down the letters Z-A-P-T-I-A-H in front of the S. "There you go: ZAPTIAHS."

"Where in tarnation did you come up with that word?" Jake asked angrily.

"In the dictionary. Means Turkish policemen. Ain't that something?"

Alabama reached underneath the table and grabbed the dictionary from Clarence. "This dictionary?"

Jake took the dictionary away from Alabama and waved it under Clarence's nose. "This is cheating!"

"I don't know, I thought that's what you called bending the rules," Sunny pointed out.

Jake dropped the dictionary in the middle of the Scrabble board. "If we're bending the rules that far, then maybe I don't want to play this game anymore."

Clarence hung his head. "I'm sorry, Jake. I ain't gonna do it no more. Promise."

"It's all right, Clarence," Alabama said, squeezing his shoulder. "Look, fellows, don't fuss. I want your visit to be something I can remember with a smile in case we don't get to do this again."

Jake looked up in alarm. "What are you talking about? You don't like our company?"

Alabama pretended to concentrate on arranging her wooden letters. "I might be moving."

Jake's eyes narrowed. "Is your son-in-law getting transferred?"

"Actually . . ." Sunny cleared her throat. "Balmy thought the living might be easier and more fun if she moved in with me at the Villas."

Jake slowly stood up, never taking his eyes off of Alabama. "You mean move to those fancy Villas in Brunswick permanently?" He leaned over the table toward her. "Please tell me you're joking?"

Clarence laughed nervously. "Of course, she's joking, Jake. Who would make us buttermilk biscuits and oatmeal cookies, if she moved?"

"I'm serious about this." Alabama bit her lower lip, surprised that Jake was getting so upset. Did he like her biscuits and cookies that much? Or could it be that he would miss her?

"No, you can't be serious, Alabama!" Jake said adamantly, as Sunny and Clarence listened in bewilderment.

Alabama blinked. Jake was not acting like the homeless man she had come to know and like. He was acting downright bossy. "What is your problem, Jake?"

"Alabama, you haven't thought this through," Jake insisted. "You know your daughter's not going to let you leave."

Alabama stuck her chin out defiantly. "If I want to go, I'll go. I'm no vegetable yet!"

"Maybe not," Jake said, cocking his head. "But you're an older woman who's dependent on her daughter. You're safe here, living with your family."

Alabama sighed. "Oh, Jake, please, I thought you would be on my side." She screwed up her face and began to cry softly.

The front door slammed and everyone in the kitchen jumped. "I'm home," Doug's voice called out from the living room. In a few seconds, he stepped through the kitchen door, lugging his book bag. "Hello, Clarence. Hello, Sunny. Hello, Jake." He looked at Alabama. "What's the matter, Grandma?"

Alabama stood up and gave her grandson a hug. "Nothing's the matter, Douglas."

"Then why are you crying? Did somebody hurt your feelings?" Jake, Clarence, and Sunny all looked down at their feet in silence.

Alabama touched Doug's face. "How about some cookies and milk?"

Doug frowned. "Grandma, you know Mom gets annoyed when you feed homeless people in her kitchen."

"What your mother doesn't know can't hurt any of us," Sunny said.

"Amen to that," mumbled Jake.

Douglas poured himself a glass of milk and took a bite out of an oatmeal cookie. "All right, but they better leave before Mom gets home."

"I hope you stayed away from Horace today," Alabama said, deciding a change of subject was needed.

"I did until soccer tryouts." Doug gulped down a swallow of milk. "But Coach Mike kept us so busy running around, we didn't have time to look at each other, much less punch each other in the face."

"Did you make the team?" Sunny asked.

Doug grabbed another cookie. "We have final tryouts tomorrow. Won't know until then."

"You have tryouts on a Saturday?" asked Jake with surprise. He looked at Alabama and raised an eyebrow.

"Oh, no!" Alabama exclaimed. "That's unfortunate."

"What's wrong, Grandma? Do you need me for something?" Doug asked.

"I'm having a little garage sale tomorrow. Your parents are going to the lake with the Schmidts for the weekend, and I was hoping you could help me." Alabama shrugged.

"Grandma, I can't miss final tryouts tomorrow."

Sunny put her arm around Doug and gave him a hug. "Of course, you can't, Doug. And no one expects you to be here. Don't worry, Balmy, I'll be here to help."

"Clarence and I can help, too," Jake volunteered.

Alabama looked up in surprise. "But I thought you two planned to dumpster-dive for aluminum cans and plastic bottles tomorrow?"

Jake put his hands in his pants pockets. "Aww, we can do that Sunday."

"All right," Alabama said. "But I insist on giving you a little something for your time and trouble."

"How little?" asked Clarence.

Jake gave Clarence a slight shove. "Will you shut up, Clarence? You don't have to give us anything, Balmy. You're always feeding us and being nice to us. We appreciate everything you do. Helping you out at your garage sale is the least we can do."

"Grandma?" asked Doug.

"Yes, Douglas?"

"Do Mom and Dad know you're having a garage sale?" Doug tilted his head and looked directly at Alabama, who avoided eye contact. Doug gasped. "Oh, Grandma, you aren't selling any of Dad's stuff, are you?"

Alabama huffed. "Young man, I wouldn't dare sell anything in that garage that didn't belong to me."

Doug nodded. "That's good. I wouldn't want us to get into trouble. 'Cause then Dad would say you are a bad influence on me." He paused. "Why're you having a garage sale?"

Alabama gave him a hug. "Your dad says my stuff has filled up the garage, and he can't get his car inside." And because I need the money to move away, but she couldn't admit that to him. Or to anyone yet. The time was not ripe.

Chapter Six

Alison Webb, dressed in her usual black Gothic attire, opened and slammed the front door. She halted abruptly, her back to the door, while her kohl-lined eyes scanned the room. Alabama, Sunny, Doug, Jake, and Clarence, who were seated in the living room, paused their conversation. Alabama thought it was a surreal moment. Like Alison was on stage, and everyone else was the audience. Averting her eyes, Alison hefted her punk rock book bag and trudged toward the hallway door.

Alabama lifted a hand in her granddaughter's direction. "Alison, wait. Did you have a good day?"

Alison didn't slow down or turn around. "It was okay," she mumbled.

"Hello, Alison," Sunny called out. "Remember me?"

"Yes, Sunny. Hello," Alison replied, disappearing down the hallway without a glance.

Alabama sighed long and loud. "Are all teenage girls this frustrating?"

"I think it's caused by those angry hormones upsetting their emotional system. Gives them lots of highs and lows," Jake suggested.

Alabama frowned. "Alison's seem to be mostly lows."

"Don't worry, Grandma," Doug said, putting his hand on Alabama's shoulder. "When I get Alison's age, I'll still be my old adorable, lovable self."

Alabama gave Doug a hug. "I'm sure you will, sweetie."

The backdoor in the kitchen opened and banged shut, causing Clarence to jump. "What was that?" he whispered.

Sara's voice called out from the kitchen. "I'm home. Can someone give me a hand?" Sara asked as she walked into the living room.

"Doug, will you please help me with . . ." She stopped in mid-sentence and stared at five people staring horrified back at her.

Jake jumped to his feet, pulling Clarence out of his seat. "Guess we better run along, Clarence, or we'll be late for the concert."

Clarence looked at Sara and balked. "What concert, Jake?"

Jake kicked Clarence and dragged him toward the front door. "Oh, yeah, the concert. Good bye, everyone," Clarence said. "Thank you. Enjoyed it."

Jake opened the door and shoved Clarence through it. "Bye, Balmy. Sunny, Doug." Jake glanced at Sara and nodded. "Ma'am." Then he was gone, softly shutting the door behind him.

While Sara glared at Alabama, Doug slipped out of the room. Not taking her eyes off of Alabama, Sara spoke calmly and quietly, "Sunny, would you please ask Doug and Alison to get the groceries out of the car and put the food away?"

Sunny, looking apprehensively at Alabama, nodded. "Sure, Sara. Be right back."

Alabama smiled grimly. "I thought you were at an all-day workshop."

"I was, but I decided to leave early and pick up groceries," Sara said.

After a long, long silence, Sara walked over to the sofa and sat down next to her mother, sighing loudly.

Alabama shrugged her shoulders. "Don't hold it in, Sara. I know when you start breathing heavy like that, I'm in serious trouble."

"Mother," Sara started softly, "what were those vagrants doing in this house?"

Alabama discreetly edged her body over to put extra space between her and her daughter. She couldn't believe she'd lost track of time. Jake and Clarence should've left the house before Doug came home from school. And Sara came home much earlier than expected. Now she had to deal with what was sure to be a bad confrontation when she'd been trying very hard to be nice and not cause problems. "They were playing Scrabble with me and Sunny."

"Mother!" Her voice grew louder and shrill. "You know I don't want those homeless men in my home! What were you thinking?"

"They're my friends." Alabama wrung her hands and tried to think of something to say that would de-escalate the situation.

"They're dirty. And they smell." Sara wrinkled up her nose, ran into the kitchen, and returned with a spray can of Lysol.

Alabama coughed and waved her hand in front of her face, as Sara turned in a circle, spraying the living room "But they showered at the homeless shelter this morning," Alabama protested. "They even wore clean clothes. And they're good company for me after everyone leaves for the day."

"They could be carrying all sorts of diseases, Mother. Like the Black Plague. Or they could be bringing lice or bed bugs into my house." Sara paused her spraying to scratch her arms and shoulders.

"Are you feeling itchy, Sara? Those two men were cleaner and less smelly than Doug. I really like them. They make me laugh." Alabama smiled.

"Mother, don't you understand?" Sara touched Alabama's shoulder. "They could rob us or slit your throat or worse."

"What could be worse than having my throat slit? Anyway, they care about my feelings. They respect me. They listen to what I have to say. They treat me like a real person with brains."

Sara shook her head. "All they care about is the free food you're obviously giving them. The thought of those dangerous men in here alone with you and Sunny makes me physically ill."

"Then stop thinking about it, because we had a great time." Alabama crossed her arms across her chest and grunted.

"The children shouldn't be around them either," Sara added.

Doug walked into the living room, passing his mother and his grandmother without slowing down. "I'm unloading the car, Mom."

Alison, following her brother, stopped in front of her mother. "Mom, I have lots of homework. Can't Doug handle it by himself?"

Alabama, who saw that Sunny had stopped in the hallway, figured her friend was probably afraid to get caught up in the middle of the fray.

Sara turned her attention from Alabama to her daughter. "Alison, it's Friday. You have the whole weekend to do homework. Go help your brother."

"Manual labor is degrading," Alison replied, rolling her eyes.

Sara jumped to her feet, pointed at the kitchen door, and shouted, "Go!"

Alison scowled and dropped her shoulders. "It's humiliating drudge work."

"Don't push me, Alison," Sara shouted. "How humiliating will it be if I ground you for the entire weekend? No cell phone, no computer, no tablet, no TV?"

Alison stomped her foot. "That's spiteful and mean!"

Alabama stood up, and reached out to Alison. "Come here, child, and let me give you a nice warm fuzzy." When Alison was a little girl and upset, Alabama could always cheer her up with a warm fuzzy — Alabama's name for a really big hug.

"Grandma, that doesn't work for me anymore." Then Alison trudged out of the living room, through the kitchen, and out the back door, slamming it as hard as she could.

After a few moments of silence, Sunny walked over to Sara. "You certainly missed out on a terrific afternoon. Balmy has the funniest friends."

Alabama shook her head at Sunny, hoping that would shut her up. It didn't.

"Did you know that Jake used to be in show business in the Sixties? He worked backstage with lighting. He's so bright and quite charming!" Sunny clapped her hands and laughed.

As Sara frowned, Alabama buried her face in her hands, and waited for the dam to burst.

"You won't believe this, Sara. Jake was friends with Mel Brooks. Can you imagine that? And Clarence dropped out of high school to join the circus. Would you believe he used to be a clown? Two great guys! It's hard to find folks like that outside of California."

Sara put her hands on her hips. "I've always heard that California is home to misfits and perverts. I guess they're right about that."

The backdoor slammed, again, and a disturbance sounded from the kitchen. "Mom," Doug yelled. "Alison isn't doing her share. I brought in two heavy bags of groceries, and she only brought in a jug of milk."

"Do you know how heavy one gallon of milk is?" Alison yelled back. "Did you want me to strain myself?"

Sara's entire body slumped. She banged her forehead with the heel of her hand and sighed. "Alison!" she shouted and trudged into the kitchen.

Sunny quietly sat down next to Alabama. "Are you okay, Balmy?"

Alabama sighed. Was she okay? She wasn't sure. "Just a little tired, Sunny."

Sunny nodded, leaned her head on Alabama's shoulder, and lowered her voice. "Listen, I'm going to slip outside and reply to this text."

As Sunny waved her iPhone in front of Alabama's face, she caught a whiff of Joy perfume. "Is he good-looking?"

"It's a she—Sally Fields."

Alabama sat up straight. Had she heard correctly? "The actress Sally Fields texted you? The same Sally Fields you met during the filming of *Smokey and the Bandit*?"

"Yes, we've kept in touch over the years. Such a nice person. She has plans to be in Savannah soon to visit friends." Sunny stood up. "I'm accepting her invitation—for both of us."

Alabama squealed. "I love Sally Fields! I read her memoir *In Pieces* last year. She's such a great and kind person." Alabama often felt jealous of Sunny's life in Hollywood, but then she remembered how much she loved her life in Georgia with Ray and raising their daughter. She had no regrets. "Do you think Sally will sign my copy of her book?"

"I think she would love to sign it," Sunny replied, heading out the front door.

As soon as the door shut behind Sunny, Alison came out of the kitchen looking upset. "Alison, sweetie, do you need some help?" Alabama asked.

"I need a new mother."

Sara's voice sounded from the kitchen. "Alison Webb! Get yourself right back in here, this instant!"

Alison turned around and disappeared into the kitchen.

Alabama slumped back into the sofa cushions. Was the Webb family falling apart today? Did she cause this negativity by inviting Jake and Clarence over to play Scrabble? Was there anything she could do to improve everyone's attitude? She was jolted out of her thoughts by Doug waving cookies in front of her face.

"Yoo-hoo, Grandma, you in there? Want a cookie?"

Caught off guard, Alabama jumped and waved her arms wildly. "Douglas Webb, don't sneak up on people. You scared the bejesus out of me."

"Sorry." He plopped down beside her. "You must have been in deep space." He stuffed half a cookie in his mouth.

"On the moon at the very least," she agreed, taking a deep breath to calm herself.

Doug handed his grandmother a cookie. Alabama accepted his offer, leaned back and tried to relax, but she couldn't. Every muscle in her body was tense. Something bad was coming. She could feel it in her very being.

"Something bothering you, Grandma?" Doug asked, his mouth full of cookie.

"Do I look bothered? Why do you ask?" She took another bite of her cookie. Not bad, she thought, savoring the taste of raisins, chocolate chips, and pecans mixed in with the oatmeal. Quite yummy, she decided. She was glad she'd baked them this morning for Jake and Clarence.

Doug gulped down his mouthful of cookie. "I don't know. You look unhappy. Like the time Dad got rid of the VHS player and you couldn't play your old Cary Grant tapes."

"Oh?" Was it that obvious she felt miserable?

He nodded. "Yeah, you haven't been yourself since Sunny showed up from California."

"Oh." Was that when things began to change for her?

"Want to talk about it?" He reached out and touched her arm.

"I don't have anything to talk about," Alabama blurted, marveling at her grandson's empathy and sympathy. Maybe he would grow up to be a counselor or a psychologist.

"Hmm. Well, if you're not in trouble, then maybe you have a friend who needs help?"

This put a smile on her lips. How many times had she used that same line of questioning to get Doug to talk about his troubles? "Let me see." She stroked her chin. "Now that you mention it, I do have this friend . . ."

Doug turned his head to look at her. "Yeah?"

"Her best friend wants her to do something. It's something that she wants to do."

"Yeah?"

"But my friend is afraid other people won't go along with what she wants to do." Alabama paused. Was that too straight forward?

"I see," Doug said. "Does your friend really, really want to do this thing? Or does she just want to please her best friend?"

Alabama twisted her mouth. Surely that wasn't the case, was it? No, definitely not. "I'm pretty sure my friend really, really wants to do this."

Doug wiped cookie crumbs off his mouth with the back of his hand, and then wiped his hand on his jeans. "Uh-huh. Would this thing really, really make her very, very happy?"

"Oh, yes," Alabama said with a nod. "It would, but it would make some other people very, very unhappy."

"Does your friend know about pros and cons?"

Alabama sighed. She was not having this conversation with her grandson. "Douglas, this is an important decision that would affect a number of lives. You don't understand the gravity of the situation."

Doug shook his head. "Are you saying my problems aren't important like your friend's?"

"Yes . . . No, Douglas. I'm saying this problem is different than whether or not you should go out for soccer."

Doug tilted his head and stared at his grandmother. "But Grandma, my problem is just as important to me, as your friend's problem is to her."

Alabama reached out and clasped Doug's hands. "You're right, and I'm sorry, if I minimized your own problems."

Alison stomped out of the kitchen with a scowl on her face. "Douglas Webb, if I strain any of my muscles or joints, you'll be sorry."

Doug looked blankly at his angry sister. "Why would I be sorry?"

"Because I will be in great pain in the ER, and you'll have to do the dishes every night all by yourself, that's why." Then Alison spun around and stomped into the kitchen.

Looking over his shoulder at the kitchen door, Doug asked, "Should I get up and help her?"

Alabama gently nudged Doug back on the sofa. "Trust me on this. She can do it. Besides, I thought you were helping me?"

"Oh yeah, that's right." He looked at Alabama thoughtfully. "Grandma, this friend you're talking about is really you, isn't it? And the best friend is Sunny, right?"

Alabama nodded. Doug was one smart boy. She was not surprised that he'd figured that out. "Yes, Douglas. That's correct."

He ran his fingers through his hair. "Does Sunny want you to go live in a cardboard box with Jake and Clarence?"

Startled at the question, Alabama let out a big belly laugh. "Heavens, no, child. What a preposterous idea!"

Doug looked visibly relieved. "Thank goodness, Grandma. Then you should write down the pros and cons just like you showed me. That will help you decide what to do."

Alabama gave Doug a big hug. "It's just not that simple."

"Why not? What does Sunny want you to do? Is it against the law? Can you be arrested?" He raised his eyebrows in question.

"Sunny wants me to move into the Villas at Kensington Grove with her." Alabama held her breath and waited for her grandson to react.

Doug frowned. "Move in with her? Move from our house to her house?"

Alabama nodded. "Yes. She has a large two-bedroom unit with a view of St. Simons and Jekyll Island."

Doug jumped to his feet. "Why would you want to do that, Grandma? Don't you like living here? We're your family."

Oh, bother, Alabama thought, studying her grandson's face. His anxiety-ridden reaction was not unexpected. She quickly considered her response to Doug. What could she say to make him understand? She reached for his hands, pulled him down beside her, and hugged him.

"It's like this, Doug. Many retired folks call the Villas their home. They get to do all sorts of fun things every day. They have art classes and exercise classes. They can play games like Scrabble and mahjong."

"What about computer games like Minecraft and Super Mario?" Doug interrupted her.

"I'm sure many residents play those games, too. But I'm talking about a special room for playing cards and board games," Alabama explained.

"Art, exercise, and board games, Grandma? That doesn't sound so great."

"How about special interest groups for everything from model trains to woodworking?" Alabama guessed that what seniors were interested in sounded dull to an 11-year-old boy.

"They have model trains there?" Doug looked excited. "What kind? HO or Lionel?"

"I'm not sure, but Sunny says there's a room full of model trains running through towns and tunnels and over bridges."

"That sounds interesting. What else?" Doug asked.

"They have mini-buses that take them to concerts, plays, and museums."

"Boring."

Alabama sighed. "Imagine being able to swim in an indoor, heated, Olympic-size swimming pool every day?"

"Now that sounds like fun. Better than going to the beach and getting eaten by a shark or stung by a jellyfish."

"Doug, the important thing is if I move in with Sunny, I won't be sitting alone in an empty house every day, while your parents go to work, and you and Alison are at school."

"But Grandma, you have Jake and Clarence to keep you company!"

Alabama reached out and rubbed his cheek. "Yes, but we know how your parents feel about that, don't we?"

Doug pulled away from his grandmother and scowled. "You know Mom won't let you do this, don't you?"

Alabama clenched her jaw. "Maybe I won't tell her."

"Even if you don't tell Mom, she'll find out sooner or later, and you know it. Are you going to run away in the middle of the night?"

Alabama nodded. That might not be such a bad idea, she thought, considering the possibility — but then there would be hell to pay.

Chapter Seven

Laughter sounded from the front porch as the door opened, and Richard and Sunny walked in from outside. "I'm home!" Richard called out. "Let the revelry begin!"

Doug ran over and gave his father a hug. "Hi, Dad."

Richard dropped his briefcase in the corner. "Hello, Douglas! Alabama, how was your day today?"

"Not too bad until late this afternoon when I was run over by a Mack truck and . . ."

Sunny sat down on the sofa next to Alabama. "Balmy Knight! How you do carry on!"

Richard smiled, shook his head, and sat down in his chair with the newspaper.

"Carry on, nothing." Alabama lowered her voice to a whisper. "Richard didn't hear a word I said. No one listens to me."

A frowning and annoyed Alison stomped out of the kitchen and dropped a stack of plates on the table with a thud. "I don't know why Doug can't set the table. It's always Alison do this and Alison do that. Poor baby Doug can't do anything."

"Alison, please!" Sara shouted from the kitchen. "Just set the table."

"Watch this," Alabama whispered to Sunny. "Alison, that's a lovely shirt. Is it new?"

Alison, ignoring Alabama, glanced at her father. "Dad, is it all right if I spend the weekend with Tina?"

Richard looked up from his newspaper. "Ask your mother."

"I already did. She said to ask you." Alison plopped down dinner plates around the table.

Alabama elbowed Sunny. "Alison, I have this lovely brooch that belonged to my mother that will go magnificently with your shirt. Would you like to see it?"

"Well, Dad? Is it all right with you?" Alison asked.

Sunny elbowed Alabama back. "All right, Balmy, you've made your point."

Richard looked at Sunny and then at Alabama. "Answer your grandmother, Alison. She asked you a question."

"Okay, but can I go to Tina's?"

Sara stood in the kitchen door. "How about you answer your grandmother, first?"

"It's all right, Sara. Grandmothers are like pieces of furniture. Easy to ignore," Alabama said.

Sunny elbowed Alabama and whispered. "That's so not true, Balmy. Sounds like sour grapes to me."

Alison motioned to her grandmother. "See, she didn't expect an answer."

"Richard, you handle this. I have to check on dinner." Sara walked back into the kitchen.

Richard folded up the newspaper. "Alison, adults deserve respect. Your grandmother is an adult, and if you can't speak to her courteously, then you absolutely cannot go to Tina's."

"Well," said Alison, stomping her foot. "I think I should get respect, too. All I get is ordered around like the hired help. Bring in the groceries, Alison. Set the table. Wash the dishes. Vacuum the rug. Dust the furniture. Child labor is against the law or haven't you heard?"

"That's it, young lady!" Richard jumped to his feet and pointed his finger at Alison. "Go to your room," he shouted. He took a deep breath and spoke softer. "But first, apologize to your grandmother for your rudeness."

Alison put her hands on her hips. "I wasn't being rude!"

"Richard, please, it's alright," Alabama said.

"Balmy!" Sunny exclaimed.

"It's not alright, Alabama," Richard said. "Alison?"

Alison turned abruptly and headed out of the living room, calling out over her shoulder, "Excuse my rudeness."

"I'm sorry you had to witness that Sunny," Richard said. "I don't know what's gotten into her."

Alabama raised an eyebrow. "Puberty. I heard that God makes teenagers act ugly so their parents will be glad to see them move out on their own."

Richard smiled. "You know, Alabama, there just might be some truth in that."

"Truth in what?" asked Sara, walking out of the kitchen and placing glasses on the table. "What was all the shouting going on in here?"

"Alison was talking ugly and mean, again," Doug reported.

Richard held up his hand like a traffic cop. "Stop it right there, Doug. That's enough." He looked at his wife. "Alison was being extremely rude to everyone. I'm sure I was never a problem to my parents when I was a teenager. She must get it from your side of the family."

Sara nodded her head. "Yes, of course. Right along with overall stupidity, $2,000 overbites, the inclination to hate mushrooms, and size 11 feet?"

Richard returned to his seat, and opened his paper. "Of course."

Doug cocked his head in thought. "Did I inherit my wimpiness from you or Mom?"

Richard rustled his newspaper loudly. "As someone who's grounded for punching another person in the mouth, aren't you pushing your luck?" He brought the newspaper closer to his face and concentrated. "Sara, are we having a garage sale in the morning?"

Sara walked out of the kitchen and sat on the sofa. "Richard, don't be silly. How could we have a garage sale and go out of town?"

Sunny tugged Alabama to her feet. "Let's go for a walk before dinner."

"I think I'll go with you." Doug slowly sidestepped out the front door behind Sunny and Alabama.

"Don't shut the door," Alabama whispered. "We need to hear about the garage sale." Sunny, Alabama, and Doug pressed against the cracked door and listened. When she purchased the ad, Alabama hadn't realized that Richard read the want ads.

Richard took a closer look at the newspaper. "I don't understand. It's a notice in the WANT ADS section. That is certainly our address."

"Most likely a typo," Sara said. "They printed the wrong house number by mistake. It's probably the Crawfords. They're always having a garage sale."

"Is it possible your mother is having a garage sale?" Richard asked. "Doug, do you know anything about this?" He looked at the sofa where Doug had been sitting. "Doug?"

Doug backed away from the cracked front door and held both hands over his mouth.

Alabama frowned at Doug and held her finger to her lips. "Shh!" Then she turned back to Sunny to listen to Sara and Richard's conversation.

Sara rubbed the back of her neck. "Mother wouldn't have a garage sale while we weren't at home, would she?"

"She certainly didn't ask us if she could have one, and this is our house," replied Richard.

"I don't know, Richard. That doesn't sound like Mother, at all."

"I beg to differ with you," Richard said. "When she and Sunny get together, Alabama does some really crazy things."

"What do you mean?"

"You haven't noticed, Sara? She doesn't act her age."

"What are you talking about, Richard?"

"She goes off half-cocked and does stupid things without checking with us."

Sara stood up. "First of all, Richard Webb, Mother does not go off half-cocked. And secondly, do you ever consult with her when you want to do something? Her money did help buy this house we're living in, remember?"

"Point taken."

"You're the one who keeps complaining about how her belongings have filled up the garage and how you can't get your car in it." Sara walked over to Richard and pulled the newspaper out of his hands. "Have you considered that she might be getting rid of everything to make you happy? Or maybe she wants money to buy Christmas presents?"

"Personally, I think she's getting senile," Richard said, as Sunny, Doug, and Alabama continued to listen through the cracked front door.

"Mother is certainly not senile!" Sara yelled.

"What about all the stupid stuff she does when we aren't home?"

Sara threw her arms up in the air. "Like asking the neighbors when they plan to cut their grass and fix their front steps?"

"Yeah."

"And inviting the mailman in for tea?"

"Yeah, stupid stuff like that." Richard stood and looked down at his wife.

"Richard Webb! People refer to that as eccentricity."

Richard shook his head. "Whatever you call it, half the time she can't remember if she's coming or going."

"Well, let's see how your memory compares with hers in thirty years," Sara yelled.

"What about her attachment to those scroungy, homeless, old men? She invites them into our home and feeds them breakfast," he pointed out.

Sara's shoulders sagged. Her voice became softer. "Okay, I agree with you. That makes me nervous. I don't like it, but she does enjoy their visits."

"Don't forget how she mumbles a lot under her breath, and I bet it's nothing nice," he reminded her.

"So, she mumbles under her breath? A lot of what she mumbles is the truth."

"If it's the truth," Richard said, "why can't she say it to my face?"

"For the same reason your father never told me to my face that I'm irresponsible for working, instead of being a stay-at-home mom."

Richard turned away in disgust. "So? He keeps his opinions to himself."

Sara jumped to her feet. "At least Mother doesn't drink or get obnoxious or smoke stinky cigars or talk ugly to guests."

"Ah, come on," Richard said, turning back to her with a scowl on his face. "It was Gertie Filmore's fault for egging him on after Florida beat Georgia. She's a sore winner, and my father's always been a sore loser. Besides, you know Dad was a little snockered at the time. He didn't remember anything he said the next day."

"So _he_ claimed." Sara paused. "My point is, Richard, Mother doesn't act any stranger or more eccentric than your father."

"But Dad doesn't live with us."

"That's right, because if he did, I wouldn't!"

They both stood in silence, glaring at each other. Finally, Richard broke the silence. "Have you thought about the future? What if she has another stroke and ends up a vegetable? What if she comes down with Alzheimer's?"

"Mother's health is fine," Sara insisted.

"That's not what she says when I ask her how she's feeling."

Sara smiled and shook her head. "Richard, Richard, Richard. That's just Mother. She does it for attention and to needle you. It obviously works."

Richard sat back down in his chair. "Before it's too late, we should start investigating assisted living places or nursing homes."

Alabama slapped her hand over her mouth to muffle her gasp. Sunny quickly pulled Doug and Alabama around the corner of the front porch.

"What was that noise?" Richard asked, pushing open the front door and looking outside. He grunted. "I don't see anything."

Sara joined Richard standing at the open door. "You're lucky Mother didn't hear you. You talk like she's a burden. She isn't. She's my mother, and I won't let you throw her into a nursing home because she grumbles and mumbles, and cuts holes in your morning paper."

Richard grimaced. "You're right, Sara. I apologize for bringing it up. I didn't realize you felt so strongly about it."

"Apology accepted," Sara said. "Tell me Richard, have you ever been inside a nursing home?"

"Only once. To visit my grandmother. It was terrible. She shared a small room with two other women. The entire building smelled like stale urine. I couldn't wait to leave."

Sara lifted her chin and raised her brows. "Then not a place where you'd be willing to live?"

"Absolutely not."

"Yet you'd put my mother in one?"

Richard spluttered. "Jumpin' Jehoshaphat, Sara! She won't be in good health forever. We need to think about the future."

"That's it, Richard Webb. This conversation is over. There will be no further discussion." Sara stomped back into the living room, followed by Richard, who slammed the front door behind him.

Alabama let out the breath she did not realize she'd been holding. Doug slipped out of his grandmother's tight grip. Sunny, who had been squished into the corner, gasped for air. It was obvious to Alabama now—after listening to the heated conversation—that Richard would be her staunchest ally when she told them she was moving in with Sunny. Even though Richard's comments hurt her feelings to some extent, she knew she had only herself to blame for that. But it was so much fun to annoy him.

Later that evening, after a take-out pizza dinner, Sara and Richard left for their weekend getaway. On their way out of town, they dropped Alison at Tina's house—making sure her parents planned to be home for the weekend.

Sunny decided to spend Friday night with Alabama instead of driving back to the Villas and returning Saturday morning for the garage sale. The two women spent the evening marking items without interference from Doug, who watched an old Spiderman movie. Armed with black Sharpies, sticky labels, a notebook, and a pen, the two best friends stood silently in the door to the garage and surveyed Alabama's belongings that filled every inch of space. Belongings that she couldn't bear to part with when Sara and Richard moved her out of the home she had shared with Ray. A home where she had raised a daughter and enjoyed a good life. Yet here she was, ready to dispose of all those memories and move on.

Sunny hugged her friend. "I know exactly what you're feeling," she said softly in Alabama's ear. "Because I went through it in California before moving to Georgia."

"How did you manage to do it all by yourself, Sunny?"

"Since I bought all new furniture, dishes, and cooking ware in Savannah, I only had to deal with clothes, accessories, and mementos," Sunny said. "It's the mementos that are the hardest to part with."

"What stuff did you keep?" Alabama asked, picking up a red boa she'd worn in a musical production on off-Broadway. The name of the show escaped her. It had terrible reviews and ran for only a few weeks before closing. She'd held onto it all these years because Ray thought she looked sexy wearing it in bed with nothing else on.

Sunny smiled and laughed. "This will sound silly . . ." Alabama raised a questioning eyebrow. "Playbills from my favorite musicals you and I performed in."

"Let me guess . . ." Alabama sucked in her bottom lip. "*South Pacific?*" Sunny nodded. "*Oklahoma?*"

Sunny nodded, again. "Also, *The Sound of Music* and *The Music Man*. They are signed by cast members, too. I also kept photo albums, but ended up throwing out lots of scrapbooks."

"Oh no! Why?"

"Mainly because the pages were turning brittle and the corsages I had pressed between the pages had rotted and molded. The scrapbooks were mostly full of napkins, menus, tickets, and sugar packets." Sunny squeezed Alabama's hand. "But it was time to let go and move on."

"Brace yourself, Sunny!" Alabama stepped into the garage and grabbed a pink princess phone. "I'm ready to move on." She wrote $1 on a label and stuck it on the receiver.

Chapter Eight

Alabama felt her spirits lift when Jake and Clarence knocked on the kitchen door around 6:30 a.m. She yanked open the door and grabbed Jake's hand. "Are we glad to see you two! Your help will make today easier for us."

Jake and Clarence went right to work. They cranked open the garage door and started dragging folding tables and chairs outside. As soon as the tables and chairs were set up, Sunny and Alabama arranged jewelry, hats, purses, and small items on the tables, while the men hauled out boxes and furniture. Already, Alabama could see folks pulling up to the curb, but whenever anyone opened their car door, Jake would shout out, "Sorry, we don't open 'til 7:30."

Huffing and puffing, Jake and Clarence carefully carried out a small, mahogany china cabinet. Meanwhile, Alabama and Sunny worked together to slide a huge cardboard box—labeled FREE STUFF—to the end of the driveway and invited everyone waiting for the sale to begin to help themselves. The box was filled with everything Alabama and Sunny deemed not worth the trouble of a price tag. Items included mismatched china cups and saucers, old hardback books, odd pieces of silverware, oddball clothing accessories, and cheesy Florida souvenirs.

Ready or not, by 7:30 a.m., impatient and hungry-for-bargains early birds dashed down the driveway and pounced. They wanted to purchase the best of everything before moving on to the next garage sale. By 8:15 a.m., the initial surge was over, Alabama was hundreds of dollars richer, and several big-ticket items—a guest bedroom suite, a like-new hide-a-bed sofa, a well-worn Persian carpet from Tunisia, and Ray's prized chainsaw—had been carted off.

Around 8:30 a.m., Doug ran out the door to leave for soccer tryouts. "Bye, Grandma! See you later!"

Alabama, seated at a table with the cash box, looked up and waved. "Good luck, Doug!"

Doug strapped on his flaming-red bike helmet, hopped on his black cyclocross bike, and started pedaling down the driveway.

"Hey, buddy, I saw that bike first." A bearded, bald-headed man — seriously on the edge of obesity — chased Doug down and grabbed the handlebars. "I'm buying that bike, so get your greedy paws off it."

"Grandma!" Doug yelled, as the man tried to pull him off the bike.

Alabama left her chair and reached her grandson just as he fell butt-down onto the concrete. She quickly pulled Doug to his feet. "What's going on here?" Hands on hips, she stared up at the man, who towered above her by at least a foot.

Still gripping the handlebars, the man glared at Alabama. "This little brat tried to ride off with my bike."

"Your bike?" Alabama put on her meanest old woman face and stretched as tall as she could. She wished now she hadn't sold that cast iron skillet. It would have made a good weapon.

"Well, I haven't paid for it yet, but I looked at it first — before the kid grabbed it. So, it's mine. How much are you asking for it?" He picked the bike up off the ground like it weighed five pounds and stared at Alabama threateningly.

"It's not for sale," Alabama said as calmly as she could, even though her knees were starting to shake and her heart was pounding. "That's my grandson's bike." Behind the scary man, she watched Jake pull a wooden mallet out of Ray's old toolbox and heft it in his hand.

The man grunted. "I'll give you $100, but I doubt it's worth that."

"She said it wasn't for sale," said Jake, looking up at the boorish man who was several inches taller and at least 100 pounds heavier than him. Jake pulled the mallet out from behind his back, squared his jaw, and smacked the mallet into his left hand.

Alabama's eyes widened and her chest tightened. This was a part of Jake she'd not seen before. He looked very fierce and so brave. She felt like a damsel in distress being rescued by her prince.

The man's eyes narrowed as he seemed to consider his options. "Fine," he yelled, slamming the bike down. "It's a crappy excuse for a bike. I didn't want it anyway." He lumbered to the street and got into an enormous honking-red testosterone truck. With tires squealing, he sped off

"Another case of sour grapes," whispered Sunny into Alabama's ear.

Trembling and shaking from her clash with the bearded man, Alabama headed back to her chair and collapsed. Jake and Sunny followed closely behind her.

"Balmy, are you alright?" Jake asked.

Alabama waved her hand. "I'll be okay. Just give me a minute." Maybe in a minute, she thought, her heart rate would slow down. She took deep breaths and coughed. Her doctor told her to do that when her heart raced. It seemed to work, only she didn't know why.

Sunny grabbed her wrist. "Did that hateful man scare you?"

Alabama nodded and coughed, again. "I think some water will help."

Jake immediately sat down next to Alabama and reached for her hand. "Sunny, I have this. Please get Balmy a glass of water." Sunny power-walked into the house, and Jake turned his attention to Alabama. "Take slow, deep breaths and try to relax." He squeezed her hand and gently rubbed his thumb back and forth across the back of her hand. "That man is gone. He isn't coming back."

"What if he does?" Alabama asked softly, enjoying the handholding, which was calming her down. But on another level, she felt herself getting excited. Something she hadn't felt, since Ray was alive.

Jake reached underneath the table and brought out the wooden mallet. He hit the palm of his hand with the mallet and scowled.

"Oh, Jake, you'll have to do better than that to scare that brute off."

Jake straightened up in his chair – growling, making an ugly face, and flexing his muscles. Alabama burst out laughing. She felt her heart soar. "I think that's it. That man would run even if you didn't threaten him with your mallet. What a ferocious face!"

Sunny set down a glass of water in front of Alabama. "Drink it. You'll feel better." She paused and looked at her friend's face. "I see some color returning. I think you're going to live after all."

"Jake, I found something for you." Clarence ran up to the table sporting a long Cleopatra wig and a golden serpent wrapped about his head. He handed Jake a crushed, dark-brown, faux-leather fedora.

Jake ran one hand inside and outside the hat, straightening out the brim, and trying to improve its sad appearance. Finally, he put it on his head.

Alabama did a double-take and her heart beat quickened. Jake remarkably resembled Harrison Ford in the old Indiana Jones movies. But Indiana Jones with long hair and a beard. How she did love Harrison Ford!

"Did I hear you say something about Alabama being in danger?" Clarence asked.

"No, no, no," said Sunny, grabbing Clarence by the elbow and steering him in the direction of the wig, hat, gloves, and purses table. "Balmy's fine, so why don't we check out this Carmen Miranda hat with the fruit on top. I think you'll really love it."

"Thank you for getting rid of that man, Jake. You were so brave," Alabama told him. "You even scared me. Were you ever in the military?" She was still trying to learn how he'd ended up homeless. She'd read statistics on the number of men who leave the military and are unable to return home to a normal life. Could that be what happened to Jake?

At first, Jake didn't say anything. He just squeezed the mallet handle until his knuckles turned white. Alabama suspected he was trying to decide if he wanted to tell her or not. He never wanted to share anything about his personal life. Could he be a serial killer on the run?

Jake cleared his throat. "Yes, I served in the Navy during Vietnam. I was a cryptographer."

Alabama shrugged. "I don't know what a cryptographer is."

Jake rubbed the back of his neck and fingered a musical-theater-themed charm bracelet in the jewelry pile. He rolled the charms between his thumb and forefinger thoughtfully, as though considering his response. "Let's just say I was a spy of sorts. I listened to communications coming from Russian ships and airplanes, and reported anything suspicious."

Startled, Alabama asked the first question that popped into her mind. "Was it dangerous?"

"Not as long as I was listening from a safe spot on the ground." He paused. "But some cryptographers did the same job from spy planes and spy ships. In 1969, just months after I arrived for duty in Japan, men I worked with were killed when their EC-121 was shot down by the Koreans. Then I heard stories about men on the USS Pueblo spy ship captured by the Koreans in 1968. They were tortured and held in prison for a year." He paused. "They weren't the same when they returned home."

Alabama let out a breath she didm't realize she'd been holding. "Holy moly! So, when you left the military, you didn't want to go home? You've been living homeless all these years?"

Jake tossed the bracelet onto the table and stood. "No—" He shook his head. "I'm sorry, Balmy, but I'm not comfortable talking about this." He strode off to talk to two men rummaging through Ray's tool box.

Alabama touched her hand to her mouth and watched Jake hand the mallet to one of the men.

"What was that all about?" Sunny asked, sitting down in the seat vacated by Jake. "I could tell it was an intense conversation."

"I think Jake is not a touchy-feely kind of guy," Alabama said thoughtfully. "He's a private kind of person, yet he shared something personal with me—and now he's regretting it." Which only makes me want to know more about him, she realized. A whole lot more.

Chapter Nine

By 2 o'clock hardly anyone was dropping by to paw through what was left in the driveway. Alabama officially declared the garage sale over. Sunny seconded the motion. Jake and Clarence folded up the tables and chairs, and put them away. Remnants of the sale were carried, shoved, pushed, or kicked back into the garage, and the rolling door was pulled down.

Alabama checked the time on her Tigger watch. Goodwill was scheduled to haul away what was left in an hour or two. She figured their truck would be making a lot of post-garage-sales stops before it pulled into the Webb driveway. In the meantime, Clarence and Jake walked around the neighborhood to remove the garage sale signs they'd put up. With the money box tucked under her arm, Alabama took one last look around the yard and driveway to make sure all evidence of a garage sale was gone. *Perfect.*

Inside the kitchen, Alabama prepared fresh-squeezed lemonade and homemade oatmeal cookies to serve to her workers. She had offered to pay Jake and Clarence for their time, but Jake said "absolutely not" and slapped Clarence's hand when he held it out. When Alabama told them to take anything they wanted from the unsold items, Jake said he wanted nothing. Clarence, however, picked out a white-straw hat and a Groucho Marx disguise, and added that to a red boa already hanging around his neck. He insisted on wearing both the straw hat and the Groucho Marx disguise.

Collapsing on the sofa later — with an exhausted Sunny — Alabama smiled and shook her head at Clarence and Jake. The two men sat at the table, busily pulling out bills and coins from the money box, and carefully counting it. Alabama and Sunny had marked down every item sold and the amount paid. Hopefully, the amount of cash and checks in the box—less Sunny's change contribution—plus a few credit card sales, would come close to matching the final tally on the written list.

"If we collected at least $1,000, I'll call it a success," Alabama said, collapsing on the sofa. "I'm bushed."

"I feel like we just danced and sang all the way to Savannah," Sunny said, half reclining back into a sofa pillow. "I didn't know garage sales could wear you out this much."

"Neither did I." Alabama closed her eyes. "I haven't been this tired since the Christmas we performed at all those military bases in Virginia."

Sunny sighed. "Yes, I remember that Christmas. I can still picture those guys now—dressed in their uniforms, sitting in front of the stage."

"And every time they let out a wolf whistle, Ray and Jeff just died."

Sunny jumped to her feet. "I'm Sunny . . ."

Groaning, Alabama stood up. "I'm Balmy . . ."

"We're here to entertain you . . ." Sunny and Alabama chorused.

"Is that the only song you know?" Clarence asked.

"More likely, the only song they remember," Jake said with a laugh.

Sunny pouted and stomped her foot. "That just happens to be the song that always opened our act."

"Yeah," Alabama said. "We remember lots of songs."

"I'd love to hear one," Clarence said.

Alabama bent over, hands on her knees. "We're too tired to perform."

"Yep," Jake said, not looking up as he counted a pile of dollar bills out on the table. "Old age just wipes out the memory banks."

Sunny grabbed Alabama's hand. "Come on, Balmy. Let's show 'em we haven't lost it yet." She began swaying and singing "Put on a Happy Face" from the musical *Bye Bye Birdie*. She paused singing and yanked Alabama's hand. "Balmy, you're not singing."

"I never liked that song," Balmy complained.

"Fine. I forgot. You choose one then."

Alabama chewed on her bottom lip and thought. What were her favorite songs. She tried hard to remember. That was so long ago. She glanced at Jake, who nodded at her and smiled. Her heart and mind seemed to come alive. She squeezed Sunny's hand. "How about this one?" She started singing lyrics from "Try to Remember."

"Now you're talking," Sunny said, and joined her in singing the popular song from *The Fantasticks*.

Jake and Clarence jumped to their feet, applauding, cheering, and whistling. "More, more!" the men insisted.

Sunny and Alabama sang the entire song before falling back onto the sofa. "Forget that," Sunny said. "I don't see you two singing along."

Clarence sat down with a thud. "Not me, I'm plumb tuckered out."

Jake sat back down. "We need to rest up before Goodwill shows up. It should be soon."

Clarence looked behind Jake's chair and picked up a nicely carved wooden sword. "Is this yours, Jake?" Jake nodded. "It sure is a really nice sword, Jake." He ran his hand up and down the sides. "I tell you what, Jake, I'll give you my hat and my disguise and my boa for it."

"No," Jake said, snatching the sword back from Clarence. "No way. I paid $2 for that."

"It was worth every penny, too," Clarence said.

Alabama raised an eyebrow. "Clarence, did you see a little boy buy that boa?"

Clarence looked down at his hands. "Yes, ma'am, I did."

"Clarence, you didn't?" Sunny blurted.

"I did not steal this boa from him, Miz Sunny. I promise. We traded."

"And what did you give him as a trade?" Alabama asked.

"Uh . . . 28 cents, a Howdy Doody ring, and an Elvis Presley bubble gum card."

"That was your own personal stuff?" Jake asked.

"Of course, it was, Jake. It was stuff I found in the park." Sunny and Alabama laughed. "What's so funny?" Clarence asked.

Alabama stopped laughing. "Oh, Clarence, I sold him that boa for 10 cents."

Jake stood up and waved his arms for attention. "Everyone, listen up, please. I have the grand total here. Drum roll, please." He banged his fists on the table and handed Alabama the money box. "Two-thousand, two-hundred, thirty-six dollars and fifty cents."

"Holy crapola!" exclaimed Clarence.

"I'm surprised we made that much money," Sunny said.

"Me, too!" Fighting off an impulse to give Jake a hug, Alabama accepted the money. "Thanks, Jake. I'll put this with what I've squirreled away. Things are looking good."

Sunny reached around the sofa for her overnight bag. "On that high note, I will bid everyone adieu and head back to the Villas. I promised Eula Mae I'd join her for dinner. It's SeaFest Night with Florida lobster, Georgia blue crab, and fried Gulf shrimp. Plus make-your-own sundae for dessert."

Alabama gave Sunny the tightest hug she could. "Thanks for your help, Sunny. I hope one day I'll be able to enjoy SeaFest Night with you and Eula Mae."

With their arms entwined, the two best friends forever headed for the front door, but froze in mid-step when Alison ran out of the kitchen screaming. "Help! We've been robbed! Call the police!"

Chapter Ten

"What?" Jake said, running towards Alison, followed by Alabama, Sunny, and Clarence.

Alison screamed and grabbed Alabama. "Grandma, they're still here!"

"What on Earth are you talking about, child?" Alabama asked.

Alison hid behind her grandmother and pointed at Jake and Clarence. "Mom warned you about them, Grandma. They stole everything out of the garage, and now they're going to kill us!"

Alabama wrapped her arms around Alison, who was shaking and tightly gripping her grandmother. "Alison, it's alright. Nobody stole anything. I had a garage sale today and sold my stuff that was stored in the garage. Since your brother had soccer tryouts, Jake, Clarence, and Sunny offered to help." Alabama caressed Alison's face and smiled. "You actually sound like the kind, concerned granddaughter I used to know."

Alison pushed back from Alabama. "Excuse me for caring." She glared at everyone and stomped off toward her room.

"Well, if the drama is over," Sunny said, hugging Alabama one more time, "I'm leaving."

As Alabama opened the front door, Doug pushed past her and Sunny. "I'm back!"

"And I'm gone," Sunny said, closing the door behind her.

Alabama hugged Doug. "Did you make the soccer team?"

"Yes, I did."

Alabama led him past Jake and Clarence to the sofa. "Did Horace make the soccer team, too?"

"Mmm, yeah, he did."

"That's great! Sit down and have some lemonade and cookies." Alabama poured lemonade into a glass and handed it to Doug with a cookie. "When is your first game? I know the entire family will want to be there."

"Don't bother. The coach is mad at me and Horace, so we won't be allowed to play." Doug took a bite of his cookie, sipped his lemonade, and stared at Jake and Clarence.

"Not another fight?" Alabama asked.

"More like a shouting match. Horace said you keep company with dangerous homeless men who're stealing our stuff and might start stealing everybody else's stuff soon."

"That's preposterous!" Jake yelled. "Clarence and I have never stolen anything from anybody."

Clarence tugged on Jake's sleeve. "Uh . . . Jake, I did eat my sister's Christmas chocolate once and got a terrible whupping for it."

"That doesn't count, Clarence."

Alabama couldn't believe what she'd just heard. Were there actually neighbors who believed this?

Doug walked briskly toward the money box on the table. "I bet the garage sale money is gone." He flipped open the lid and dumped the contents on the table. Doug's eyes widened in surprise. "That's a lot of money."

Jake handed the list of items sold at the garage sale to Doug. "Here, kid. Count the money. Check the list and tell me how much money we stole."

Doug shook his head and waved the list away. He slowly returned the cash to the box. "I'm sorry, Jake. It was wrong of me to believe what Horace said. Especially after how you stopped that mean man from stealing my bike."

Jake moved over next to Doug and squeezed his shoulder. "It's all right, kid. Horace is a bully who uses untruths to try and destroy folks who intimidate him. You shouldn't believe everything you hear or read. Be objective. Be a fact-checker."

Alabama stared at Jake. Her heart quickened. He had surprised her, again. There was more to him than she thought possible. She decided she needed to talk to him more about his past life and how he'd ended up living in a cardboard box under a bush.

"Balmy, I think Clarence and I will head out before anyone else shows up." He nudged Clarence toward the front door.

Alabama followed them. "Thanks for your help, fellows. Have a good evening." She shut the door and turned to face Doug. "I think I'll go to my room and lie down. If the Goodwill truck arrives, will you please raise the garage door and show them what to pick up?"

"Sure, Grandma. Is it okay if I have more lemonade and another cookie?" He was already pouring lemonade into his glass before Alabama could answer.

She laughed. "Doug, you may finish off the lemonade and the cookies." She yawned and headed toward her room.

Doug settled on the sofa with his drink and cookies, and turned on the TV. He was switching channels from golf to hunting pythons in the Everglades when the back door slammed and he heard his dad yelling in the kitchen. "I can't believe it! The whole garage has been cleaned out!"

An agitated Sara walked into the living room. "What happened to everything that was in the garage, Doug?"

Doug switched off the TV, stood, and stretched. "Hi, Mom. Dad. You're home early. I just got in from soccer tryouts myself." He started trotting toward the hallway door. "I think I'll go to my room and rest up."

"Douglas Webb, you stop right there, young man. Did your grandmother have a garage sale this morning?"

"Dad, I wasn't here. Soccer tryouts, remember?"

"Is the Salvation Army picking up what she didn't sell?" Richard asked.

"No, Dad, Goodwill. Uh-oh." Doug covered his mouth with both hands.

"Thank you, Doug. You may go to your room now," Sara said.

Doug hesitated. "Hey, I made the soccer team."

"That's nice, Doug," Sara said and sat on the sofa.

"Yes, Doug, that's absolutely great news," Richard said.

"I don't understand why she had to have a garage sale?" Sara mumbled.

"I'm not complaining. We now have room for our cars in the garage." Richard grinned. "Isn't that the best news?"

"By the way, Alison might not be here for dinner tonight," Doug said casually.

Sara didn't glance at Doug. "Thanks, Doug." She sighed and looked at Richard. "I guess we'll have to talk to Mother about this."

"What's this 'we' stuff? She's your mother, not mine," Richard said.

"For your information, Alison won't be home for dinner because she's eloping with Tiger Tim, the punk rocker," Doug said, matter-of-factly

"All right, Doug, thank you for telling us," Sara said. "Richard, I'm not talking to Mother alone."

Doug shrugged, sighed, and took a step toward the hallway door.

Sara and Richard jumped to their feet. "Punk rocker? Douglas?" Sara shouted.

"Just kidding. I wanted to see if you were listening to me." Doug turned and disappeared down the hall.

A truck horn sounded out front. Doug ran past his parents and out the door. Before Sara and Richard could take one step, Doug had raised the garage door for the Goodwill workers to haul off what was left of the garage sale. "My grandma says to take it all!"

Chapter Eleven

Alabama stood on the front porch and watched four men hauling leftover items from the garage sale out to the Goodwill truck. Sara and Richard stood next to the open garage and watched.

"You should be happy now, Richard," said Sara, her arms crossed in front. "There will be plenty of space for our cars."

Richard smiled and nodded. "That's true." His eyes widened. "Hey, that looks like my old fishing boots." Richard stopped the man carrying the boots and snatched them from his hands.

Sara looked at the boots. "My gosh, Richard. Let the man haul them away. There are more holes than rubber. Water would seep in everywhere. Why would you want to keep them?"

Richard looked at his wife in disbelief. He spluttered the obvious, "Because they're mine!" He elbowed Sara. "My heart won't break to see that disgusting lamp with the cupids and hearts leave here."

"What?!" Sara looked around to locate the lamp. "Not the one Aunt Edna left me in her will?" She spotted the man carrying it and ran after him.

Alabama leaned back against the front door and shook her head. "Guess I better go straighten out this mess," she muttered and headed toward a man with a clipboard in his hand. Since he wasn't doing anything but watching, he was obviously the man in charge. Screams from the garage stopped her in her tracks.

"Grandma! Help!"

Alabama turned to see a worker pushing Doug's bike toward the truck with Doug desperately trying to take the bike back. Alabama and the clipboard guy ran over to referee, just as Richard yelled, "Oh no you don't. That's my stuffed Tasmanian Devil and you aren't taking it."

"Sir," Alabama touched the clip board, "Please, you're only supposed to take the stuff leftover from the garage sale." She indicated several boxes and larger items on the concrete floor. "My grandson's bike, the lawnmower, the rake, hoe, shovel, power tools, and everything on the shelves and hanging on the walls stay here."

The man-in-charge nodded. "Yes, ma'am. I'll explain it to my men."

Alison grabbed Alabama's arm. "I don't know what's going on, but Dad is in the back of that truck, fighting with some man over an ugly stuffed thing, and Mom is egging him on. Parents are so weird."

"Richard, just give the man five bucks for it, and get out of the truck," Sara yelled.

"I'd say that's the pot calling the kettle black," Alabama said to Alison.

"If that's your way of saying I'm weird, I'm not weird!"

Alabama raised her eyebrow. "Purple hair, kohl-lined eyes, and five holes in each ear lobe isn't weird?"

"No, Grandma, it's just different, that's all."

Alabama smiled and nodded. "I see. You're merely trying to make a statement, right?"

"I guess so. Maybe."

Alabama gave her granddaughter a knowing look. "Like what?"

Alison shrugged. "Like everyone treats me like a child, and no one understands how I feel. I'm showing my individuality."

"Alison, my dear child," Alabama said, placing her hand on her granddaughter's shoulder. "Both of your parents were teenagers once."

"Hmph. You'd never know it."

"They remember being teenagers, trust me," Alabama said. "I even remember being a teenager."

Alison looked surprised. "Really? Your memory goes that far back?" She paused. "Oh. Sorry." Another pause. "What is something you remember about being a teenager?"

Alabama sucked her lower lip. "Well, let me jog my old memory banks. I guess my best memory would be me and Sunny running away to New York City."

"No, your parents wouldn't have let you do that." Pause. "Really? I mean, that's pretty cool. I knew you and Sunny performed on stage in New York, but I did not know you ran away from home. Were your parents mad you did that? Weren't they scared something bad might happen to you?"

Behind her, Alabama heard Richard talking loudly to Sara. "Come on, Sara. Let them have the bird cage and the fish tank. We're never ever going to buy another parakeet or a goldfish."

"You can bet your bottom dollar on that, Alison," Alabama said. "They were very worried that I wasn't going to stay in Savannah, marry a hometown boy, and procreate for them. But once they heard Sunny and I were rooming at the Y and working at decent jobs, they felt better."

"I thought you and Sunny sang and danced on Broadway?"

Alabama sighed. "Eventually, but it took a long time, hard work, and persistence to break in. One day, before I leave, I'll tell you what your mother was like as a teenager."

"Mom always says she was never a problem teenager." Alison looked hopeful. "Was she pure trouble? Wait . . . Leave? What do you mean? Are you going somewhere?"

Rubbing the back of her neck, Alabama wanted to slap herself for her slip of the tongue. "Sunny wants me to move to the Villas and live with her."

"Did Mom say that's okay with her?" Alison looked at her grandmother's placid face and shook her head. "No, Mom would never agree to that."

"I haven't mentioned this to your mother. I'm sure she'll think it's a terribly bad idea for many reasons," Alabama said. "You know how you feel when your mom tells you no, you can't do something you want to do?"

"Happens all the time. I just want to break things and slam doors and scream."

"Exactly." Alabama took a deep breath. "That's because you're growing up and getting ready to become a strong, independent young woman. You want to cut the old apron strings. You think you're too big to have your mother tell you what you can and can't do."

"You're right, Grandma!" Alison said. "You so get me. Mom won't let me do anything fun. She treats me like a baby!"

Alison and Alabama both turned to look at the back of the truck where Sara and Richard were in a death grip with an old photo enlarger that Richard had used in college to make his own black and white prints for photography class. "Richard Webb, you are being obstinate and stubborn. You sold all of your film cameras. We have only digital cameras. You have no need for this now." Sara yanked the enlarger out of Richard's hands.

"But it's mine! You just don't get it!"

Sara dropped the enlarger on the truck bed. Then she went over to Richard and gave him a hug. "I do get it, Richard," she spoke soothingly. "You love it because it reminds you of your good old youthful days. It's going to be all right." She took his hand and led him toward the house.

Alabama turned back to Alison. "My dear granddaughter, you've reached the point in your life when you think you're smarter than your mother. But speaking from experience, I can tell you that the older you get, the smarter your mother will get." Then softly to herself, she muttered, "Then one morning, 40 or 50 years later, you'll wake up and believe your mother has lost her mind."

"What do you mean?" Alison asked.

"I'm sorry, I merely digressed a little," Alabama said softly, placing her hand on Alison's cheek. "Oh, yes, about your mother. By the time she left for college, your mother was driving me and your grandfather crazy — hanging out with the wrong kids, staying out until the wee hours, skipping class, making bad grades . . ."

Alison started giggling. Her giggles turned to loud laughter. "Mom did all of that?" Alabama nodded. "Did you fuss at her and boss her around and make her help around the house?"

"Indeed, I did. Of course, she whined and complained and carried on just like you do. Especially when she had to clean the bathroom."

"Who likes to clean bathrooms?" Alison said and laughed.

"When your mom left for college, she told me she was happy to leave home because it meant she would never ever have to clean another toilet. Years later, after your parents married, your mother told me that she finally realized that I was right about everything I'd told her, and she was wrong."

"That's hysterical!" Alison said with a shake of her head. "Hard for me to picture Mom as a troublemaker."

The man in charge of the Goodwill pickup walked over to Alabama and handed her a receipt. "Thank you, ma'am, for your donations. Sorry about any misunderstandings."

"Thank you for picking up our stuff," Alabama told him, watching his men shut the back of the truck. The man ambled back to the idling truck, jumped into the passenger seat, and slammed the door shut. The truck was out of the driveway and down the street in less than a minute.

Alabama focused on her granddaughter. "Alison, as a teenager, I thought my mother was mean to me. I bet my own grandmother bossed my teenage mother around, too. And when your own children become teenagers, you'll do the same."

"Nope, not gonna happen. I'm not getting married, and I'm definitely not having any kids."

"Ha!" Alabama said. "I remember one day when your mother was really being a pain in the butt. I looked at her, and I said, 'Sara, you just wait. One day you'll get your just rewards.' And she told me the exact same thing – 'I'm not getting married, and I'm not having kids.'"

"Well, I mean it, Grandma! Don't expect any great-grandchildren from me."

"Believe me, dear Alison," Alabama said, "you'll change your mind the minute the right young man comes along. Then one day, your teenagers will sass and aggravate you. Later, when they become middle-age adults and you grow old, they'll talk to you like you're a child."

Alison stood silently and stared at Alabama, as though letting her grandmother's words sink in. "That's depressing." Pause. "But Mom loves you, Grandma. She wouldn't be able to bear the thought of you moving away, because she doesn't want anything to happen to you. If you leave and something happens to you, she'll feel very bad."

"Yes, you're right, and knowing that doesn't make my decision any easier to make. My point to this soul-baring conversation is this —

your parents love you very much. They're not trying to torture you or make your life miserable. They don't want anything to happen to you."

Alison looked down at her feet. "Somehow, I knew you would turn this around and get back to me." Alison moved over to her grandmother and gave her a hug. "I love you, Grandma. I don't want you to move away, but I understand." Alison looked up into Alabama's face. "I'm sorry if I acted like a bratty teenager to you."

Alabama stroked Alison's hair. "It's all right, child. I love you, too, even when you act like a bratty teenager. Now I think we better check on your parents." They walked into the garage and found Sara and a disheveled Richard huddled around a pile of leftover garage sale items.

"Look what we rescued from the Goodwill," said Richard, holding up a broken accordion and a bent saxophone. A moth-eaten Davy Crockett cap sat catawampus on his head. "I hate to think what sort of good stuff you sold out from under us."

Alabama stood with her hands on her hips. "Oh, just all that good stuff you and Sara couldn't persuade me to part with when I sold my house."

"Did you really sell Uncle Don's rocking chair?" asked Sara, holding a box of old puzzles and games.

"I sure did. It was missing one arm piece. Man paid me $10 for it. I think he planned to use it for kindling."

"Mother!"

"What about Ray's old raccoon coat?" Richard asked.

"To a young boy for a dog bed—$8. Plus boxes of costumes, the bed Ray and I slept on for 45 years, and a unicycle. I made close to $2,500."

Sara and Richard looked surprised. "Thank you for emptying out our garage," Richard said. "I appreciate it."

Doug pushed his bike into the garage. "It really does look empty now."

"What do you plan to do with the money?" Sara asked.

"Use it when she moves out, right Grandma?" Doug said.

"What?" Sara and Richard chorused.

Alison gave Doug a big shove. "Douglas Webb, you got the biggest mouth."

Alabama looked from Sara to Richard, not sure how to respond. She could put on her innocent face and claim she didn't know what Doug was talking about, but it was probably too late for that.

"Grandma wants to live with Sunny at the Villas," Doug said. Sara gasped. "And I don't blame her one bit. It's better than being thrown into some smelly nursing home. Living in a cardboard box in the park is better than that."

Chapter Twelve

All eyes turned from Doug to Alabama, who wasn't sure if she should run screaming toward the kitchen door or stay for what was sure to be an uncomfortable confrontation with her daughter.

"Mother," Sara said loudly. "What is Doug talking about?"

Alabama took a deep breath. You can do this, she told herself. Who's the parent here? She let out a short little laugh. "It's nothing, dear. No big deal. Sunny wants me to move in with her at the Villas, so we can have fun and enjoy each other's company."

"That's absolutely out of the question." Sara said.

Alabama rubbed her forehead. This wasn't going well, she thought. "You know, suddenly I don't feel well. I think I'll go to my room and lie down. I have this kink in my neck and this awful pain in my head that shoots down my backbone and explodes in my spine." She slowly headed for the door. "I feel faint and there's all sorts of red dots and squiggles dancing in front of my eyes and loud noises are going off in my ears and it feels like a thousand camels stampeding inside my stomach and . . ."

Sara caught up with Alabama and grabbed her shoulder. "Stop right there, Mother. You know moving to the Villas is not a good idea."

Alabama turned around to face her daughter head on. "What's so wrong about me moving into the Villas with Sunny?"

"Your health for one thing," Sara spluttered. "You're not in good health, and those retirement communities are nothing but petri dishes. One little virus could swoop in and wipe out every old person living in the Villas."

"Hmph!" Alabama said loudly and walked back into the living room, followed by the rest of the family. Carefully considering how to respond, Alabama stopped in front of the sofa. "Dr. Baker checked me out last week and said I'm fine, did he not?"

"He said you had improved a lot," Sara admitted.

"He said my lab work looked great, and that I had the blood pressure of a young woman."

"Mother, I'm not talking about blood pressure," Sara pointed out. "Look at yourself. Would you want Sunny to end up taking care of you? You know that would cramp her lifestyle, right?"

"Or be a burden to her like I am to you?"

Alison and Doug gasped. Richard took a step toward Sara.

"Right . . . No . . . Mother, you're not a burden to us," Sara insisted.

"So you say now." Pulling a folded sheet of paper out of her pocket, Alabama sighed loudly and sat down on the sofa. "I knew you wouldn't be happy with the idea, but Doug helped convince me I should do this."

"Douglas Webb, what have you done?" Sara asked him.

"I only told her to make a list of pros and cons before making a decision," he said, running over to the sofa and sitting next to his grandmother. He whispered, "Don't worry, Grandma, you can do this."

Sara placed her hands on her hips. "I'm sure the cons won out— too old, too sick, too feeble . . ."

Alabama waved her list in the air. "Here are the results."

"It doesn't matter, Mother. We aren't even going to consider your moving to the Villas."

Richard came up behind Sara and put his hands on her shoulders. "Let's not be hasty, sweetheart. To be fair for everyone involved, we should at least listen to what Alabama has on her list."

Sara's eyes narrowed. She looked at Alabama.

"Mom?" pleaded Doug. "It can't hurt to hear her out, can it?"

Sara sat down in the overstuffed armchair across from the sofa and folded her arms across her chest.

Alabama's hands trembled as she smoothed out the paper on her lap and spoke in a soft voice. "First off, I listed why I shouldn't go and I could only think of two reasons: I'd miss seeing my family every day, and I would feel guilty about having so much fun with Sunny."

Sara leaned forward toward Alabama. "Mother, I can think of plenty more reasons for you not moving to the Villas. For one thing, packing up and moving will put too much stress on a woman your age and with your health conditions."

Alabama lifted her chin. "And being forced to give up my home, my car, and my independence aren't stressful? I managed to survive that without dropping dead."

"She does have a point, Sara," Richard said.

"Richard, you stay out of this. Mother, we bought this larger home so you could live with us. We love you, and we want to keep you safe."

"Sunny loves me, too. We've been bosom buddies since our sandbox days. We had something great when we lived together in New York. Even though we were scrimping and barely getting by, we had more fun than I've had any time since."

"Mother, if you move, you could have another stroke and drop dead."

"My dear Sara, I could just as easily drop dead here tonight!" Alabama said. "They have access to doctors at the Villas. When your time's up, your time's up!"

Sara leaped to her feet and pointed her finger at Alabama. "That's true, Mother, but would you douse yourself with gasoline and light a match to prove your theory?"

"Hey, everybody, let's calm down," Richard said, walking over to Sara.

Doug wrapped his arms around Alabama. "Why is everyone shouting? I don't want Grandma to leave either, but it's her life. Shouldn't it be her choice?"

Alison, who'd been standing in the hallway door, stepped into the living room. "Doug, you need to stay out of this."

Doug turned to face his sister. "Maybe you're okay with Grandma moving out, Alison, but I like her company. She bakes me cookies when I've had a bad day. And she talks to me and makes me feel better."

Alabama put her arm around Doug. "My sweet Douglas, I love you so much. We can still have daily talks on FaceTime. You can keep me updated on your quarrels with Horace."

"I can bake your lousy cookies," Alison said. "Don't be such a baby."

Sara and Richard listened to the conversation, but didn't interrupt.

"Thank you, Alison, but let me handle this." Alabama lifted Doug's chin. "Doug, you're a big boy now. You'll be able to manage without me being here every day. You'll be at soccer practice every afternoon, and in the evening, you'll rush home to do your homework."

"And as soon as you reach puberty, Doug," Alison said, "you'll be thinking that Grandma and Mom and Dad are stupid, anyway."

"Alison!" Sara and Richard both shouted.

"Mother, I've heard your list, but my answer is still no. You need to stay here with us."

"Let's not be hasty, Sara." Richard licked his lower lip. "We haven't heard your mother's list of pros. Alabama, why do you want to move to the Villas?"

Alabama cleared her throat and glanced down at her list and began reading. "During the day, everyone goes off to work or school. I'm left here all alone with nothing to do."

"Nothing to do?" asked Richard. "What about those homeless men you invite to the house to steal my stuff?"

"Richard, stay out of this," Sara said. "Let Mother finish her list."

"But Grandma, you have lots of stuff to do here." Doug said. "You can watch old movies, work on your scrapbook, bake me cookies, walk around the neighborhood . . ."

"But I get bored. I have no independence," Alabama protested.

Sara sighed. "Mother, you have plenty of independence. You can do anything you please."

"So, if I stay here, will I get to drive my car and leave the house?" Alabama raised an eyebrow.

"That's a bad idea, Mother. You know I can take you any place you need to go."

Alabama snorted. "Yeah, right! If the time is right? If it's absolutely necessary? If there's no way to get out of it? If it suits you?" Alabama shook her head. "At the Villas, I would have friends to talk to and lots of daily activities to participate in. They even have field trips to shopping areas and museums and tourist attractions. Every day would be filled."

Sara stood and threw up her hands. "That's enough, Mother. The answer is no. I will feel better and the family will be happier, if you stay here with us."

Richard grimaced. "Could we be democratic and put it to a vote?"

Sara turned around. "Absolutely not, Richard. End of discussion."

Alabama got to her feet and pulled an envelope out of her pocket. She sighed. "I was afraid that would be your answer, Sara. Here." She handed a pink envelope to her daughter. "Sunny said I should give this to you, if you were having any negative feelings about my moving in with her."

When Sara opened the envelope, the smell of lavender wafted through the living room. She pulled out a card covered with drawings of purple flowers and opened it.

"Read it out loud, Sara, so everyone can hear," Alabama suggested.

Sunny Day

Cordially invites the Webb family

To spend the day

At the Villas of Kensington Grove

Next Friday from 10 a.m.-4 p.m.

Lunch will be served at Noon

RSVP Regrets Only

A note from Sunny was written on the opposite page of the invitation:

Dear Webb Family,

I'm inviting you to see the Villas in person. I know you love Alabama as much as I do and are worried about her safety and well-being. I think by touring the Villas yourself and experiencing what it's like to live here, you'll feel better about Alabama's decision to move in with me. I know you'll enjoy lunch. The chef came to us from a Michelin Three-Star restaurant in California. If you want to bring your swimsuits, the Villas is home to a saltwater, Olympic-size swimming pool. Alison will love the art studios. Doug will go bonkers over the model railroad train room. From my fifth-floor apartment, there is a great view of the boats on the river, and you can see all the way to the Atlantic Ocean.

Of course, there is always the possibility that Alabama herself might not like the lifestyle at the Villas. Therefore, I would like for her to spend the weekend with me to see what she thinks before any final decisions are made. I want her to meet my friends and soak up the ambiance. Everyone should keep an open mind while exploring and experiencing the Villas at Kensington Grove.

Looking forward to seeing the Webb family on Friday morning.

Love, Sunny

"Oh boy, oh boy!" Doug ran over and hugged Sara. "Can we go, Mom? Huh? Please?"

"I think it would be interesting," Alison said. "The Villas is right there on the water and near the beaches."

"I don't know . . . What about school?" Sara said.

"It's a work day for teachers," explained Alison. "No school."

"How fortuitous!" Richard said. "I take that as a good sign. I can take the day off myself."

Alabama walked over to Sara. "How can it hurt? Aren't you the least bit curious? It would be a nice outing for the family." Alabama could see that Sara was weakening. Probably hoping that I'll hate the place, Alabama figured.

"All right. Fine," Sara agreed. "We'll go. Just to check it out, but no promises that I'll change my mind."

Well, Alabama thought, that will be a start. How could she ask for anything more?

Chapter Thirteen

Alabama passed through the automatic double-glass-door entrance to the Villas at Kensington Grove and came to an abrupt stop. Her mind flashed back to her and Ray's 40th wedding anniversary trip to the Gaylord Opryland Resort in Nashville. Nine acres of indoor gardens, cascading waterfalls, and an indoor river with boats.

The Villas' jaw-dropping, cavernous atrium lobby was nothing close to the Gaylord. Still, beneath an opulent-domed ceiling, sunlight filtered through cut crystal and stained glass, and shone on six separate seating areas. Plants and small trees scattered around the entire lobby made her feel like she was standing in an outdoor garden. Alabama couldn't believe her eyes. Sunny kept telling her the Villas was exquisite, but she never expected a lobby that looked like this.

"Wow!" exclaimed Doug, coming up from behind Alabama and clasping her hand. "This looks like a queen's palace."

Alison, carrying Alabama's overnight bag, trotted over to a white Steinway grand piano centered under the massive dome and looked up. She squealed and dropped the bag. "This is absolutely unbelievable!"

Alabama followed Alison's eyes upward to beveled stained glass and crystals sparkling in the sunlight like diamond jewels. This was surreal, she marveled. How could this be a retirement complex? This was a five-star resort. Alabama turned, as she heard the glass doors open.

Sara and Richard, in the middle of a heated discussion, walked through the lobby doors and stopped in mid-sentence with their mouths agape. Their eyes widened in surprise as they took in their first glimpse of the lobby at the Villas at Kensington Grove.

A wide smile stretched across Richard's face. "Well, Sara, now what do you have to say about this? Do you smell stale urine? Do you see any sad, pathetic old people sitting in wheelchairs with drool running down their chins?"

Sara shook her head in bewilderment and walked over to Alabama, placing her hand on her shoulder. "Well, Mother, I never expected anything like this," she said softly.

Alabama placed her hand over Sara's. "Me, neither."

"It's beautiful, Mother, but I can't picture you living here. It would be quite a change from the relaxed feel of our living room," Sara said.

Alabama nodded. "That it would." No mad scramble with everyone rushing out the front door to work or school, she thought. No yelling or fussing over school fights, eating on the sofa, turning up the TV too loud, or cutting up the newspaper. She glanced with envy at residents sitting around the lobby, conversing with friends, reading books or newspapers, drinking coffee, and simply enjoying the moment.

"If the rest of the Villas looks like this, I might consider moving in, too," Richard said.

Douglas ran over to his dad. "Really? Could we move here? It does have that Olympic-size swimming pool."

"Indeed, it does, Doug. A heated, salt-water pool. Did you bring your swimsuit?" Sunny reached out and gave Doug a big hug. "I remember how much you love model trains. Wait until you see the model train layouts in the workshop here."

Alabama didn't know who looked more excited about the trains, Richard or Doug.

"Would we be able to run the trains ourselves?" Doug asked.

"I think you'll have to talk about that with the men who built the train layout." Doug's smile faded. "But I bet they could be talked into it."

Sunny grabbed Alabama's hand. "Hello, dear friend! I'm so glad you made it here. And you brought the whole family, too."

"Mom wanted to make sure we weren't leaving Grandma in a bad place," Doug said.

"Doug!" Sara said. "That's not true."

Alison cleared her throat. "I believe your exact words were 'I won't let Mother stay in a disgusting dump, even for a few days.'"

"It's far from being a dump," Richard said. "This lobby looks like a five-star resort."

Sunny laughed. "And you've only seen the lobby. Come on, everyone, allow me to give you the grand tour of the Villas at Kensington Grove. Our first stop will be the front desk, where you will sign in and get your visitor's tag. We are very careful about who we let in here."

After everyone was officially signed in and their visitor's tags in place, the next stop was Sunny's apartment on the fifth floor, via one of four high-tech elevators. "Watch this," Sunny said, approaching a computer screen adhered to the wall. She touched the number 5 and a voice sounded, "Elevator C, please."

Sunny herded the group toward the "C" elevator just as the doors opened with a loud ding. "Okay, everyone inside."

Doug stepped in and turned around 360 degrees. "Hey, where're the buttons?"

"We don't need buttons, Doug," Sunny explained. "The elevator knows where we're going."

Alison edged closer to Alabama. "But what if it bypasses the fifth floor and doesn't stop."

"This isn't *Charlie and the Chocolate Factory*, Alison." Sunny said. "Besides, that hasn't happened to me yet."

Even though Alabama had laughed at Sunny's elevator joke, she still felt a little bit uncomfortable about being in a closed box—big enough to hold a stretcher from an ambulance or funeral home hearse—with no buttons to press, except for a discreetly-placed red emergency one. But it was a smooth ride to the fifth floor, where the doors opened—just as Sunny said they would—and everyone piled out.

Sunny touched what Alabama thought was a Fitbit bracelet to a metal plate on the door of her unit. When a green light flashed on, Alabama realized it was a high-tech bracelet like what guests at Disney World once used to enter their rooms and the theme parks. The new high-tech thing now for Disney guests was using cell phones and special apps.

Pushing down on the handle, Sunny opened the door. Doug was the first one through. He dashed from the foyer and across the living room to the wall-to-wall, floor-to-ceiling windows and pointed outside. "Look, you can see the whole world from up here."

Alison dropped Alabama's bag on a chair and joined her brother at the window. She looked straight down. "I see walking trails below, Grandma."

Doug pressed his forehead against the window. "And a boat on the river!"

Sunny, followed by Alabama, Sara, and Richard, walked over to the windows. "Yes, that's the Brunswick River down there. If you walk over to that small park at the foot of the Sidney Lanier Bridge, you can have a picnic and watch the boats go under the bridge."

Doug pulled back from the view. "I could stand at this window and look all day long."

"I think the newness would wear off in no time for you," Sara said.

"Is that the Atlantic Ocean way in the distance?" Richard asked.

"Yes, that tiny streak of blue is the ocean. To your left," Sunny pointed, "is St. Simons Island. And on the other side of the bridge is Jekyll Island. We are close to the Golden Isles beaches, too."

"This is impressive," Alabama said, admiring the bookshelves that ran the length of one wall. A niche in the middle of the bookshelves framed a high-res, 50-inch TV. A four-person sofa and two over-stuffed chairs were on the opposite side of the room. "Could we see the rest of the apartment?"

"By all means," Sunny said. She started with the large kitchen/dining room area that opened out onto a shaded screened-in porch with a patio table and chairs. "I like to sit out here in the morning, drink my coffee, and read the Savannah paper on my tablet."

Alabama walked back into the kitchen, where Sara was standing. "You know, Mother, this kitchen is bigger than ours. You could cook a gourmet dinner for eight in this kitchen. I never expected anything this big."

"I didn't either," Sunny said. "The dining room area is so large, I turned half of the room into an office area with a desk, computer, and printer. There's plenty of room left for a second desk." She looked at Alabama questioningly.

Alabama frowned and shook her head to silence Sunny. Getting Sara to "allow" Alabama to spend the weekend with Sunny had taken lots of convincing and effort. And even then, only on the condition that the Webb family accompany her to make sure the Villas was clean and nice enough for Alabama to stay for a few days.

While Alison and Doug stayed by the windows and marveled at the view, Sunny led everyone else to a bright, airy room with a walk-in closet, ceiling fan, queen-size bed, two bedside tables with lamps, a chest of drawers, and vanity with mirror. "This is the guest room. Across the hall is the guest bathroom. Please notice that all doors are wheelchair width, and the bathroom has a walk-in shower with safety bars and an emergency call button located by the comfort-height toilet."

"Looks like they thought of everything," Richard said, looking sideways at Sara.

Halfway down the hallway, folding doors opened to reveal a laundry room with washer, dryer, and storage cabinets. The master suite—Sunny's room—was at the end of the hallway. Much larger than the guest room, Sunny's bedroom had an intimate sitting area with two recliner chairs and another large wall TV. Double doors led outside to a private balcony with two chaise lounges.

"I'm so lucky to have an apartment facing the coast," explained Sunny. "I get the morning sun, but not the hot, afternoon sun. That means in the heat of the day, this balcony's in the shade and gets a cooling breeze."

Richard and Sara walked out on the balcony to see the view. "It feels nice out here in the sun," said Sara.

Sunny hugged Alabama. "Well, Balmy, what do you think?"

A tear rolled down Alabama's cheek.

Sunny grabbed her friend's shoulders. "Balmy, what's wrong? Are you feeling all right?"

Alabama wiped her tear away and smiled at Sunny. "These are tears of joy, dear friend. This is like heaven, but I know I'm not dead yet." Suddenly Alabama felt deliriously happy.

Sunny shook her friend gently and laughed. "Eula Mae says the Villas is God's waiting room. If that's true, then it's the perfect place to wait."

Alabama looked through the balcony door at her daughter, who was laughing and pointing towards the bridge, and hoped she would be able to join Sunny in God's waiting room. She glanced back at Sunny. "Who's Eula Mae? I think you mentioned her already. Was she one of the women who went on the cruise?"

"Yes, that's right, Balmy," Sunny said. "You'll love her! She's the funniest resident I've met here. Very down to earth. A person who calls it like she sees it. I can't wait to introduce you to her."

"Then I have to meet her. Will I get to see her today?" Alabama watched Sara and Richard open the balcony door.

"Definitely. We'll be joining her and several of her bridge friends for dinner tonight. They want to tell you about their Caribbean cruise. It was one exciting adventure," Sunny said.

"Adventure?" Sara asked, shutting the balcony door behind her. "Isn't everyone living in the Villas too old for adventure?"

Sunny laughed. "Why, Sara, a little adventure every now and then keeps your adrenaline pumping and makes you feel younger and invigorated."

Sara opened her mouth to reply, but was interrupted by a very excited Doug. "Mom, Dad, come quick. You have to see this yacht coming down the river. There's a naked lady lying on the deck." He grabbed his father's hand and pulled him down the hallway.

Laughing, the three women followed Richard and Doug. Alabama, pulling up the rear, was thinking how the Villas could be the answer to her dreams. She only had to convince Sara of that.

Chapter Fourteen

Alabama stood in the end of the huge aquatic center, which housed the Villas' heated saltwater swimming pool—complete with separate lap, diving, and therapy pools. She watched an ongoing water aerobics class of mostly women marching in place and moving their arms back and forth through the water. A perky young brunette stood on the deck, shouting encouragingly, while demonstrating the movement.

"Grandma, look!" Douglas squealed behind her and pointed to the diving board.

Sara, Richard, Sunny, Alison, and Alabama turned their attention to a balding, pot-bellied man in red swimming trunks standing on the edge of the diving board. While he stood and stared at the water below, two other men stood at the bottom of the diving board yelling at him.

"Go, Sidney! You can do it!" called out an Asian man in plaid trunks.

A second man—good-looking and muscular with thick, gray hair—spoke loudly, "Be careful, Sid. Keep your head down."

Sidney nodded, bounced on the board once, and threw himself into the air, hugging his knees for the long fall toward the water.

"Wow!" shouted Doug, as Sidney hit the water like a cannonball. The loud splash reverberated to the far end of the pool, causing the entire water aerobics class to turn around. A torrent of water gushed out of the diving pool, sending Sunny, Alabama, and her family scurrying back from the pool's edge.

As the two men began hauling Sidney out of the water, a woman shrieked from the pool entrance, "Charlie Chan, what are you doing?" Then a beautiful Asian woman hurried toward the three men. "Did you make Sidney jump off the diving board, again?"

"No, we did not," the Asian man answered, as he and the other man pulled a coughing Sidney to his feet, handed him a towel, and slapped him on the back. "Great job!" Charlie told Sidney.

Alabama admired the Asian woman's long, jet-black hair, her immaculately made-up face, and the exquisite gold jewelry she wore around her neck and on her wrists. Remembering the time-consuming effort it took to apply her own makeup prior to each stage performance, Alabama marveled that the woman went to such trouble while living in a retirement community.

Shaking her head, the Asian beauty turned towards Sunny with a wide smile. "Sunny! Good to see you! Is this your friend Balmy?"

Sunny stepped forward. "Yes, it is. Balmy, meet my new friend Yasuko." Alabama and Yasuko shook hands. "And this is Balmy's family—her daughter Sara Webb, her son-in-law Richard Webb, her granddaughter Alison, and her grandson Douglas."

While everyone was shaking hands, the three men ambled over to their group. "Hello," the Asian man said, reaching out to shake hands with Alabama. "I'm Yasuko's new husband, Charlie Chan." He held up his hand. "And before you say anything about my name, I just want to say my mother was a great fan of the old Charlie Chan movies."

"Who?" asked Richard. "I never heard of Charlie Chan."

"Oh, wait," Doug butted in. "Was he a famous Chinese ninja assassin?"

Alison rolled her eyes. "If you're thinking about that really old *Ninja Assassin* movie that came out before you were born, dummy, the answer is no. Ninja are Japanese martial arts experts."

"Also, Doug," Sara said, "Chan is Chinese, not Japanese."

Charlie crouched down in front of Doug. "Charlie Chan is a fictional Honolulu police detective in a series of mystery novels published back in the 1920s. Way before your grandparents were born. Mr. Chan traveled around the world, investigating mysteries and solving crimes."

"Way before my time, too" Richard said. "No wonder I didn't recognize the name."

"Was he like an Asian Sherlock Holmes?" Sara asked.

Charlie stood up and laughed. "I guess you could say that. Anyway, Charlie Chan books and movies were very popular in the 1940s."

"I used to watch those old black and white Charlie Chan movies on Armchair Playhouse when I was growing up," said the other man. "Hello, I'm Ron Williams." He shook hands with everyone.

When Ron took Doug's hand, Doug nodded and said, "You have big muscles. Were you ever a ninja assassin or a secret agent like James Bond?"

Ron laughed. "Hardly, young man, but my new wife Carolina calls me her Hunky Spy. Does that count for anything?"

Alabama glanced at Sunny and smiled. She'd already heard about Ron and Carolina from Sunny. All about their cruising adventures in the Caribbean while onboard the *Emerald Dream*. Such an unbelievable tale of stowaways, smugglers, and kidnappers.

After everyone was introduced to the cannonball diver, Sidney Downs, Sunny gathered her group around her. "How about lunch at Le Bistro?"

"Not us, I'm afraid," said Yasuko. "We're meeting Lilly and Archie for lunch in the main dining room. We'll see you later."

Sunny watched Yasuko and the three men walk away. "What about the rest of you?"

"Yay! Lunch!" Doug shouted. "How about a grilled cheese sandwich and a chocolate shake?"

Alison shrugged. "Sure."

"I'm starved," Alabama said.

"Yes, I could definitely do lunch," Sara said.

"Count me in," said Richard, but not very enthusiastically.

Sunny picked up on his lack of enthusiasm. "We have reservations at Le Bistro. It's a smaller dining area with a different menu from the main dining room. Richard, you'll be glad to know you won't have to eat mac and cheese or lime jello. Unless you really want to order that?"

Richard seemed to perk up at the news. Alabama tried not to laugh. Sara told him before they left the house that if he was served mac and cheese or lime jello at lunch, he should not complain.

Apparently, Sara believed that's what residents in retirement communities ate for lunch most every day.

• • •

A hostess seated the Webb family and Sunny at a round table for six next to a large window. Sunshine filtered through white, sheer curtains for a cheerful, airy feel. Alabama watched Sara run her hand over the damask tablecloth and finger the high-quality stainless silverware. Richard sipped from a stemmed water glass and slipped a linen napkin across his lap. When he looked at the menu, he raised his eyebrows in surprise. "They have prime rib on the lunch menu?"

"Yes, that's right," Sunny explained. "Many of the residents like to eat their big meal of the day at lunch. Then they will have leftover lunch in their apartment or a sandwich or something small for supper."

"This is my kind of restaurant," Alison said happily. "Lots of awesome-sounding vegetarian dishes."

Doug frowned. "I don't see anything I want to eat."

"Douglas Webb, watch it," Sara warned him. "There's plenty of food on this menu. A variety of entrees, soups, and sandwiches. How about a croque monsieur? I'm pretty sure that's a fried ham and cheese sandwich."

A waitress, who had arrived at the table to take their orders just as Doug had started his tirade, smiled at him. "All right, young man, tell me what you want for lunch that isn't on the menu?"

Douglas closed his menu and looked at the waitress. "A grilled cheese sandwich?"

"Cheddar or Swiss or both?"

"Both, please."

"White bread, multi-grain, whole wheat, or rye?"

"White."

"Fries, chips, or onion rings?"

"Chips. And a chocolate shake?"

She smiled broadly. "You got it!"

Alabama closed her menu. "Make that for two, please."

A stunned Alison said, "I don't get it. You look at this splendid French food and you order grilled cheese sandwiches? Well not me. I'm eating the *ratatouille*."

Sunny laughed out loud. "You three are hilarious! But I'm going with the Marseille-style shrimp stew."

The waitress looked at Sara. "And you, ma'am?"

Sara bit her lower lip. "The *confit de canard* with baked potato and asparagus."

"What's that?" Doug asked.

"It's duck," Alison replied proudly. "I learned that in French class."

"Yuck! I'll stick with my grilled cheese," Doug said. "What is Dad having?"

Everyone chorused at once, "Prime rib!"

* * *

After a dessert of *soufflé au chocolat* and chocolate truffles, Sunny led everyone out of Le Bistro. "Well, what did you think of Le Bistro?"

"My prime rib was delicious. How does this place differ from the main dining room here?" Richard asked.

"It's smaller and quieter. With the French menu and ambience, it is a perfect place to bring guests. We also have a very small eating area called Bubba's. They serve comfort food, like pizza, burgers, hot dogs, sandwiches, fries, and shakes."

"Le Bistro was an excellent choice for me," Richard said. "Is there much more to see in the Villas? We need to get on the road no later than 4 o'clock. Savannah rush hour traffic is especially bad on Fridays."

"That won't be a problem," Sunny said, halting in front of a glass door. "This is our model train room."

Doug looked through the door at a train layout that filled the entire room and yelled, "Dad, have you ever seen such a big layout?"

Richard took one look, pushed open the door, and ushered Doug into the room. Two men wearing traditional striped train engineer's hats, turned and grinned. "Howdy, fellas!" greeted a large, jovial man.

"Welcome to Kensington Grove Railroad. I'm Kevin Archer and this is my train buddy, Mike Bakowski."

Alabama nudged Sara. "I think they're both in hog heaven."

Sara nodded. "I think you're right." She looked at Sunny. "Doug and Richard share a love of trains. Is it possible for them to stay here while the rest of us finish the tour of the Villas?"

Sunny yelled, "Hey, Kevin, is it okay to leave our men here for about an hour or so?"

"Oh, sure, Sunny. They look content. I think they won't mind staying with us a might longer." Richard and Doug didn't look up. They were busy listening to Mike explain about the four different types of trains running throughout the layout.

Sunny continued down the hallway, pausing only briefly at the door to the woodworking workshop, but when the group reached the entrance to the arts and crafts suite, Alison's face lit up. "Oh, please, could we go inside?"

The art suite area was made up of several studios, including a general studio for a variety of artwork, from drawing to making jewelry; a painting studio for working with oils, watercolor, and acrylics; and a ceramics studio with wheels for throwing, a glaze room, and a kiln room. "This is where I would spend my time," Alison said. "If I were old and lived here," she added.

The group walked by a combined library and computer room, a hair salon and barber shop, and a game room, where residents could be seen playing board games and cards, and working on jigsaw puzzles. Zig-zagging from one hallway to another, Sunny stopped in front of large, wooden double doors, which opened into a huge ballroom with a stage on the far end. "This room seats 1,200 guests for plays, musicals, and concerts, or about 500 guests for special dinners and dancing with music by the Kensington Grove orchestra and band," Sunny pointed out. "We use the space for art exhibits and the annual authors book festival, too."

Sara glanced down at her watch. "It's almost 3. We need to round up the boys and head back to Savannah. But thank you for showing us around. The Villas at Kensington Grove is quite impressive."

Alabama pulled up the rear as the group followed Sunny back to the train room. She hugged herself and sighed happily.

It was difficult for Richard to pull Doug out of the model train railroad room, now that Kevin and Mike were allowing him to run their trains through a miniature village with vehicles, farm animals, and people. As soon as the men told Doug he could return anytime and run the trains himself, he thanked them and reluctantly followed his dad out of the room.

●　●　●

Outside the entrance to the Villas' lobby, Sara gave Alabama a big hug. "This appears to be a nice place, Mother. I hope you and Sunny have a great weekend. I can't believe all the fun things to do. We'll be back Sunday to pick you up."

Doug hugged Alabama tightly. "If I were staying here this weekend, I would spend it in the train room," he said. "But I'm sure you won't go near it. That place would be a total waste on you, Grandma. You'll probably spend your time doing stupid stuff like arts and crafts or playing card games or something dumb."

"Probably so, Doug, but I will enjoy whatever I do. You be good this weekend, promise?"

"Okay, Grandma!" He followed Alison into the SUV and waved from the window.

Richard tooted the horn, and drove away.

Sunny threw her arms up in the air, tilted her head back, and yelled, "Woohoo!" She did a little victory dance in a circle around Alabama, who was bent over, laughing and crying. "Well, Balmy, we sure got rid of them party poopers. What do you think? Did we score any points?"

Alabama straightened up and wiped her eyes on her sleeve. "They were definitely surprised at what they saw." The lobby doors automatically opened for the two women to enter the Villas. "They were expecting to see a bunch of old folks pushing walkers or sitting forlornly in wheelchairs around the lobby."

"Only in the assisted living wing," Sunny said, putting her arm around Alabama and giving her a hug.

"They were literally shocked at the size of your beautiful apartment," Alabama continued. "They expected the rooms to be small and claustrophobic."

"And don't forget, Richard expected to eat mac and cheese and lime jello for lunch," Sunny said with a laugh. Their arms entwined, the two best friends headed toward the elevators. "Sounds like we scored some serious points with them."

"With Richard for sure," Alabama said, touching 5 on the computer pad. "He feels less guilty about me moving in with you because the Villas at Kensington Grove are much better than he expected."

"Elevator B, please," a voice sounded. By the time Sunny and Alabama turned around, the doors of Elevator B opened, and they stepped in. The elevator doors closed, and the elevator began to rise.

"I bet after Richard ate that last bite of prime rib, he was thinking that he wouldn't mind living here," Sunny pointed out.

"I agree," Alabama said, as the elevator doors opened on the fifth floor. "As for Sara, I'm not so sure. Only time will tell."

Chapter Fifteen

"Well, my dear friend, what would you like to do now?" Sunny asked, pressing her bracelet key against the right spot and opening the door. "It's too early for Happy Hour. And to be honest, this is the time of day that many residents take a rest before dinner."

Alabama crossed the spacious living room to the floor-to-ceiling windows and looked down at the river below. No boats in sight at the moment. "How about a glass of something wet? Then I'd like to sit and rest in one of the chaise lounges on your balcony, if it's not too chilly. Enjoy the view, relax, and have a pleasant conversation with my best friend."

"You got it, Balmy! I'm good with your suggestions." Sunny headed to the kitchen and opened the fridge. "Iced tea, cranberry-ginger ale, lemonade or water?"

Alabama followed her friend into the kitchen. "Cranberry-ginger ale works for me."

A few minutes later, Alabama was settled down on a comfy chaise lounge, a frosty glass on the table next to her. "This is the life. A little sunshine. A nice breeze off the water. I could get used to this." It was definitely cooler on this fifth-floor balcony, she thought, than it had been in the parking lot. Even in late October, the Georgia coast could be warm and humid. She closed her eyes and felt her entire body relax — something she wasn't able to do much of the time at the Webb house. "I can't believe that Halloween is next weekend."

Sunny sipped her drink. "I can't believe that you won't be here for the big costume shindig."

Alabama glanced at her friend. "You're having a Halloween party?"

Sunny nodded. "In the ballroom. Prizes awarded for best costumes."

"What kind of prizes?" Alabama asked. "I played bingo once with my friend Ethyl Baer at the senior center on Tybee Island. Their prizes were bananas and body lotion for small bingos. The grand prize for a full blackout on your bingo card was boxes of Fig Newtons, Oreos, and animal crackers."

Sunny grinned and stared at Alabama. "After what you've seen of the Villas today, you think our prizes will be fruit or cookies or toiletries?"

Alabama shrugged and felt embarrassed. Sunny was right. The Villas at Kensington Grove was definitely an uptown retirement community—on a much higher tier level than any senior center in Savannah.

"The grand prize is tickets for two for the Villas weekend mini-bus tour to the Biltmore House in December. Four runners-up get dinner for two at the popular Captain Ahab's Seafood Restaurant in Brunswick."

"They sound like decent prizes," Alabama said, relieved to hear the quality of the prizes.

Sunny laughed. "Of course, they're decent prizes. The Villas is a first-class joint. But I suspect that Richard and Sara would probably expect the prizes to be apples and spray cologne."

Alabama laughed along with Sunny. "Yes, as you say, this is one first-class joint. And that really concerns me, Sunny." Alabama took a sip of her drink and wiped the condensation off the glass with her napkin. "The Villas looks like one very expensive place to live."

"Yes, and worth every penny, too." Sunny reached over and gently touched Alabama's forearm. "Are you already worried about money, Balmy? You should focus on moving in with me. Then we can talk about money."

Alabama sat up straight and swung her legs off the chaise lounge. "The Villas is much more luxurious than I expected. I hate to think what the monthly fee is to live here. Not to mention what huge amount of money you had to pay up front just to move in. It's obvious to me that I could never afford to live here with you."

"What are you talking about?"

"But that's okay. All this talk of moving in with you has just upset my family." Alabama paused and rubbed her hands together. "I'll be fine living right where I am until they carry me out of that house in a wooden box. Besides, Sunny, I wouldn't fit in here."

"Oh, Balmy, that's just sour grapes. You know you would love to live here with me, and the monthly fee isn't all that bad."

"If that's true, then just how bad is 'not all that bad'? Because I'm really starting to think I can't afford to live here in this little bit of heaven with you." Alabama wiped at a tear running down her cheek.

Sunny turned to face her friend and grabbed both her hands. "Oh, my goodness, Balmy. Please don't cry. Talk to me. We can work this out. You must have some money coming in? Social security?"

Alabama sniffed and pulled back a hand to wipe her other eye. "A little bit more than that. You know how you and I left home after high school and headed to New York City to star on Broadway?"

"We were so naive, weren't we?" Sunny laughed.

"But determined."

"We had to work those dismal jobs for minimum wage, while auditioning and hoping for that big break," Sunny said.

"I wish we'd been smart like Ray," Alabama said.

Sunny looked puzzled for a minute. "Oh, right, he went to college at the University of Central Georgia. What did he get his degree in?"

"Education. He loved children. He wanted to be a middle school teacher."

"Oh, yes, I remember the story now." Sunny stood and stretched. "He took dance classes for PE credit and music classes for electives."

"Then he auditioned for the music department's spring musical his freshman year and got the Will Parker role in *Oklahoma!*" Alabama said. "After that, every spring he performed in the department's musical — *Annie Get Your Gun, Kiss Me Kate*, and *South Pacific*."

"Then he met Jeff when they both performed in *Carousel* at the Macon Little Theatre," Sunny added.

Alabama stood and walked over to the balcony railing. "After graduation, Jeff convinced Ray to hold off on teaching school and go with him to New York. Of course, by this time, Ray was so enthralled with the theater glamor, it didn't take much convincing."

Sunny gave Alabama a hug. "Aren't you glad he did, Balmy? Think how different your life would be if Ray had stayed in Georgia to be a middle school teacher?"

"Yes, I know," she said softly. "In the end, he did fulfill his dream of becoming a teacher."

"Plus, he encouraged you to get an education degree, too."

Alabama nodded. "And that is why each month I get a teacher's retirement check, a social security check, and survivor benefits from Ray's teacher retirement."

Sunny squealed. "Balmy, that's so marvelous," she said, breaking into the memorable song from the musical *Funny Face*.

"What?" Alabama thought Sunny might be losing it.

Grabbing Alabama's shoulders and giving her a gentle shake, Sunny explained what she was talking about. "Listen up, Balmy. You have more than enough money coming in to cover the monthly fee for living here with me."

"Surely not," Alabama said. "It must cost thousands of dollars each month to live here."

Sunny linked elbows with Alabama. "All we have to do is follow the yellow brick road!" Alabama joined in as Sunny began skipping and singing "We're Off to See the Wizard" through the bedroom and down the hall. They halted at Sunny's desk. She opened the top middle drawer, pulled out a blue folder with the Villas logo on the front, a notepad, and pens. "Let's sit down at the table and play with some numbers."

Alabama pulled a chair up to the table next to Sunny, who was pulling information sheets out of the Villas folder and spreading them in front of her. One sheet showed the layout for the "Deluxe" two-bedroom apartment with its extra-large living room, dining room, and master suite, plus balcony and screened-in porch. "Is this your apartment?"

Sunny smiled and nodded. "See the list of monthly fees? I pay a little over four-thousand dollars a month."

Alabama gulped and sunk back in her chair. "That's a lot of money. It would take nearly everything I have coming in to pay that amount of money each month."

Sunny pointed to the second line under monthly service fee charge: "Second person in deluxe two-bedroom apartment ($650)."

"How can that be?" Alabama asked with a sharp intake of breath.

"Listen, Balmy. Let me read to you what the monthly fee covers for one person: 'All expenses except phone line; includes all utilities, cable/Internet, weekly housekeeping, scheduled transportation for appointments, and one meal a day in the main dining room.'" She paused. "'Fee for second person in apartment covers one meal.'"

Alabama frowned. "I understand that, but a second person would still use her share of utilities, cable, Internet, and other stuff. If I lived here, I would want to pay for my share of that. What would that be?"

Sunny brought up the calculator on her smart phone and pressed in the numbers. "$2,500."

Relief flooded through her. "I could certainly swing that easily," Alabama said.

"But since I live in the very large master suite, it's only fair I pay more for the extra space. So, let's drop your share down to $2,200?"

Alabama's head was spinning with all of these figures. "I don't know, Sunny. Somehow, that still doesn't seem fair to you."

"Fine! Then you can live in the master suite."

"What?" Alabama choked out. "No, no, no."

"Does that mean that $2,200 now sounds acceptable to you? Plus, you need to consider that each year the monthly fee will go up 3 percent."

Taking a deep breath and feeling a little bit manipulated, Alabama exhaled slowly to calm herself. "All right. But what about the money you invested to buy into this apartment? I should pay for my share of that, too."

"Oh, Balmy, Balmy, Balmy. That will not be necessary."

Alabama straightened herself up as tall as she could and still be sitting down. "I'll have you know, I'm not some charity case. I have my own money. Even though we had to sell my house and Sara's house to buy a home big enough for all of us, they used their equity and only part of my money to pay for the new house in full."

"All right, I hear you . . ."

"Wait, don't interrupt me. I'm not finished yet."

Sunny plopped her arms across her chest. "Sorry. Please continue."

"Sara returned any money they didn't use to buy the house. My financial adviser invested it in additional stocks, bonds, and mutual funds. Sara said that's my emergency fund — my rainy-day money — in case I need it later." She grimaced and shrugged. "You know, to pay for a bed in a memory care unit or a nursing home, should I reach a vegetative state before I drop dead."

"Are you done now?" Sunny asked.

Alabama nodded. "I'm done. Your turn."

"You definitely won't be needing to spend your rainy-day money yet," Sunny said.

Alabama lifted her hand and opened her mouth.

"No, you don't! It's still MY turn. Now I get to have my say." Sunny raised an eyebrow and glared at Alabama. "A few years after Jeff and I moved to California, we saved up enough money for a down payment on a 1920s two-bedroom/one bath bungalow on a postage-stamp lot in a nice neighborhood near several studios. By the time we bought the house, we'd joined the Union and signed with a great agent, who kept us working steadily as supporting actors in movies and TV shows. Because we were reliable, hardworking, didn't cause problems on the set, and got along with everyone, we had steady employment."

"But—" Alabama interrupted.

"Nope, not finished yet." Sunny shook her head; Alabama shut her mouth. "Thank you. As I was saying, Jeff and I lived frugally and invested wisely. Over the years, we renovated and enlarged the kitchen, added a Florida room, a covered patio, and a large master suite. Remember me telling you that my realtor had three offers the first day?" Alabama nodded. "Well, I finally accepted the highest offer of $1.2 million."

Alabama's jaw dropped. "That's absolutely unbelievable. Ray and I paid $52,000 for our three bedroom/two bath home off Victory. It sold for $675,000."

Sunny grunted. "In my old neighborhood, a house that big with a decent lot would have sold for $2 million or more."

"It's all about location, location, location," Alabama said with a nod.

"After I bought this apartment, I took the leftover money and did exactly like you did—invested it in more stocks, bonds, and mutual funds for my portfolio. And thanks to my Union—the Actors' Equity Association—I also get a monthly pension check," Sunny explained. "Do you have any questions?"

"Why can't I contribute to the cost of buying this apartment?"

"Because it's all mine, Balmy. If I decide to leave here for any reason . . ."

"Like move to Paris?" Alabama remembered how Sunny used to talk about doing just that. She'd even taken French lessons from a Parisian actress who performed with them in *Irma La Douce*. That had been a good gig. It was later made into a movie starring Jack Lemmon and Shirley MacLaine. She would have loved to have performed in the movie, but alas, it was not made as a musical.

"Oui! Peut-être que bientôt nous irons à Paris?"

"Stop it, Sunny! You know I don't understand that gobbledygook."

Sunny let out a light-hearted giggle. "Yes, I know, dear Balmy! I do remember that. You told me once that you were behind the barn door when they passed out the foreign language gene." She paused. "I said that maybe soon we can visit Paris."

"I would like that, but only if you agree to interpret and translate everything for me, and we always go Dutch. Just like when we lived together in New York." If Alabama did move in with Sunny, she wanted it known she would always pay her share. She did not want to accept charity. She did not want to become a burden to Sunny. Something that she often felt she had become while living with her daughter.

"I agree to abide by your rules. Just know that if we both decide to move to Paris, I get 90 percent of my money back." She reached out and covered Alabama's hand with her own. "And if I die, then I'm leaving this apartment to you, so you won't have to worry about moving back in with Sara and Richard."

Alabama spluttered. "Sunny, you should leave this to your brother. What if I decide to move to Paris or drop dead first?"

"Then I plan to leave it to my goddaughter, Sara. Maybe by then, she and Richard will be ready to retire to the Villas at Kensington Grove."

Alabama tried to picture Sara and Richard living at the Villas. Richard would spend his time in the model train room and eating prime rib for dinner. As for Sara, Alabama figured she would sit on the balcony or the screened-in porch and read and enjoy the river view. Doug would visit a lot, too. Maybe Alison, occasionally. "That's nice of you to think of Sara, but you seriously aren't leaving anything to your brother?"

"Trust me, Balmy, Derik made a ton of money as a plastic surgeon in Atlanta. He and his third wife Clara — she's twenty years younger — have no children. They have a second home in the Hamptons and a cottage in the French countryside. Derik doesn't need nor is he expecting anything from me. His estate will most likely be left to a dozen nonprofits — if he outlives Clara. If he goes first, then I'm pretty sure Clara will remarry and manage to spend it all on jewelry and gigolos."

"Well, okay, then," Alabama said, picking up a folder titled Confidential Application for Villas at Kensington Grove. She couldn't think of anything else that was holding her back. Sunny had answered her questions and brushed away all of her concerns. "I have to fill out all four pages?"

Sunny nodded. "Yes, ma'am. You can turn it in before you leave here on Sunday. Are you ready to move forward with the rest of your life?"

Alabama's eyes widened. Could it be true? Could she really afford to live in the Villas after all? She didn't have to think twice. "Hand me a pen." She would worry about Sara's hurt feelings later.

Chapter Sixteen

The Villas' main dining room was huge. The size and elegant decor reminded Alabama of her first cruise with Ray to celebrate their tenth wedding anniversary. She had been seasick the entire cruise. The ship's doctor gave her Dramamine, which kept her too groggy to leave the cabin. But every time the ship docked and stopped rocking, Alabama's queasiness ended. Unfortunately, as soon as the ship reached Nassau, Ray began suffering from traveler's diarrhea. Unable to leave the ship, he'd insisted that she go ashore without him.

"We saved our money for two years to pay for this cruise, Balmy. If you don't get off this ship and see these Caribbean islands after all of your seasick days, then all will have been for naught. So, get your sun hat and your sun glasses, and go. Take lots of pictures and give me a full report."

Ray had hugged her tightly and pushed her out the cabin door at each port to explore the sights of Nassau, San Juan, St. Thomas, and Antigua. After such a disastrous first cruise experience, most normal people wouldn't have ever considered taking another cruise, but Alabama and Ray did—after discovering scopolamine patches and Imodium.

Alabama's thoughts were interrupted by a smiling hostess— Isabella Finch, according to her name tag—who greeted them at the dining room door. She was a little bit fluffy around the edges, but looked good in her well-fitted dark-blue skirt and jacket.

"Good evening, Mrs. Day," Isabella spoke to Sunny. Then she nodded toward Alabama and asked, "Is this your guest for the weekend?"

"Yes, Isabella. This is my friend Alabama Knight."

Isabella's smile broadened into what Alabama called a "Martha Raye" smile that spread from ear to ear. She bet that every person living in the Villas was old enough to remember the popular comic actress and singer who had had seven husbands.

"Welcome to the Villas, Mrs. Knight," Isabella said. "Mrs. Day, your friends are waiting for you at table 24 in the far back corner."

Sunny thanked Isabella and led Alabama through a sea of tables of various shapes and sizes—round, rectangular, and square—that seated from one to eight diners. All tables were covered with a white linen cloth. Each place had a linen napkin, good matching silverware, and a stemmed water glass. A small vase of real-live flowers was centered on each table.

This is so uptown, Alabama mused. So elegant. It had a much more formal feel than the smaller Le Bistro, where they had eaten lunch. Immediately, Alabama was glad Sunny had insisted on changing into dressier clothes for dinner. Otherwise, she would have felt very much underdressed. Sunny had combed and styled Alabama's hair into a bun for the occasion and insisted that she put on lipstick. Alabama felt all gussied up and giddy. Like a teenage girl going on a first date. Like an excited old lady ready to meet Sunny's new friends, who might one day be her friends, too.

When they reached the table for eight in the corner, Alabama was pleasantly surprised when three men stood up. Back in the old days, it was considered good manners for men to stand when a woman entered the room. She thought that had died out with the Boomer Generation, but then this room had to be full of Boomers like herself and Sunny, plus members of the Silent Generation, who were now in their 80s and 90s.

"Hello, again, Charlie Chan," Alabama said, as he helped seat her at the table. "Thank you." She watched as Ron Williams assisted Sunny. Such nice manners, she thought, and the men looked good, too. Charlie wore a white-linen jacket over a white-collar shirt, open at the neck; Ron, a casual blue-denim blazer over a pale-blue, snug-fitting tee; and the third man—quite distinguished looking—a slim-fit navy blazer over a pin-stripe dress shirt, open at the neck.

All three gentlemen sat down, and everyone began introducing themselves. Seated to Alabama's left were Charlie and Yasuko, whose face once again appeared flawless. No dark circles or blemishes or wrinkles under her twinkling, black eyes. How did she do that, Alabama wondered. Tonight, Yasuko's long black hair was carefully pinned up with a trio of elegant Asian hair sticks.

Sunny was seated to Alabama's right. Seated on the other side of Sunny were newlyweds "hunky spy" Ron and his wife Carolina, organizer of the Caribbean cruise adventure. Alabama was fascinated by her frizzy, silver hair. She wondered if Carolina had any problems keeping the frizz under control like she did.

Eula Mae Davis, seated directly across the table from Sunny, introduced herself. She was everything Sunny said she was and more. Not only was she the queen bee and matriarch for this group of friends, she also kept everyone smiling with her Southernisms and unbridled straightforwardness. Eula Mae turned to her right and introduced Geoffrey Winston Churchill, an extremely handsome gentleman with a stock of white hair and black-framed glasses. An image of the late Cary Grant when he was 80 popped into Alabama's mind.

"Did all of you cruise together on the infamous *Emerald Dream*?" Alabama asked, spreading her linen napkin across her lap.

"Lordy, Lordy, Lordy," Eula Mae said. "Butter my butt and call me a biscuit. Sunny Day, have you filled Balmy's head with our exploits before we've had a chance to properly introduce ourselves?" Everyone at the table laughed.

A waiter—dressed in a white shirt, red tie, and dark blue trousers—walked up and handed each person a burgundy, leather-bound menu. "Good evening, ladies and gentlemen," he said. "Mrs. Day, I see you have a visitor this evening."

"Yes, indeed, I do, Diego." Sunny motioned toward Alabama. "This is my friend, Balmy Knight, who wanted to visit the Villas this weekend to see what life is like living here. Balmy, this is Diego Diaz. He just became a new U.S. citizen this week."

"Where were you born," Alabama asked. She had never met a naturalized citizen before.

"Cuba, Mrs. Knight," Diego said. "I came to America as a child with my parents in the 1960s. Back then, Cuban immigrants enjoyed preferential treatment, and my parents were given legal permanent residence in Miami. Eventually, they became naturalized citizens. And now I follow in their footsteps."

Geoffrey cleared his throat loudly. "Congratulations, Diego," he said. "I, too, am a naturalized citizen. I'm very proud to be an American."

Sunny leaned over and whispered in Alabama's ear. "Don't you just love his deep-bass voice?"

"And that sexy British accent," she whispered back. His accent reminded her of Patrick Stewart and her favorite old TV series, *Star Trek: The Next Generation.* Of course, she also had a thing for the Irish actor Pierce Brosnan and the late Scottish actor Sean Connery, who had played the James Bond character so well.

"Jolly good, Geoff, old boy," said Charlie with an obvious fake British accent. He reached over and playfully slapped Geoff on the back.

Diego took a step back and smiled. He made a slight bow. "I'll give you a few minutes to read over the menu and return for your drink orders."

"Diego is the manager of the main dining hall and Le Bistro," explained Sunny to Alabama.

"He's married to Bernita, a nurse in our medical center," Carolina said.

"Lordy, Lordy, Lordy," Eula Mae spoke up. "They have Eleanora's *Gateau a la Crème de Coco* on the dessert menu, again."

"What's that?" asked Alabama and Sunny together.

Yasuko took a sip of water. "The chef takes menu suggestions from residents. Two months ago, Georgette Fasquelle submitted this recipe to the chef for his consideration. It was a dessert that her grandmother in Nice used to make for special family celebrations."

Ron put his fingers to his lips and kissed them. "The chef enlarged the recipe to feed everyone. It was a huge, lip-smacking success. My mouth is watering now, just thinking about it. It's to die for!"

"This ultra-moist cake oozes creamy coconut milk, and is topped with sweetened whipped cream, covered with coconut," Carolina said. "If you like coconut, you have to give it a try."

· · ·

By the time Diego returned to take their orders, Alabama had found several entrees she wanted to try, including the Dover Sole Meunière and Blue Crab Mornay. One of the nice things about living on the Georgia coast was the abundance of fresh seafood. Ray loved to buy shrimp and fish right off the fishing boats and bring them home for her to cook for dinner. No doubt about it, Alabama decided, living in the Villas might be dangerous to her waistline.

Diego paused at Alabama's elbow. "What would madam like for dinner tonight?"

"Too many tasty choices, Diego, but I've decided on the Dover sole."

"Excellent choice, madam."

Alabama looked up from her menu. "With the coconut cake for dessert."

"What would you like to drink?" Diego asked. "Perhaps a nice white zinfandel?"

"May I recommend the Kim Crawford sauvignon blanc?" Geoffrey suggested.

Alabama glanced at Geoffrey and thought that sounded much too fancy pantsy for her tastes. And too pricey. She and Ray didn't start drinking wine until the early 1970s. Even then it was only a bottle of Almaden white zinfandel or cabernet sauvignon to celebrate special occasions. But in the 1980s, Ray started taking an interest in wines and even took her on a week-long trip to visit California wineries in Sonoma. She looked up at Diego. "Do you have a California chardonnay or a soft white Bordeaux?"

Diego rubbed his chin. "Mmm, I think we may have a bottle of Château Smith Haut Lafitte white Bordeaux. I will check, madam."

"If you do have such a bottle," said Geoffrey, who had ordered pan-fried, spotted sea trout, "I'll give it a go, too."

Ron ordered the crab entrée and thumped his menu on the table. "Diego, isn't that vineyard known for its organic winegrowing?" Diego nodded. "Then I'll also have a glass. And to show what a generous fellow I am, I'll order the whole bottle. Diego, please put that on my tab."

Well, well, well, thought Alabama. Looks like this dinner is off to a good start.

Diego was back at their table with the last bottle of Château Smith Haut Lafitte white Bordeaux. Since Ron was paying for the bottle, Diego poured some into his glass. Holding the glass by the stem up to the light, Ron rolled the liquid around the glass, gave it a deep sniff, and sipped it. He closed his eyes and swished it around his mouth before swallowing. He smiled and opened his eyes. "It's more citrus and floral than grassy and herbal." After Diego poured more wine in his glass, Ron took another sip. "The flavor is not as tropical or peachy as California sauvignon blanc. I declare this will go perfect with our seafood tonight."

"Hear, hear!" Geoffrey lifted his wine glass. "Cheers to our jolly good fellow, Ronald Williams!" He took a sip, followed by everyone at the table—even Eula Mae, with her class of iced tea, and Yasuko, with her glass of Takara plum wine.

Alabama and Geoffrey locked eyes briefly. She waited for him to start singing "For he's a jolly good fellow," but his opportunity passed.

"I say, there, Balmy," Geoffrey started the table conversation, "I hear that you, Sunny, and your mates performed on Broadway and in night clubs together?"

Alabama had just taken a sip of her wine and nearly choked. She coughed several times into her napkin and frowned at Sunny. "I don't know what Sunny told you, but we only sang and danced in the chorus of a few splashy musicals."

"No need to be modest, my dear," Geoff said with a wink.

"Please fill us in," Yasuko begged. "Name some of the musicals you performed in."

"Would you settle for any musical in which we might have hummed a few bars?" asked Sunny.

Everyone nodded. "Go for it," Ron egged Sunny on. "Tell us the nitty-gritty of performing on Broadway."

"It was gritty, all right," Alabama said. "When we first got to New York City, we shared a room at the Y, worked at menial jobs to survive, and went to as many cattle-call auditions as we could find."

"What kind of work did you find?" Yasuko asked.

"Legal, I hope," interrupted Charlie with a chuckle.

"Fortunately for me," Alabama said, "my mother made me take typing and shorthand in high school. I was able to get a job as a clerk with a large insurance company, where I worked in a cavernous office with dozens of other young women. Later, after three months of classes, I was promoted to insurance underwriter."

"I wasn't so lucky," Sunny admitted. "But I did manage to get a job at the Automat in midtown Manhattan. I worked myself silly during the lunch crowd. When a customer removed a dish, it was my job to replace it. The banana cream pie was very popular."

"Boring!" Yasuko exclaimed. "I want to hear about the singing and dancing part."

Alabama sighed. "It took a long time before we got any breaks."

"We did a lot of work in off-off-Broadway productions at small theaters and performing halls like the New Bowery or York Playhouse or the Orpheum," Sunny said.

"We finally got our break with *Fiddler on the Roof*," Alabama said. "We were like understudies or something. We only actually performed a couple of nights."

"But it looked good on our resumes," Sunny said. "And that was the toe in the door we'd been hoping for. After that we were able to get small singing or dancing roles in musicals like *This Was Burlesque, South Pacific, The Music Man, The Man of La Mancha* . . ."

"What about the night clubs?" asked Charlie. "I must have missed that conversation."

"Yes," said Carolina, "please tell us more about performing in the club scene after you were married. Sunny said you called your act 'Knights and Days'?"

"I'm sure it sounds glamorous to you, but it was a job for the four of us. We worked hard to get up on that stage night after night and perform," Alabama said. "The mood of the crowd affected our performance. Any night we didn't get boos or heckles was good. Nights we received applause and standing ovations were even better."

"Which night club was your favorite?" Geoffrey asked.

"I would have to say the Copacabana, even though it was the scariest venue as far as I was concerned. It was the only place we performed that I actually threw up from stage fright." Alabama looked sideways at Sunny. "Don't you agree?"

"Definitely. The night club was very much uptown. A first-class joint, where celebrities went to hang out with other celebrities and eat expensive dinners," Sunny said. "I remember the week that we performed there, Ray and Jeff decided we should eat dinner before the show." She waved her fingers in front of her face. "Ooh la la. You wouldn't believe the prices! Nearly four dollars for filet mignon or sirloin steak. Three dollars for lobster. Fifty cents just for a bowl of tomato soup."

Everyone at the table, who had been listening intently to Sunny, burst out laughing.

"Huh? What did I say that was so funny?"

"Sunny," Alabama spluttered, trying to stop laughing, "I know those prices seemed exorbitant to us back in the Sixties, but think about how much a bowl of soup or a steak or a lobster cost today?"

Geoff, who had been quietly listening, spoke up, "I think that Sunny and Balmy should sing and dance for us. We'd like to hear you sing a song from one of your musicals or see a dance number from your night club days."

Alabama spluttered. "Excuse me? That was way over fifty years ago. I doubt seriously if either of us would be up to entertaining you tonight."

At that point, Sunny quickly steered the conversation toward the great Caribbean cruise adventure. "Carolina, tell Balmy how you met the stowaway on the ship," Sunny said, taking a bite of her last hushpuppy.

Carolina wiped her mouth with her napkin. "I caught this young woman stealing my strawberries, so I chased after her to get them back."

"Bless her heart," butted in Eula Mae, "and just as she was fixin' to catch that gal and get back her strawberries, Carolina collided with the ship's purser and bloodied his nose."

"I didn't do it on purpose," Carolina explained.

"He was madder than a wet hen!" Eula Mae laughed and pushed back from the table. "Lordy, lordy, lordy, my belly's as full as a tick. I think I'm calling it a night. It's been a busy day, and I'm worn slap out. If you'll excuse me, I'll be heading to the barn."

The three men stood, Geoffrey helped Eula Mae to her feet, and then he escorted her out of the dining room. As soon as they were gone, Alabama asked, "Are they a couple?"

"Why do you ask?" Yasuko asked. "Are you interested in him?"

Alabama felt her cheeks warm. "What? No, I was curious about him, that's all. I mean, he's so very British and she's so . . ."

"Southern?" Carolina asked.

"Opposites attract?" Sunny asked.

Ron and Charlie looked at each other and laughed. "I think Geoffrey uses her as a safe port in the storm," Ron said, gleefully.

Alabama shook her head. "I don't understand."

"It's quite simple, really," Ron explained. "When Geoff moved into the Villas, many of the women became interested in him."

"What Ron is saying is that Geoff became the prize stud," Yasuko said. "Geoffrey, who hails from Rustington, England, is a very young and spry 80. With his thick, white hair and rugged good looks . . ."

"He reminds me of Cary Grant in his older years," Sunny added with a sigh.

"Or Patrick Stewart with lots of white hair," Alabama said.

Yasuko nodded and ran her finger around the rim of her wine glass. "Yes, and the man works out in the gym and swims to stay fit. He drives a new Mercedes and his bass voice with that sexy British accent keeps the women circling his wagon."

Charlie leaned toward Alabama and lowered his voice. "Because Eula Mae didn't make goo-goo eyes at him or drop off home-baked goodies on his doorstep or act like she wanted to strip him naked and ravish him, he befriended her for safety reasons. Now the women have backed off and leave him relatively in peace."

"Smart man," Alabama said.

"But I saw the way he was looking at you tonight," pointed out Yasuko. "I bet if you move to the Villas, you two could become friends. Really good friends."

"Yes, but we've heard things about him that are troubling," Carolina quickly spoke up.

"Oh? Things like what?" asked Alabama.

Yasuko leaned toward Alabama and lowered her voice. "Like he might be a heartbreaker. Or worse."

• • •

Alabama took a bite of the sweet, oozy cream of coconut cake. It was one of the most delicious desserts she had ever tasted. She sighed and thought about what Yasuko had said. Would she want to become friends with Geoffrey? She felt faint stirrings in her abdomen. Stirrings she'd not felt since before Ray died. And then, *ping*, Jake's face popped into her mind.

Chapter Seventeen

The next morning, the first thing Alabama did after putting on her robe was to calm her wiry hair with a smattering of Odessa's Taming Serum for frizzy, dry hair. Then she walked into the kitchen and pressed the coffeemaker ON button. Within minutes, the smell of dark-roasted coffee wafted through the entire apartment. She closed her eyes and breathed deeply, remembering the many mornings Ray had awakened her with a cup of *caffè latte*.

It was during an anniversary trip to Florence, Italy, that Alabama first tasted and fell instantly in love with the Italian coffee. Every morning, during their week in Florence, she had *caffè latte* for breakfast with a variety of sweet cakes and pastries or bread with butter and jam. Somehow, before they checked out of the hotel, Ray managed to get the recipe for making the special *caffè latte*: 1/3 espresso, 2/3 heated milk, and a little foam.

After Ray died and the espresso machine stopped working, Alabama compromised with faux *caffè latte*. She'd heat herself a cup of hot milk in the microwave, then pour in a spoonful of dark roast coffee and a little bit of sugar. She missed the espresso and foam, but she still found her version better than drinking regular, boring American coffee.

Sipping her hot latte, Alabama sat at the table and pulled out her application for living at the Villas and a pen. By the time Sunny walked into the kitchen, Alabama was finished. She stacked the pages neatly together, inserted them in the folder, and handed it to Sunny.

"What's this?" Sunny asked.

"My application."

Sunny tapped it against her chin. "You filled it out completely?" Alabama nodded. "Then after breakfast, we'll drop it off at the office."

Alabama took another sip of her latte, which was starting to cool. She placed her cup in the microwave and gave it 45 seconds. "If I get approved to live here, this might be an important deciding factor."

After a quick breakfast of cinnamon-raisin bagels and cream cheese, Alabama followed Sunny down to the director's office on the first floor where she met Dottie Brashear, a petite, pixie-cut brunette with very large eyes and a heart-shaped mouth. Alabama thought she looked twenty-something. Wouldn't it be better, she wondered, to have at least a forty-something person in charge of a retirement community? An older person who could better relate to retirees? But Dottie exuded youth, enthusiasm, vitality, and energy. Maybe that's exactly what's needed, she decided.

When Dottie stood, she wasn't much taller standing than when she was sitting. She stretched up on tiptoe and reached out across her desk to shake hands with Alabama. "It's my pleasure to meet you, Alabama. Sunny says you're interested in sharing her apartment?"

"Most definitely," Alabama said, handing her the folder. "Here's my application. So far, I love everything I've seen about the Villas. I heard at dinner last night that this is the perfect place to live out your golden years."

Dottie laughed. "You must have met Carolina Cunningham. Oops, excuse me. I mean Carolina Williams. Too darn many women in the Villas getting married lately and changing their names." She winked. "Carolina's always going on and on about how the Villas is the perfect place to live out your retirement years." Dottie looked at her watch. "My goodness, ladies, it's almost 10 o'clock. You better hurry or you'll miss the great pumpkin-carving contest."

"What pumpkin-carving contest?" Alabama asked, glancing from Dottie to Sunny.

Dottie started nudging them toward her office door. "I'm surprised Sunny didn't tell you about it. The residents are carving pumpkins for our Halloween costume party next Saturday. The pumpkins will be party decorations displayed around our ballroom. In addition, the staff will choose the four best-carved pumpkins. First, second, and third place winners will receive prize ribbons; and the grand prize winners will each receive a $25 VISA gift card."

"That sounds like fun," Alabama said. "I always loved carving pumpkins with my daughter Sara, and later with my grandchildren."

Dottie walked Alabama and Sunny out her office door and closed it behind her. "I will be sure to put your application on fast-track, Alabama." She paused. "It's a good thing you want to room with Sunny and not have your own apartment."

"Why is that?" Alabama asked.

Dottie raised her eyebrow. "Because our waiting list is over two years long."

• • •

When Alabama and Sunny reached the ballroom, they found a short line at the entrance, where Yasuko and Carolina were handing each person a pumpkin-carving kit. "What a surprise," Yasuko greeted them. "We thought you two might have driven to Jekyll or something."

"No," Sunny said. "Balmy wants to experience activities going on at the Villas. How else will she know if this is the perfect place to live?"

Yasuko laughed and handed Alabama a kit. "I think you'll enjoy the pumpkin carving. It will be an opportunity to meet some of the other Villas residents."

Carolina smiled. "Yes, you should participate in everything this weekend, so you'll know what life here is really like."

Inside the ballroom, Alabama and Sunny walked down a long row of tables with all sizes of pumpkins. While Sunny picked one of the smaller pumpkins, Alabama chose a medium-sized one. She had really wanted a larger one, but Sunny was quick to point out how much longer it would take to scrape out a large pumpkin and carve it.

Ron and Charlie greeted Alabama and Sunny as soon as they selected their pumpkins and escorted them to a paper-covered carving-station table in the center of the ballroom. Then Ron and Charlie sliced off the top of each pumpkin.

"Use the large metal spoon to scrape out the pumpkin seeds and flesh," Ron explained. "Toss it all into that huge red plastic tub," he said, pointing at the one in the center of the table.

"Okay, you two, go for it!" Charlie said. The men gave Alabama and Sunny the thumbs up and headed back to the pumpkin tables to assist other residents.

Alabama sorted through other tools in her pumpkin-carving bag. She found a serrated knife to create a hole in the bottom of the pumpkin. That way, the candle or other light source would sit level and the pumpkin could be lowered over the light or candle. She also found several different sizes of small paring knives, something that reminded her of the ice picks from the old days, and half a dozen stencils of simple images to carve on a pumpkin—outlines of a cat, a bat, an owl, a wolf with full moon, and a spider.

Sunny tentatively poked her scoop into her pumpkin and brought out a mass of orangey flesh sprinkled with seeds. She shrugged and dumped it into the tub. "What are you waiting for, Balmy? Apparently, you're the experienced pumpkin carver. This is the first pumpkin I've ever carved."

"You gotta be kidding me!" Alabama replied. "You never carved a pumpkin when you were young?" She started rapidly digging the insides out of her pumpkin. She had forgotten how satisfying it felt to stab and scoop and toss. She closed her eyes, inhaled the smell of the raw pumpkin, and thought of her mother cooking down the flesh that would later be used to make the family's Thanksgiving pumpkin pies. She wondered if the chef at the Villas ever made pumpkin pies.

"My mom never made pies. She didn't even like to cook," Sunny said. "If it didn't come in a can, then she didn't know how to cook it." She looked carefully at the inside of her pumpkin. "I think I'm ready to start carving." With help from Alabama, Sunny was able to trace the outline of a bat onto her pumpkin. Then she selected a carving tool and went to work.

Passing on the stencils, Alabama etched in and carved a tombstone with an arching, toothy cat on top. Slowly, she added a moon and creepy, leafless tree branches. As an afterthought, she carved a skeletal hand rising from the grave. She stepped back from her pumpkin to see if she needed to add further details and stepped on someone's foot.

A deep-bass voice of a man yelped. Alabama jerked around in surprise and found Geoffrey with a pained expression on his face.

"That smarted!" he exclaimed, gingerly rubbing the toes protruding from his black slides. "You didn't signal you were backing up, my dear."

"I'm so sorry. I didn't realize you were standing behind me," Alabama apologized to Geoffrey, who was standing there in a pair of red-and-blue plaid swimming trunks and an unbuttoned, British flag-themed shirt that exposed silvery chest hairs. A Tower Bridge of London beach towel hung around his neck. She looked him up and down. "I see you're dressed in high-fashion this morning."

"That's being a bit cheeky, Balmy." He laughed softly. "I was on my way to the pool for a few laps before lunch. Thought I'd stop by to see who was participating in this phenomenal event." He glanced from Sunny's pumpkin to Alabama's. "Creative and simplistic!" He ran his fingers around the edges of Sunny's bat and tapped lightly on Alabama's cat-topped tombstone. "Definitely not traditional American pumpkins with eyes, nose and mouth."

Sunny struck a diva pose and pouted. "I don't see you in here carving a pumpkin." She tapped her foot.

"Two reasons why, lovely ladies."

"And what's that?" asked Alabama, wondering if Geoffrey was showing his royal snooty side this morning. Of course, she really didn't know him that well.

"First of all, luv, I have no artistic talent. Secondly, I'm one of the judges for the pumpkin-carving contest." He winked and smiled.

Alabama was startled. *Geoffrey had dimples.* Why hadn't she noticed that last night? Ray had had dimples. Then she wondered if Jake shaved his beard, if he might have dimples, too. She shook the thought from her mind. "Geoffrey, I accept your reasons for not participating."

"I don't have any artistic talent, either," Sunny admitted, "but Dottie said this was a fun thing to do."

"Not a doubt in my mind that this Halloween will be the bee's knees! Mark my word!" Geoffrey said.

"I'm looking forward to the costumes," Sunny said.

"I'm disappointed that I won't be able to make it," Alabama said.

"What?" exclaimed Geoffrey. "Why not? When are you moving in?"

Sunny tilted her head toward Alabama, as though waiting for her response.

"I just turned in my application this morning."

Geoffrey threw his hand out to the side. "Tosh! Not a problem for you, dearie. You'll be officially approved by tomorrow."

Alabama sighed. "It's a little bit more complicated than that . . ."

"Tell you what, you can tell me all about it at lunch, and I'll tell you all about Guy Fawkes Day." He headed toward the exit at a fast trot.

"But—" Alabama started to respond.

He looked over his shoulder and waved his hand. "12:30 in Le Bistro. Don't be late!"

Alabama's eyes widened in shock. "Who does that man think he is?"

Sunny chuckled. "The king rooster in the hen house."

"Well," Alabama huffed. "We'll just see about that." And he thought she was cheeky? Why he was just like Rex Harrison in *My Fair Lady*! If only she had yelled out after him with Audrey Hepburn's memorable line: *Just you wait, Henry Higgins, just you wait.*

Chapter Eighteen

Alabama thought Le Bistro was darker, quieter, and smaller than she remembered from Friday's lunch. Not to mention she'd been so caught up in the lunch frenzy with her family on Friday, she'd not paid that much attention to her surroundings. Today the tables were covered with burgundy cloths and decorated in the center with fabric pumpkins and rustic natural raffia. Compared to the main dining room, Le Bistro had an intimate, chic, Parisian feel. It had atmosphere.

Geoffrey stood and waved at them from across the room. He grinned as Alabama and Sunny approached the table. Alabama was immediately fascinated by how white his teeth looked. Her own dentist had whitened her teeth twice in six months, but they'd never looked anywhere near as bright as Geoffrey's. She figured he had dentures, until Sunny assured her that those were his real teeth. If that were true, perhaps he'd had his front teeth veneered? And what about that thick head of white hair? Sunny said it was not a toupee or creative hair styling. Did that impress her? Of course, it did. Not too many 80-year-old men could claim that.

"I'm glad you two could join me for lunch," Geoffrey said, seating Alabama next to him. The hostess, who had followed them to the table, helped seat Sunny next to Alabama, recited the chef's special of the day—*Huîtres au Four Au Camembert*—and explained it was baked oysters on the half shell, smothered in French camembert. Then she left.

By the time the waitress returned and began pouring water into long-stemmed glasses, the three were ready to order: Steak and frites for Geoffrey and French *Quiche Lorraine* for Alabama and Sunny. "May I take your dessert order now, too?" she asked.

"Do you have any of that delicious coconut cake left from last night?" Alabama asked, remembering the gooey, creamy, sweetness, but not the name of the dessert.

"Oh no, madam. That dessert was served in the main dining room," the waitress said. "If you dine there tonight, they may have some left, but go early before it's all gone."

"In that case, I'll try the French macarons," Alabama said. "With a cup of *caffé latte*."

Sunny handed her menu to the waitress. "*Crème brûlée* for me, please, and a cup of black coffee."

Geoffrey shook his head. "You two are a pair of lightweights. I'll have the *sauerkirsch-erdbeer-baiser-galette* with coffee, please."

"What in the world is that?" Alabama asked, as the waitress took their menus and left. She'd taken French in college, but she only recognized *galette*, meaning a small, round cake.

Geoffrey wiped his mouth with his linen napkin. Alabama wondered if he did that to cover up his smirk.

"Translation, ladies: sour cherry-strawberry-meringue cake. It's a much more substantial and tastier dessert than macarons or *crème brûlée*." He raised one of his dark-brown eyebrows. "But I like your dessert choices, too."

"That's good, Geoffrey, but I'm not sharing mine with you," Alabama shot back.

Geoffrey threw back his head and laughed loudly. "That's a jolly good comeback, Balmy," he said, wiping the tears from his eyes. "I like a good woman with a wry sense of humor."

Was that what she had, Alabama wondered—a wry sense of humor? She opened her mouth to make another wisecrack, but Sunny grabbed her wrist and whispered, "Let it go." Then Sunny leaned toward Geoffrey. "What was it you were going to tell us at lunch? Something about Guy Fawkes Day."

"Oh righto, I was indeed." He smoothed his napkin in his lap. "Your American Halloween has always reminded me of our Guy Fawkes Day in England."

"You go trick-or-treating on Guy Fawkes Day?" Sunny asked.

"Not exactly, but there is some similarity. Blimey! I need to start at the beginning, but if I do, it will be *absobloodylutely* boring."

Alabama and Sunny giggled. "Start wherever you need to start," Alabama said.

"I'll do just that." He cleared his throat. "How much do you two know about Catholicism in England during the reign of Queen Elizabeth I?"

Alabama grimaced. "World history was not my best class in college. Was she the one they called the Virgin Queen because she never married?"

Geoffrey smiled and nodded. "Yes, that's the one."

"Was she ugly or did she have a terrible disposition or something?" Alabama asked.

"Look at who she had as a father figure and role model." Sunny said. "Henry VIII had six wives. He killed Elizabeth's mother—his second wife, Ann Boleyn—when Elizabeth was a toddler. Maybe thinking about getting married left a bad taste in her mouth."

Alabama's eyes widened, as something clicked in her mind, and she felt a strong desire to raise her hand and yell, "Pick me!" She grabbed Sunny's wrist, bursting with a eureka moment. "Yes, I remember now. She had lots of male friends like Walter Raleigh and Francis Drake. Lots of prominent suitors wanted to marry her."

Geoffrey rubbed his hand over his face. "Ladies, please. Elizabeth's marriage status and her lovers are not what's important here."

"What could be more important than that, Geoffrey?" Sunny asked.

"She established Protestantism in England and got rid of the Catholics."

Alabama frowned and thought about that. "Are you saying she murdered the Catholics and turned her subjects into Protestants?"

"You know what Eula Mae would say if she were here?" asked Sunny.

"Lordy, Lordy, Lordy!" the three of them chorused and laughed out loud.

Alabama rubbed her chin thoughtfully. "What does this have to do with Halloween?"

"I'm getting there," Geoffrey said. "Don't get your knickers in a knot." He took a long swig of water and wiped his mouth with his napkin. "After Elizabeth died, the new ruler of England, King James I, didn't like Catholics, either. So, a bloke named Guy Fawkes and associates decided to kill the king and his leaders by blowing up the Houses of Parliament."

"My goodness, Geoffrey, this isn't boring at all," Sunny said, just as their food was served.

"No, it sounds like the political squabbling that's always going on in Congress," Alabama said. She leaned over her quiche and inhaled the richness of cheese and bacon. "This quiche smells so good." She took a small bite and chewed slowly to enjoy the creamy, buttery goodness.

"Oh yum!" exclaimed Sunny, savoring her first bite of quiche.

Alabama glanced curiously over at Geoffrey's plate of steak and frites with a few pieces of arugula for decoration. The round piece of steak was about three inches in diameter and two inches thick. Geoffrey's knife sliced through the rare meat like it was butter. With the fork in his left hand, he pierced one small bite, plopped it into his mouth, closed his eyes, and sighed happily.

Geoffrey swallowed and opened his eyes, which locked on Alabama's. He smiled. "Sorry, dear lady, but it's near impossible to get a beef tenderloin filet this tender in England. I always take my time and enjoy the moment whenever I can order it here."

"It's quite alright," Alabama said. "I do love to watch a man enjoy his steak." Ribeye was always Ray's favorite cut of steak, she remembered. He was willing to eat beans and chicken for weeks, if he could have a good ribeye steak once a month.

Sunny sipped from her water glass. "What's alright?"

"It's alright for Geoffrey to enjoy his steak and *pomme frites*," Alabama explained.

After Geoffrey devoured his last piece of potato, he pushed his plate back. "That was scrummy! Best lunch today." He swigged down a mouthful of water and wiped his mouth with his napkin. "Now, where was I?"

"You were talking about Guy Fawkes wanting to blow up Parliament," Alabama said, finishing her last bite of quiche and thinking how *absobloodylutely* boring this piece of British history was getting.

"Righto! So, during the opening of a new session of Parliament, Guy and his friends planned to blow up the king, his eldest son, the House of Lords, and the House of Commons. Then they would kidnap the king's daughter, crown her queen, marry her off to a good Catholic, and restore the Catholic monarchy." He paused and took another swig of water.

"I realize I slept through a lot of world history class, but I don't remember any of this," Alabama admitted.

"Probably because it didn't come to fruition," explained Geoffrey.

"All that planning went awry?" asked Sunny.

"Afraid so," Geoffrey said. "The authorities found Guy Fawkes in his cellar with matches and barrels of gunpowder. Everyone involved in the plot was either arrested or died in a shootout with English troops."

"This story didn't have a happy ending," Sunny said.

"That depends on whose side you were on," Geoffrey said.

"The Catholics lost and King James won, obviously" Alabama pointed out. "And what happened to Guy Fawkes?"

"I'm sorry to report he was sentenced to be hung, drawn, and quartered, but committed suicide by leaping off the scaffolding," said Geoffrey.

"That's just unimaginable," Sunny said with a shudder.

"Totally disgusting, Geoffrey. But I still don't understand what that has to do with Halloween?" Alabama asked.

"In order to remember this infamous day, Parliament designated November 5 as Guy Fawkes Day—a time to get together with friends and family, set off fireworks, light bonfires, attend parades, and burn effigies of Fawkes. When I was growing up, my brothers and I wore Guy Fawkes masks and pulled an effigy of him around in a wagon, demanding a 'penny for the Guy.'" Geoffrey rocked back in his seat and crossed his arms across his chest.

Alabama smirked. "I do believe Guy Fawkes Day was one of your favorite holidays as a child, right?" She leaned back as a bus boy began clearing dirty plates and silverware from the table.

Geoffrey chuckled. "Yes, yes it was. After the war, American troops stationed at bases throughout Great Britain, brought their families with them, along with American culture. British children were fascinated by Halloween, the fanciful costumes, and the distribution of candy to trick-or-treaters. It didn't take long for me and my friends to create our own unique way of marking the spookiest of holidays."

"Do English children carve pumpkins?" asked Sunny.

"Bloody yes! We grow millions of pumpkins in the UK every year. Most of them are hollowed out to create ghoulish lanterns."

"Excuse me, madam," said the waitress to Alabama, as she set down her *caffè latte*. Then she poured coffee into large cups for Sunny and Geoffrey. The conversation paused long enough for desserts to be placed in front of the proper diner. "Does anyone need anything else?" the waitress asked. Everyone shook their head and said no.

Sunny poured a little bit of cream into her coffee and a few grains of sugar before stirring it. "Pumpkins aside, Geoffrey, do British children go trick or treating or do they prefer Guy Fawkes Day?"

Geoffrey grimaced. "Let's just say British children find the American Halloween much more appealing. In England, Halloween is hot right now. The children have bloody well embraced it. Houses and shops are decorated with images of witches and pumpkins, and even pets are dressed in silly Halloween costumes. It's become ridiculous." He rolled his eyes up.

Sunny scraped the last of her *crème brûlée* from the dish and licked the spoon. "So, tell me Geoffrey, are you dressing up as Guy Fawkes for the Halloween party?"

"Bloody hell, no," he spluttered. "What about your costumes?" He glanced from Sunny to Alabama.

"I'm thinking about coming as Sylvia," Sunny said.

"Sylvia?" Geoffrey asked.

"Surely not?" blurted out Alabama, remembering how much Sunny loved Anita Ekberg's role in the old movie *La Dolce Vita*. "She's not serious, Geoffrey. I'm sure you're old enough to have seen *La Dolce Vita*?"

Geoffrey leaned his head back and kissed his fingers. "Oh, that Sylvia. That was one hot actress." He winked at Sunny. "How about you, Balmy? Wait, let me guess. Eliza Doolittle?"

"No, though I would have loved to have performed that character in the original Broadway production, but Sunny and I missed that musical coming and going," Alabama said sadly. "The stage musical with Julie Andrews and the movie with Audrey Hepburn."

"If you loved it so much, why didn't you audition for a role when it was on Broadway?" Geoffrey asked.

"We arrived in New York too late," Sunny said. "The production closed in 1962 after over 2,700 performances."

"We arrived five years too late," Alabama said. "By the time the show was revived in the mid-1970s, we were gone. It has always been my very favorite musical, but I won't be dressing up as Eliza."

"Marilyn Monroe?"

"No!"

He shrugged. "I give up. Surprise me."

"I'm headed back to Savannah tomorrow. I won't be here next weekend," Alabama explained.

"Blimey! I'm bloody gutted!" Geoffrey exclaimed. "I thought for sure you'd be approved and moved in for the party Saturday night? What's the problem?"

Alabama was starting to feel a little annoyed and frustrated. "First of all, I have not been approved. Even if I were approved tomorrow, I wouldn't be able to move in immediately. My—uh—life is complicated."

Sunny pushed back from the table and stood up. "And on that note, Balmy and I must dash, Geoffrey, or we'll be late for mahjong class."

That was news to Alabama, but she silently thanked Sunny for the rescue. "Yes, we hate to eat and run." She started to follow Sunny toward the door, but was caught by Geoffrey.

"I'm sorry you won't be here for the Halloween bash, but if things should change . . ." He hesitated. "If things work out for you and you can come, then I have a deal for you."

Alabama paused. Her interest was piqued. Would he offer to distance himself from her if she came for the party? She was really starting to feel uncomfortable with all of his attention. "What sort of deal?"

"If you come, I will dress as Cary Grant, and you can be my Grace Kelly."

Sunny stifled a laugh, but Alabama stared back at Geoffrey, her eyes narrowing. "Seriously? Then I think you better have a default costume plan, Geoffrey Winston Churchill, because the chances of my being here on Saturday night are slim to none."

Chapter Nineteen

Sunny and Alabama paused in the door of the Villas' game room. Through four large windows, Alabama could see an outside garden with shaded benches under old oak trees dripping with Spanish moss. Inside, the game room was packed with men and women sitting at square wooden tables.

Sunny nudged Alabama and pointed at Yasuko and Charlie sitting alone at one of the tables. "There they are."

As Alabama zig-zagged with Sunny through a sea of tables, she noticed that nearly half of the residents were playing cards. The other half—like Yasuko and Charlie—were pushing around small rectangular tiles that clicked softly against the black-leather table tops. "They're playing mahjong," Sunny explained.

In one corner of the room, Alabama saw a hexagonal-shaped table with four women and two men. They were huddled over a game board covered with cards, playing pieces, and dice. It reminded Alabama of the weekends when Sara's high school friends came over to play Dungeons and Dragons. Hearing them laughing and shrieking in the dining room, Alabama thought the teens were playing a fun game. But after ten minutes of observing them play, she decided watching paint dry would be more exciting.

"These folks are into crazy board games." Yasuko said, walking up beside Alabama. "See the woman with the pink and white polka-dotted glasses and purple hair?"

"Impossible to miss," said Alabama. "Is she somebody's granddaughter?"

Yasuko laughed. "Hardly. That's Lilly. She's the youngest woman living at the Villas. She's Archie's second wife. He's the balding, older fellow sitting on her left. Lilly is the resident computer guru. When we were on our Caribbean cruise, we connected with her through a special app. That way, we knew what was going on at the Villas, and she knew about our adventures."

"She definitely looks like someone who would introduce new board games to folks living here," Alabama said. "Are they playing Catan?" Alabama followed Yasuko to the card table where Charlie and Sunny were sitting.

"Yes, they are," Yasuko said, sitting down. "Are you familiar with the game?"

Alabama took the remaining seat. "My granddaughter Alison and her friends play that game occasionally. That and one called Ticket to Ride. I like that game because it has a colorful board and plastic playing pieces shaped like trains." But I'm not sure I'll like mahjong, she thought, running her hands over the small rectangular-shaped tiles scattered across the table. They felt cool and smooth to her touch, but didn't look all that exciting.

Picking up an ivory-colored tile with a red "E" and a black Chinese character on top, Alabama rubbed the surface with her fingers. She could feel where the character seemed etched into the tile. A thin veneer of bamboo covered the back of the tile. She pointed to the surface of the tile. "Is this ivory?"

"No," Charlie said quickly. "Polystyrene."

"What?" she asked.

"For goodness sakes, Charlie," Yasuko cut in. "Make it simple. Call it plastic."

"Fine, call it plastic," he said. "But it's really synthetic polymer. Very cheap and popular in the 1930s and 1940s."

"I do like the Chinese characters," Alabama said, picking up a tile with the red number 9 and two characters, one black and one red.

"Actually," Charlie said and cleared his throat, "these are Japanese mahjong tiles."

Yasuko elbowed her husband's upper arm. "It's doesn't matter, Balmy," she explained. "This set is mine. I brought it back from Japan a few months ago, when I went home for a visit. It belonged to my great-uncle."

"Please tell her the whole story," Charlie said. "She dragged me to Japan so her aunt and uncle, and her cousins, could meet the new husband and get us blessed by a Shinto priest."

"That sounds so romantic!" Alabama gushed. "A man and a woman from two different cultures bonded together in marriage."

"Did you also go to China to get blessed and meet Charlie's family?" Sunny asked.

"It would've been the fair thing for her to do, don't you think?" He winked at Yasuko, as she smacked his arm. "Alas, as far as I know, neither of my parents have any relatives still living in China. My ancestors all immigrated to America—San Francisco to be exact—in the mid-1800s. They came to work in the gold mines or on the transcontinental railroad or simply for a better life."

Alabama frowned. "So, Charlie, you don't have a Chinese mahjong set?"

Charlie and Yasuko both laughed. "Mahjong originated in China in the late 1800s. In Shanghai, they believe," Charlie said.

"But a Japanese soldier brought the game to Japan in the 1920s and started a mahjong club in Tokyo," Yasuko explained. "About that same time, an American man saw the game being played on a ship on the Yangtze River. He created a version with Arabic numerals and Western letters and sold the game to Americans."

Sunny, Alabama, Yasuko, and Charlie began turning the tiles over to expose the images on the front. "The first mahjong tiles were made from bone and bamboo backs or occasionally from jade," Charlie explained.

"They're beautiful," Sunny said.

"These are obviously not the American ones," Alabama observed. "These are Japanese, you said. What do Chinese tiles look like?"

"Exactly like these," Charlie said. He held up his hand as Alabama opened her mouth. "Let me explain. Japanese and Chinese share the same characters. For example," he picked up one tile with a blue character at the top and a red one on the bottom. "The blue character—the box with two lines inside—represents the number four in Japanese and in Chinese. But in Japanese, four is called *shi*. In Chinese, four is called *si*."

Yasuko pointed to four tiles with beautiful blue characters on them. "These four tiles are called the Winds. The character on this tile translates in English as East wind. The Chinese say *dong* and the Japanese say *azuma*."

Charlie moved three tiles together. One had a red character on it; a second tile had a green character; and the third one was solid white. "The Chinese and the Japanese know these tiles represent the red, green, and white Dragons."

"The same characters, the same meaning, but they're called different names in Chinese and Japanese?" asked Alabama.

"Yes!" Yasuko and Charlie chorused.

"So, even if Charlie couldn't speak Japanese and Yasuko couldn't speak Chinese, you would be able to read the characters?" asked Sunny.

"You could read signs in a train station or a menu in a restaurant," Alabama said. She felt like this was another eureka moment. "That must have worked well for you, Charlie, when you went to Japan?"

"In some cases," Charlie agreed. "But not always."

Alabama looked over the tiles and started pulling aside tiles that had circles on them. "These tiles look like they belong together."

"Yes, you're correct. We call them dots." Yasuko gathered up the tiles that had stick images on them. "These tiles are called bamboo." She pointed to a bird on one tile. "This is the one of bamboo. This is the two of bamboo."

Charlie picked up the tile with one single large circle on it. "This is the one of dots."

Alabama felt yet another eureka moment coming. "I get it! The dots, the bamboo, and the characters are like card suits!"

Yasuko grinned like a happy teacher whose student just solved a difficult math problem. "That is mahjong in a nutshell. Visualize these tiles as cards that stand on end and are not held in your hand."

"How do you shuffle these tiles?" Alabama asked.

"How do you stack them for a drawing pile?" Sunny wanted to know.

Yasuko smiled. "Players make a four-sided wall, two tiles high. North, South, East, and West. You throw the dice to see who goes first and take turns drawing tiles from the wall."

Alabama frowned. "This sounds complicated."

"Not really," Yasuko said. "Just different."

"How about this?" asked Charlie. "Do you two know how to play rummy?"

Alabama nodded. "Of course."

"Me, too," said Sunny.

"Then let's play rummy," Yasuko said, as she and Charlie turned all the tiles face down and moved them around to mix them up. "It's a simple way to get a feel for playing mahjong. I promise we won't even keep score."

"Yasuko!" A voice shouted from the direction of the door.

Alabama turned to see Carolina and Ron making their way towards them. Carolina was waving a magazine excitedly in the air. "You have to see this!" she shouted, plopping down the magazine between Yasuko and Charlie. "See? This is us!"

"What's this?" asked Charlie.

"It's a feature article in *Coastal Georgia* magazine about the Villas having the best activities in retirement communities in the state," explained Ron.

"The writer spent a year visiting retirement communities in Georgia and interviewing residents. Remember that time a writer came here with a photographer?" asked Carolina.

"Wait," Yasuko said. "That was right after we returned from our cruise."

"Yes, that's right," Carolina said. "Ron and Charlie were here for the weekend, checking out the Villas."

"And the Villas was voted the best." Yasuko handed the magazine across the table to Alabama and Sunny.

Alabama smoothed out the magazine pages and glanced at full-color photos of the Olympic-size, saltwater swimming pool, the model train room, the woodworking shop, residents boarding the mini-bus for a weekend road trip to the Biltmore House in North Carolina, and the game room showing residents playing bridge, Scrabble, and mahjong with Carolina, Ron, Yasuko, and Charlie smiling and laughing in the forefront.

"The Villas at Kensington Grove wins hands down," proclaimed the headline. Alabama looked closely at the thumbnail photo of the writer—a distinguished-looking older gentleman in suit and tie—with the name Jacob Weatherby printed in small letters underneath. He was clean-shaven, with a thick head of graying brown hair and a twinkle in his eyes. Like he felt really passionate about his work. How odd, Alabama thought. He looked familiar to her, but she couldn't remember ever seeing him before. She looked closer at the photo. He looked like someone trustworthy. Someone she would enjoy getting to know.

Chapter Twenty

Participating in a full day of activities at the Villas left Alabama exhausted. When Sunny told her that Yasuko, Charlie, Carolina, Ron, Eula Mae, and Geoffrey were expecting the two of them for dinner in the main dining room, Alabama collapsed on the sofa. She sighed, thinking how she spent most of her day at the Webb house reading, watching movies, or napping. Here at the Villas was a whole other world.

Alabama's adrenaline had been running on high the entire weekend. Stimulating conversations, invigorating and fun activities, delicious meals, delightful company, and so much more. She hadn't expected it to leave her totally worn out. It was like she'd spent the day walking around EPCOT or shopping at the outlet malls. Alabama realized that if she moved to the Villas, she would have to get into better shape. She would have to become stronger.

"I just don't think I can do it, Sunny. I'm not used to being constantly on the go. Can't we relax and have a quiet meal for just the two of us?"

"Not a problem." Sunny picked up her cell phone and texted Eula Mae that they wouldn't be eating with them.

"Thank you for understanding, Sunny. I'm just not used to being this active."

"One of the many great things about living at the Villas is that if you want excitement or company or fun activities, there's plenty of that to go around. But if all you want to do is curl up with a good book, watch a movie, or take a nap, no one will criticize you for doing just that."

Sunny headed for the door. "Let's go get us some comfort food at Bubba's. If the breeze off the river isn't too chilly, eating on the balcony will be a pleasant way to end Saturday evening at the Villas."

Alabama followed Sunny out the door and down the hallway to the elevator. "Thank you, Sunny. I hope Bubba's isn't too far away."

Sunny touched the computer screen for the lobby. "Elevator C, please," a cheery, digital voice responded from above. Elevator C doors opened. Sunny and Alabama entered, the doors closed, and the elevator began to descend.

"Bubba's is right off the lobby," Sunny explained. "It's open from 7 a.m. to 7 p.m. At breakfast or mid-morning, you can grab a cup of coffee and a pastry. For lunch or dinner, they have a small menu with hotdogs and burgers, sandwiches, shakes, soft drinks, and fries."

The entry to Bubba's was near the front door to the lobby. No signage on the outside to indicate what was inside. Alabama couldn't believe that the entire Webb family had walked by the door on Friday and not noticed it. But to be fair, everyone had been focused on the enormous, jaw-dropping lobby at the Villas of Kensington Grove.

Bubba's was quite small. Literally a hole in the wall the size of a small living room. Inside were four small tables, each with four chairs. Four gray-headed older women sat at a far table eating burgers, fries, and chocolate shakes. They were so involved in their conversation no one looked up as Alabama and Sunny entered.

"Why are there only four tables?" Alabama asked.

"First of all, "Sunny began, waving her hand around the room, "there's not enough space for more than four. Secondly, Bubba's is more of a take-out spot, than a hang-out place."

"Okay, I see that now," Alabama said, checking out the small room. The left side of the room had an open bin full of cold drinks. The right side was lined with open shelves containing cookies, chips, and chocolate bars. On the back wall was a menu board listing available hot food choices—burgers, hotdogs, grilled cheese, and fries—and milk shakes. Not a lot of choices, thought Alabama, but perfect for what she felt like eating at the moment.

A red-headed, freckle-faced young man—most likely a local high school student, Alabama thought—smiled at them. He wore a navy-blue polo shirt with "The Villas" embroidered on the upper left side. "May I help you ladies," he asked.

"Two Chicago dogs with fries and two chocolate shakes to go," said Sunny, touching her band to the small screen on the counter.

"What?" Alabama piped up. "I was leaning toward the grilled cheese."

"Trust me, Balmy," Sunny said. "You'll love it!"

· · ·

Later, back upstairs in the kitchen, Sunny unboxed the hotdogs and placed them on plates with fries. Alabama looked over Sunny's shoulder and stared. "What in the world is all that stuff on my hotdog?"

"Everything but the kitchen sink," Sunny explained. "Mustard, a dill pickle spear, chopped onions and green peppers, fresh tomatoes, and pickle relish."

"And terrible indigestion later this evening," interrupted Alabama.

Sunny rolled her eyes, handed Alabama one plate and one chocolate shake. "Balmy, just turn around and head out to the balcony."

Alabama did as she was told. Plopped her plate and shake on the small table and sat down in one of the two chaise lounges. "I'm not eating this disgusting thing."

"Balmy, Balmy, Balmy." Sunny slid her own plate and shake onto the table and sat down in the other chaise lounge. "Do you remember the time Ray insisted that we celebrate our first anniversary at that sushi bar in the West 40s?"

Alabama smirked. Oh, yeah. She remembered that night. It was the first sushi bar to open in New York City, and Ray wanted to give it a try after reading about it in Hungry Gerald's newspaper column. Ray had always been very adventurous when it came to food. He relished nothing better than finding a "mom and pop" restaurant in an ethnic neighborhood. He had taken Alabama to eat Chinese, Italian,

Indian, Thai, Dutch, Indonesian, Greek, and Russian food. Suddenly Japanese sushi rose to the top of his dinner list.

Sunny and Jeff were not enthusiastic. Jeff was a meat-and-potatoes guy, and Sunny herself had a preference for vegetarian dishes. They both said, "No raw fish." The kimono-clad hostess suggested they try the California roll — rice stuffed with cucumber, cooked crab meat, and avocado.

When Alabama's salmon *donburi* — slices of fresh, raw salmon artistically arranged on vinegary rice with Japanese pickles and seaweed — arrived at the table, Sunny glanced at the small bowl. "That's pretty," she said. "It looks like a work of art."

"Trust me, Sunny. Take one bite of this fish. You'll love it!" Alabama couldn't remember exactly how she had coaxed Sunny into taking a bite of raw salmon, but she did remember the surprised expression on Sunny's face after she tasted it.

"My goodness, Balmy, that's delicious," she'd said. "Mmm. Sort of a buttery flavor. Almost melts in your mouth." Before the end of the meal, Sunny had swapped half of her California Roll for half of Alabama's salmon *donburi*.

Alabama stared down at the hotdog. She knew how Sunny must have felt that evening looking down at the raw salmon. She sighed, picked up the hotdog with both hands, and took a bite. A big bite, because the hotdog — plus all of the toppings — was almost too big to fit in her mouth. She closed her eyes and concentrated on the many flavors bursting inside her mouth as she chewed. Sweet and sour and salty and spicy and hot-doggy. Everything, all together in her mouth at once. She finally swallowed and opened her eyes. "Not as bad as I thought it would be," she admitted.

"But you aren't going to fight me for mine?" Sunny asked, nibbling on a French fry.

Alabama laughed. "Hardly. It's different, but my favorite will always be a slaw dog with a side order of fried onion rings."

Sunny's cell phone dinged that she had a text message. She wiped her fingers on her napkin, picked up the phone, and checked. "It's my brother. He's inviting me over for Sunday lunch."

"That's nice of him. Don't worry about me. Sara and Richard will be here to pick me up at 10 in the morning."

"I realize that, Balmy, but if I'm driving to Tybee in the morning, I could drop you off on my way. Save them a trip to the Villas."

Alabama sucked the last of her chocolate shake through the straw. "Yes, sure, that would make Richard happy. As long as it won't take you out of your way."

"It's between I-95 and Tybee. Not a problem at all." She paused. "As long as you can hop out, grab your overnight bag, and step back before I back out of your driveway or I might run over your skinny old ass."

"You are such a crotchety, old woman. How about I sit with my overnight bag in my lap? When you reach my house, you just slow down to a crawl and I'll jump out."

Sunny and Alabama laughed until they cried. It felt so good. If she could only move into the Villas, she reasoned, then she would become a new woman. She'd miss seeing her family every day, especially Doug, but there was always FaceTime and weekend visits. But what about Jake? She'd become quite fond of his company. Would he miss her buttermilk biscuits? Or would he even miss seeing her at all?

Chapter Twenty-One

Alabama stood on Sunny's balcony, sipping her morning *caffè latte* and watching a cabin cruiser meander down the Brunswick River toward the ocean. She was glad she had on her jacket. A cool breeze blew across her face, bringing with it a whiff of rotten eggs. Actually, sulfur from the paper mill in Brunswick. But she knew that if the wind shifted directions and came in from the marsh, the smell would change to that of mud, salt, and dead crustaceans—a completely different smell from wood pulp.

Sunny came from behind and gave her a hug. "One final look at the great view?"

Nodding, Alabama turned to face her friend. "It's a great view to see first thing every morning."

"Carolina says it's the 'perfect view.' That the Villas is the 'perfect place to live.' That everything at the Villas is 'perfect' and why would anyone want to live any place else?" Sunny chuckled. "What do you think, Balmy?"

"If the Villas is so perfect in every way, then why did they take that Caribbean cruise on the *Emerald Dream*?" Alabama asked and grinned impishly. "What were they looking for?"

Sunny shrugged. "Lilly said Carolina was looking for a little bit of adventure, Yasuko wanted to meet the King of Bridge, and Eula Mae just went along for the ride."

"Sounds like all three of them got more than they bargained for," Alabama said with a laugh. "I love listening to their adventures. Someone should write a book about it."

"Maybe one day someone will," said Sunny. "If you're ready, let's get moving."

Alabama followed Sunny down the hallway to the foyer and grabbed her overnight bag. "I'm ready."

They took the high-tech elevator down to basement parking. "What did Sara say when you called and told her you had a ride home?" asked Sunny.

"Richard was really happy," Alabama said. "Sara's working two open houses today, so he was the chosen one to pick me up. This, of course, meant he wouldn't be sleeping in like he usually does on Sundays."

The elevator doors slid open, revealing a smiling Geoffrey sitting on a nearby bench. He stood up and walked over to Alabama. "Good morning, Balmy! I knew you were leaving this morning, so I thought I would give you a proper send off." He reached for her overnight bag. "Please, allow me to carry that for you."

For one second, Alabama considered not letting him have her bag, but a glance at Sunny convinced her to give it to him. "Thank you, Geoffrey. Were you waiting here long?"

"Not long at all. Sunny gave me a heads up when you two left the apartment."

Alabama glared at her friend, and Sunny gave her a smirky, innocent smile in return.

Sunny popped the trunk of her car, and Geoffrey dropped in Alabama's overnight bag. Then he held the passenger door open, so Alabama could get in. "Balmy, my heart will burst with absolute joy if you'll return for the Halloween Gala on Saturday," Geoffrey pleaded, shutting the passenger door.

As Sunny pushed the power button to start the car, Alabama lowered her window. "Thanks for your help, Geoffrey. My life's complicated at the moment. I seriously doubt I'll be able to make the party."

Looking like a deflated balloon, Geoffrey stepped away from the car. "Too-da-loo, Balmy. I shall remain optimistically expectant." He gave her a smart salute.

Sunny backed the car out of her parking space and headed for the garage exit. "You really know how to break a man's heart, Balmy,"

Sunny said, turning onto the Golden Isles Parkway and heading toward I-95 and Savannah.

"Oh, goodness gracious! That man is all posh! He has at least a dozen women dying for his attention."

"Maybe so," Sunny said, "but he's giving his full attention to you at the moment. Doesn't that count for something?"

"He's not my type," Alabama said.

"Oh? And what type is that?" Sunny turned her signal on to zip around an 18-wheeler creeping along. "What don't you like about Geoffrey?"

Alabama sighed. "He's just not Ray."

"Honey, Ray was one of a kind. There'll never ever be another Ray Knight. Geoffrey's good-looking. He has a great personality. He's kind and considerate. He's . . ."

"I know, Sunny," Alabama spluttered loudly. "He's perfect, is that where you're going?"

"No, he's certainly not that. You've heard some of the rumors about him."

"Then, please, let's drop this topic," Alabama insisted. "I don't want to talk about Geoffrey Winston Churchill anymore."

Sunny glanced sharply at her friend. "I get it, Balmy, and that's fine with me. Let me know what subject is safe to talk about, and that's what we'll talk about."

"Thank you." Alabama set her jaw. Not another word was spoken for 20 minutes. Alabama didn't understand why she had snapped at Sunny. If Sunny had been the object of Geoffrey's attention, Alabama would have been happy for her.

On the surface, Alabama thought, Geoffrey appeared to be a perfect catch. He was a mix of David Niven and Cary Grant rolled into one with a dash of Rex Harrison at his misogynistic worst. He was oh-so-charming. Maybe a little bit stuffy and stiff around the edges. But he was missing something—like fun and spontaneity. He just wasn't a free-spirited, cheery person. He lacked a funny bone or something. Geoffrey did not seem like the kind of fellow who would enjoy a good food fight or a person who would love to watch her favorite laugh-out-loud movies like *Legally Blonde* or *9 to 5* or *Trading Places*. He probably didn't eat buttermilk biscuits or play Scrabble, either.

Alabama sighed loudly, again. "I'm sorry for snapping at you."

"Wasn't the first time," Sunny said, blowing her horn at the driver of a red SUV trying to cut in front of her. "Remember in sixth grade when we made plans to see the new John Wayne movie?"

Alabama bristled. That was a very long time ago, but she hadn't forgotten that day. Forgiven her — yes, eventually — but not forgotten. Angie Pinkworth, the third grader who lived down the street from Alabama and Sunny, had called that morning and invited Alabama to go with her family to Tybee Beach for the day. Alabama wanted badly to say yes. The Pinkworths had a large, striped beach canopy and folding aluminum chairs. This meant they could sit in the shade and enjoy the ocean breeze, while playing card games. They always had a picnic hamper full of RC Colas, baloney sandwiches, potato chips and Moon Pies. Angie also had a very cute seventh-grade brother with curly, blond hair. But Alabama had already committed to seeing the movie with her best friend Sunny.

After reluctantly telling Angie she had other plans, Alabama had busied herself getting ready to meet Sunny. She'd combed her hair and asked her dad for a quarter for the movie and a dime for popcorn. Then she called Sunny's house to tell her she was ready to leave. There was nothing she hated worse than walking into a dark theater after the movie had already started.

"Please tell Sunny to meet me out front in two minutes," Alabama told Sunny's mom when she answered the phone.

"Alabama, Sunny isn't here," her mom said.

"She's already outside?" Alabama asked, surprised, because Sunny was always late everywhere she went.

"No, darling, Sunny went to the beach with Angie. I'll tell her you called."

Alabama remembered the sick, hurt feeling in the bottom of her stomach, and how she had stood there holding the receiver, stunned. Then she had slammed down the receiver and run screaming into her bedroom, slamming the door behind her.

"You screamed and yelled at me the next day," Sunny said. "You hurt my feelings."

"Good," Alabama said. "You're lucky that's all I did. It was my plan to never speak to you, again."

"You never apologized for shouting at me," Sunny said.

"You didn't deserve an apology. That was the meanest, most despicable thing you ever did to me." Alabama glanced out her window. Sunny was exiting I-95 onto I-16. It wouldn't be long now before she'd be home. And it couldn't be soon enough. "I don't know why you had to bring that up."

"Because if we're going to live together, we're going to get annoyed with each other for one thing or another," Sunny said. "Just like you and Ray, and me and Jeff. We always had our little disagreements, but we always managed to makeup because we loved each other."

"You and I are not getting married."

"Not unless we've both changed a lot more than I think we have over the years." Sunny giggled. "I'm thankful for that. I want to make sure you and I both realize we will . . ."

"Get pissed off at each other now and then?" Alabama asked and laughed.

"Exactly, but because we love and respect each other, our friendship will be everlasting."

Alabama wiped her eyes. "Stop it. Now you've gone and made me cry."

"Sorry, I didn't mean to do that, Balmy." Sunny sniffed. "Now you've got me getting sappy."

Alabama pulled two tissues out of her purse and handed one to Sunny. "Here. Let's talk about something funny. I need a laugh."

Sunny wiped her nose. "Okay, how about this. If you can manage to come to the Villas next weekend for the Halloween Gala, I want us to dress up like divas from the 1960s and perform."

"Like who?"

"I don't know. How about Nancy Sinatra?" suggested Sunny.

"I can see you singing 'These Boots Are Made for Walking' with no trouble at all. But I would want to dress up as Eliza Doolittle and sing 'I Could Have Danced All Night,'" Alabama said.

"You've always been hung up on that musical," Sunny said, turning into the Webb driveway. "I'm sorry we didn't ever get roles in any of the productions." She stopped the car by the garage, turned off the power, and popped the trunk.

As Alabama opened the passenger door, Doug ran out the front door yelling, "Grandma!" He grabbed her around the waist and hugged her tight. "I missed you, Grandma."

"I missed you, too, Doug." Alabama said, hugging him back.

Sunny handed Alabama her overnight bag. "Here you go, Grandma!" She gave her a hug, after Doug loosened his grip. "Okay, Balmy, I'm off. Good luck. Let me know when you decide about next weekend."

Doug grabbed the bag and carried it to the front door. Alabama turned and waved, and watched her best friend back out of the driveway. Then she followed her grandson into the house, where Richard was waiting by the door.

"Welcome home," Richard said, shutting the door behind her. "Did you enjoy your weekend?"

Alabama smiled. "Yes, I did. I met lots of the residents, ate too much rich food, learned to play mahjong, carved a pumpkin, and hung out on Sunny's balcony."

"I knew you would have a good time," Richard said. "To be honest, I was very impressed with the Villas. If I could retire from my job tomorrow, I would start packing to move."

"If you liked the prime rib that much and the perfect lifestyle the Villas offers, then you should start planning now because the wait period is over two years."

"Over two years?" Richard rubbed the back of his neck and shook his head. "That must be one popular retirement community."

"Yes, it is. It's one incredible, glorious place to live out your golden years."

Richard put his arm around Alabama and squeezed. "I'm backing you all the way, Alabama." He patted her back. "Say, how do you feel about some lunch? Nothing as great as what you ate at the Villas, but I just popped a lump crab quiche in the oven. Should be ready in about 15 or 20 minutes."

"Is it Angelina's of Maryland?" That was Alabama's favorite quiche.

"You got it."

"Will Sara and Alison be joining us?"

"Sara says she's grabbing a bite at the open house and will be home late this afternoon with dinner in hand," Richard said. "As for Alison, she's at the mall with Tina doing who-knows-what. So, just the three of us."

"Then I'll go freshen up before we eat." Alabama headed to her room, her brain in overdrive. She had a lot to think about this week. Life at the Villas with Sunny. Geoffrey's adoration. Her family. Her true feelings about Jake. The rest of her life lay before her. And she had choices and decisions to make.

Chapter Twenty-Two

After lunch, Richard sat down to watch a football game on TV. Alabama was unpacking her overnight bag and thinking about an afternoon nap, when Doug ran into her bedroom. "Grandma, there's a homeless man at the back door."

Dropping clothes she'd pulled from her bag, Alabama walked quietly past Richard into the kitchen with Doug. She smiled at the thought of seeing Jake and telling him all about the awesomeness of the Villas. But when she opened the backdoor, she found an agitated Clarence and not Jake. She stepped quickly through the door—followed by Doug—and shut it behind her. The last thing she needed was Richard getting upset at seeing Clarence.

"What's wrong, Clarence?" she asked.

"Balmy, something's happened to Jake," he answered, appearing distressed.

Her heart raced as possibilities went through her mind. Did a wild animal attack him while he slept in his cardboard box? Did a policeman arrest him for vagrancy? Or did he have a heart attack? Several times she had tried to tell Jake he was too old to sleep outside, but he insisted he wouldn't be able to sleep in a bunk bed in a room full of men snoring or talking to themselves. "What happened? Do I need to call 9-1-1?" She tried to push past Clarence. She needed to get to Jake. "Doug, you stay here."

"No," Doug said. "I want to help, too."

"No," Clarence said, holding her arm. "You don't understand. He didn't come back last night, and I don't know what happened to him."

Alabama felt her knees start to weaken. She backed up against the door and willed her heart to slow down. "What do you mean, Clarence? Where did he go last night?"

"I'm not sure, Balmy. Once or twice a week, after we eat lunch at the mission, Jake takes off to do his own thing. He says he likes to walk along River Street or just sit in St. John's and meditate. He tells me to take a shower at the mission and get some clean clothes. I been working with folks there to get training with life skills and stuff so I can get a job."

Alabama tried to follow what Clarence was saying, but her brain was screaming for her to go find Jake. "Does he meet you back at the mission later?"

"No, but he's usually back at the park later in the evening, wearing clean clothes, smelling nice, and in good spirits. Sometimes he brings back a surprise for me, like a box of Oreos or a bag of M&Ms." Clarence hung his head. "But he didn't come back last night, and this morning, he wasn't in his box."

Frowning, Alabama shook her head. None of what Clarence said made much sense. She never really thought about what Clarence and Jake did after they left her house or even what they did all day when she didn't see them. She figured they just sat around the park and watched the people go by. But that would get boring. She was glad to learn that they were able to get a hot meal, a shower, and clean clothes. She made a mental note to donate money to the mission.

"First of all, Clarence, let's go to the park and see if Jake is there. Meet me on the sidewalk out front in two minutes." Alabama and Doug went back inside. She grabbed her jacket, slipped the door key into her pocket, and tiptoed toward the front door. "Doug, you stay here with your dad," she said softly. She was glad that Richard had the sound on the TV turned up loud.

"No, Grandma, you can't go without me."

"Why not?" she asked, pausing with her hand on the doorknob.

"Because if Dad asks where you are or if Mom comes home, all sorts of stuff could spill out of my mouth. Stuff you wouldn't want me to say. But if I'm not here, then later we can say you and I went for a walk to get some fresh air." Doug smiled the smile of an innocent child who has one-upped an adult.

"Oh fine!" Alabama was too worried and stressed to argue her grandson's logic. She opened the door and they headed toward the park with Clarence.

• • •

When they reached the park, Alabama spotted Jake sitting on a bench with a middle-aged woman. She felt her heart leap out of her chest. Was Jake married? Did his wife come to the park looking for him?

As soon as the woman saw them, she jumped up and ran in their direction yelling, "Clarence!"

Jake grinned from ear to ear and headed toward the woman. She grabbed Clarence so ferociously, he almost fell over backwards.

Alabama was overcome with relief. That woman was obviously looking for Clarence.

"Clarice?" Clarence asked in disbelief, his mouth hanging open. "How did you find me?"

Clarice continued to hug Clarence, the tears streaming down her face. She grabbed his shoulders and shook him gently. "Mama and I've been looking for you everywhere. We thought you were dead."

Jake sidled over to Alabama and Doug. "My good deed for the day."

Alabama watched as Clarice and Clarence walked over to the bench, talking and hugging.

"Is that Clarence's wife?" Doug asked.

"They look like brother and sister to me." Alabama glanced at Jake for confirmation.

Jake nodded. "Twins, actually."

"Did you have anything to do with this reunion?" she asked.

Jake shrugged, hands in his pockets, rocking back and forth on his heels. "Maybe a little bit."

Alabama, who had been angry at Jake for scaring her and Clarence, felt herself calming down. "How did you manage that?"

"Old-fashion detective work. Clarence said the family left New York and moved to Brunswick. That he worked on the shrimp boats. One day during a rain storm, he slipped and fell while pulling in the nets. He said he hurt his back, had to have surgery, and ended up hooked on painkillers." Jake sighed. "Next thing he knew, poor guy lost his job and got evicted from his apartment. There he was, no job, no place to live, addicted to drugs, and too embarrassed to ask his family for help."

"How did he end up in Savannah?" Alabama asked, unable to take her eyes off Clarice and Clarence.

"A doctor in Brunswick found him nearly dead on the streets from a drug overdose and saved his life. The doctor took a special interest in him because his own son had died of an overdose a few months earlier. He didn't want what happened to his son to happen to Clarence. Fortunately, he was able to find a place for Clarence in a rehab center in Savannah. Even drove Clarence up to Savannah himself."

"That's quite a story," Alabama said. "He was given a second chance. Let me guess, after he was released from rehab, he was still afraid to call home?"

"You know what I would've done?" Doug spoke up. "I wouldn't have taken any more drugs, and I would have gotten me a job."

Jake knelt down in front of Doug. "That's exactly what he tried to do, Doug, but he had no place to live, he couldn't find a job, and he didn't want to disappoint his family, again."

"Is he going to live with his sister now?" Doug asked.

"Unfortunately, Clarice doesn't have room for Clarence because their mother already lives with her, her husband, and two children." Jake stood up.

"We didn't have room for Grandma to live with us either," Doug said. "So, we bought a bigger house that would hold all of us."

"That was only possible because I sold my house to help buy a bigger one," Alabama pointed out. "Clarence doesn't have a house to sell."

Jake ruffled Doug's hair. "But don't worry about Clarence. There are several halfway houses in Brunswick. Clarice found one in a nice residential area that has a vacancy."

"What's a halfway house?" Doug asked.

"It's a place where recovering alcoholics or drug addicts can live and learn the necessary skills to support and care for themselves," Jake explained. "Clarence can live there until he's able to live on his own, but he must decide if that's what he wants to do."

Doug frowned and looked up at Jake. "You mean he might want to stay here in the park with you?"

"That wouldn't be a good choice for Clarence," Jake said. "I think he's ready to get his life back."

"I still don't understand how you found Clarice?" Alabama asked.

"Don't you know about that stuff, Grandma? Jake probably got his DNA and found his sister on Ancestry." Doug snapped his fingers. "Just like that. Happens all the time."

Jake and Alabama howled with laughter. "Yeah, that's just about how I did it," Jake said, sobering up. "Actually, it was much simpler than that. Clarence told me about his sister and her family living in Brunswick. I simply went to the library one evening, sat down in front of a PC, and looked up her name on the White Pages. Then I gave her a call. She bawled over the phone when she heard he was alive and well."

Alabama reached over and took Jake's hand. "You're a good man, Jake. What you've done . . ." She swallowed hard. "What you've done is an unselfish act that could turn Clarence's life around."

Jake looked at Alabama, and squeezed her hand. "Thank you, Balmy. I knew I wouldn't always be here for Clarence. I'm hoping that once he's feeling his sister's love and support, everything will work out for him." Then he released her hand and walked toward Clarice and Clarence.

Alabama watched Jake walk away and wondered what he meant when he said he wouldn't always be here? Was he thinking about moving into a halfway house himself? Or maybe he was tired of being homeless in Savannah? And just where did he go all those nights after he left Clarence at the mission? Why didn't he want to talk about how he ended up homeless in the first place?

• • •

Jake helped Clarence pack up his personal effects and put them in the trunk of Clarice's Honda. "Balmy, before they leave, would you mind taking a photo of me with Clarice and Clarence?"

"I'd be glad to do that, Jake," Alabama said. Jake reached into his pocket and—to her surprise—pulled out a cell phone. Not an old android, but a smart phone.

Doug took the phone from Jake and handed it to Alabama. "Sweet!" Doug said. "Is this Apple's newest model with the zoom camera that shoots ultra-wide photos?"

"Is this your iPhone?" Alabama asked, turning the cell phone over in her hand, the silver metallic back with the Apple logo shining in the sun.

Jake simply shrugged. "I didn't steal it, if that's what you're implying. It was given to me by someone getting a newer model." He looked at Doug. "This iPhone is old, but the camera takes decent photos."

Alabama nodded. She remembered Richard and Sara arguing with Alison about wanting one for her birthday. Richard had yelled that if anyone in the Webb family was going to get an expensive iPhone, it would be him. Richard told Alison that buying a smart phone was just the beginning. Apparently, a monthly iPhone plan could cost a hundred dollars. So, Alabama had to wonder how a homeless man like Jake could afford to own such a phone? But she'd seen plenty of folks walking around with cell phones who looked like they couldn't afford "a pot to pee in"—one of her mother's favorite expressions.

While Clarice, Clarence, and Jake arranged themselves for their group shot, Doug showed Alabama how the camera worked and what spot to press. She shot several photos of the threesome before handing the phone back to Jake and smiled. "You know something, Jake? I think I want to buy a smart phone with my garage sale money."

"You've never had a cell phone ever?" Jake asked.

"No, Ray and I only had a land line. I never felt a need for one after he died. Sara and Richard both have one, and Alison has been campaigning for one. She says all her friends have one."

Doug ran over and hugged Alabama. "Grandma, if you do buy a smart phone, make sure to buy one that's good for playing games."

"Why would I want to do that?" Alabama asked.

"So, I can play them, of course." Doug paused and look at his grandmother. "Uh . . . so you can play them and have fun, too."

Jake laughed. "I still can't believe you don't own a cell phone, Balmy."

"I never needed one," she explained. "My landline worked fine. Never had to worry about charging it or losing it."

Clarice pulled a pink smart phone from her purse. "Look at mine. I bought this special Minnie Mouse cover for it at Disney World last spring." Clarice turned on her phone and handed it to Alabama. "Here are some of my games." She touched an icon and a Scrabble game appeared on the screen.

Alabama's eyes widened. "You can play Scrabble on that tiny screen?"

"Yes, but my favorite is Solitaire." Clarice touched another icon and cards were quickly distributed into the familiar Solitaire lines.

Alabama stroked her chin. "You can send and receive email?"

Doug grabbed Alabama's wrist. "And you can search the Internet for images of sexy old men."

"Douglas Webb!" Alabama yelled.

"Show her Google Earth, Clarice," Jake suggested. "Google River Street in Savannah."

Five adults huddled over Clarice and her phone as Google Earth worked its magic. "Unbelievable," Alabama said, as the historic River Street—paved with 250-year-old cobblestones—popped up on the screen. Here was where the Colony of Georgia was founded in 1733. Here was the location of the original Port of Savannah.

Clarice touched the screen in several places and the river front shops showed up at street level. "Look, Grandma! There's the River Street Sweets shop!"

Alabama hugged herself, remembering the many homemade pralines she had eaten over the years. Every time Ray and Alabama took Sara down to River Street as a little girl, Ray would always buy a box of the pralines. Then they would sit and watch the container ships and river boats sail up and down the river while they ate their sweets. "Yes, this is what I want," Alabama said excitedly. She only needed to find someone willing to drive her some place to buy one.

Jake looked thoughtfully at his phone and handed it to Clarice. "Before you go, would you mind taking a photo of me, Balmy, and Doug?" He glanced at Alabama. "Is that all right with you, Balmy?"

Alabama nodded, pleased that Jake wanted a photo of her. With Doug standing in front of her, Alabama stepped close to Jake and smiled. Maybe he could text a copy of the photo to her new smart phone—if she ever bought one. Then she'd have his phone number and a way to reach him. She smiled at the thought.

Clarice and Clarence said their good-byes and waved as the car headed down the street in the direction of I-95, the fastest road to Brunswick. Alabama glanced at Jake and thought he suddenly looked weary and very sad. "You're going to miss Clarence, aren't you?" she asked Jake.

He must have been lost in his thoughts, as she had to repeat herself before he responded. "What? Oh, yes, I'll definitely miss him. Now that they're gone, maybe we can sit and talk about your weekend at the Villas. Also, I have something very important I need to tell you."

Alabama turned to follow Jake to the bench, when Doug grabbed her elbow. "Grandma, Grandma." He pointed at his Spiderman watch. "It's almost 5. We need to get home before Mom comes home or we'll have to do a lot of explaining."

Alabama looked at her own watch and knew Doug was right. "Jake, I'm sorry, but we need to get back to the house. Would you like to come over in the morning for coffee and biscuits?"

"Tomorrow?" He seemed to pause and think about it.

This hesitation surprised Alabama. "Is there something else you need to do?"

"Oh, no, of course not. Yes, by all means. I can never turn down any of your buttermilk biscuits. I'll be there. The usual time?"

"Yes. Just make sure Sara and Richard have left for the day." Doug grabbed Alabama's hand and started pulling her down the sidewalk. "See you in the morning, Jake," she called out over her shoulder. She couldn't wait to tell him everything about the Villas. Including all about Geoffrey.

Chapter Twenty-Three

When Sara walked through the door with a special white-tomato-basil pizza and a large Greek salad from Screamin' Mimi's, Alison and Alabama had already set the table for dinner. Like five hungry pigs headed to the trough, the Webb family quickly sat down, Richard distributed pizza slices, Sara divvied up the salad into bowls, and soon the only sounds heard around the table were sounds of pleasure.

"Mom, thanks for making my day," mumbled Doug with his mouth full of pizza.

"Yeah, Mom, this is the best supper you've made us all week," Alison said.

Alabama watched Sara's smile turn upside down. "As much as I love Screamin' Mimi's pizza," Alabama said, "I think the Italian meatloaf and mashed potatoes Sara made Wednesday night was quite delicious."

Sara's smile returned. "Thank you, Mother. It's always good to know when one's cooking is appreciated."

Richard plopped another slice of pizza on his plate and Doug's. "Did you enjoy your weekend at the Villas? I have to say it—that was one impressive place. It exceeded my expectations."

"Mine, too," Alabama said. "I met many of the residents at dinner Friday night. On Saturday, Sunny and I carved pumpkins for the Halloween Gala this weekend, and I learned how to play mahjong."

While Richard and Doug fought over the last slice of pizza, Sara quietly left the table and went into the kitchen. She returned with a box of cannoli. "Mother, you get the first one." Sara placed one on Alabama's plate. "We're glad you had such a good time, but we're happy you're back home where you belong."

Richard cleared his throat and passed his plate to Sara for his cannoli. "What's this Halloween Gala?"

"Oh, does everyone dress up in costume and go trick or treating?" Doug asked, taking a bite of his own cannoli.

"Doug, please don't talk with your mouth full," Sara said. "Adults do not go trick or treating. Even your sister is now too old to do it."

"Mom! I'm not staying home to give out candy," Alison announced loudly. "Tina and I have plans. We're going through the Shriners' haunted house."

Richard's head shot up. "What!? I heard it's the best haunted house in Savannah."

"It is, Dad," Doug said. "Jack and Miller went last year. They said it was awesome scary and the monsters had super cool costumes. Lots of blood, guts, and gore. Can I go with you, Alison?"

"Absolutely not, young man." Sara stood up and started collecting the dishes. "You will either do your usual trick or treating around the neighborhood or you can stay home and give out the treats to Spiderman, Wonder Woman, Captain Marvel, and Mandalorian."

"Aw, Mom."

Sara sighed. "Please, Doug. The only reason I've agreed to allow Alison to go with Tina is because I know I can count on the Shriners to make it a safe and fun event—not to mention, the money goes for a good cause."

"Back to the Halloween Gala at the Villas," Richard said, wiping cannoli filling off his chin. "What exactly will all those old folks be doing?"

"I don't know all of the specifics," Alabama admitted, "but everyone dresses up in costume. They award prizes for the best costumes and the best carved pumpkins, of course. Some of the residents will perform and entertain. The Villas Band will play music for dancing, and there will be lots of food and fun activities."

"Sounds like a great evening," Sara said, returning from the kitchen to collect the empty pizza box. "Too bad no one here will be able to drive you to the Villas for the party." A muffled cell phone ring sounded from Sara's purse on the sofa. "Now who could that be?" She rummaged through her purse and pulled out the ringing phone.

"Hello? Yes, this is the Webb household." Sara glanced at Alabama and frowned. "One moment, please." She handed the phone to her mother. "It's for you. Geoffrey Winston Churchill? Who's that?"

"A man wants to talk to Grandma?" asked an astonished Alison.

Alabama stared at the phone in her hand. She couldn't believe Geoffrey had called her. How had he gotten Sara's phone number?

"Grandma, aren't you going to talk to him?" Doug asked. "We studied Winston Churchill in history. I thought he was dead."

"What? Oh, of course." Alabama lifted the phone to her ear. "Hello?"

"You scared me, Balmy," Geoffrey's deep-bass, British accent sounded in her ear. "I was afraid you hung up on me."

Alabama glanced around the table at four pairs of eyes, staring wide-eyed at her. "I was just surprised, Geoffrey. I didn't expect to hear from you. How did you get my daughter's number?"

Geoffrey laughed. "I'm afraid I charmed it out of Sunny, but please don't be angry at her. She could see that I was desperate to reach you. I can't believe you don't have your own phone."

I can't believe that either, she thought. "Why'd you want to talk to me?" Alabama considered walking out of the room with the phone, but what did she have to hide? After all, it was Sara's phone. And now owning a cell phone moved up to number one on her wish list. Right up there with a tablet and a sports car with 5 in the floor and a take-off from zero to 60 mph in 8 seconds.

"I want you to be my date for the Villas' Halloween Gala, Balmy."

Alabama looked sharply at Sara, who was standing by the table, holding the empty pizza box. "Thank you, Geoffrey. I would love to go to the Halloween Gala, but I don't have my own car, and everyone in this family is tied up with Halloween activities. But thanks for asking me."

"Stop! Wait!" Geoffrey shouted. "Balmy, please say yes, and I will personally drive to Savannah in my brand-new Mercedes to get you. Sunny says you can bring an overnight bag to stay with her, and I will return you to Savannah before lunch on Sunday."

"I don't know, Geoffrey, that sounds like such an imposition for you drive to Savannah to get me and then bring me back on Sunday."

She couldn't believe he was offering to do that. Alabama looked around the table at four pairs of eyes continuing to stare at her.

"It's no imposition, Balmy. I simply don't want you to miss the party." He paused. "I really enjoy your company."

Alabama looked at Sara, who was shaking her head in a negative manner. Suddenly, Alabama felt annoyed and irritated. Dang it all, she was a grown woman and not an irresponsible teenage girl. Did she want to go to the Halloween Gala or not? If Geoffrey was willing to be her wheel-man, why should Sara care if she went or not? Alabama pursed her lips. "All right, Geoffrey, I'd love to be your date for the Halloween Gala."

"You've made me a happy man, Balmy Knight. How about I collect you Saturday morning around 10 o'clock?"

"Sounds good, Geoffrey! It's a date. See you Saturday." Alabama touched the disconnect spot, smiled, and handed the phone to her daughter.

Doug threw his arms in the air and jumped out of his chair. "Grandma's got a date!" He ran over and gave her a hug.

"You rock, Grandma!" Alison said, giving her grandmother a high-five.

Richard smiled. "I did not see that coming, Alabama. Congratulations. I know you'll have a great time at this Halloween Gala."

Sara slammed the pizza box down on the table. "I don't think this is a good idea, Mother. You don't know this man. He could be a serial killer or worse. I won't allow it."

"He's been vetted by the Villas and given their stamp of approval. He's a well-mannered British gentleman. Every woman living in the Villas is lusting after him." Alabama paused. She couldn't believe she was defending Geoffrey. She blamed it on her frustration at Sara's response. "And, another thing Sara, I don't care if you won't allow it or not; I'm going."

"Mo-other!" Sara spluttered.

"Dad, what is 'lusting'?" asked Doug.

Alison grabbed Doug and pulled him away from the table. "Come with me, Doug, and we'll talk about it."

Richard pushed back from the table and jumped to his feet. "Sara, calm down, it's only a party. Your mother's a grown woman. She wants to have a little bit of fun while she's still physically able. What's your problem?"

Alabama was astonished that Richard was coming to her defense. Suddenly, she was feeling guilty about every ugly thing she ever thought about him. She walked over to her daughter and clasped her hands. "My dear, sweet Sara. Take a deep breath. Let's sit on the sofa and talk about it. Quietly."

Sara allowed Alabama to hold her hand and lead her over to the sofa. They sat in silence for a few seconds, looking at each other. "Mother, I don't want anything to happen to you. I know you think I'm being overly protective."

Alabama patted and caressed her daughter's hand. "I understand, Sara. But you need to understand how I feel. This is all about my independence. You really can't understand what independence is until you've lost it." Alabama squeezed Sara's hand. "You see, sweetheart, when your independence is gone, so is your self-esteem. You become like a child, again."

"But I don't treat you like a child, Mother."

"Sure, you do, Sara. Does any of this sound familiar? Mother, don't eat on the sofa. Don't invite anyone into my house and have fun. No, Mother, you can't go to the store with me. No, Mother, you can't drive. No, Mother, you can't have a date and go to a party. No, Mother, you can't move into the Villas with Sunny and enjoy the rest of your life."

Sara pulled back from Alabama. "Mother, you make me sound like mean person. I care for you. I love you. I only want what's best for you."

"Then stop treating me like a sullen, irresponsible teenage daughter going through adolescence," Alabama said. "I'm your mother! I carried you in my womb for nine months and endured 18 hours of labor. I held you in my arms all night when you were sick. I comforted you when you came home from school in tears after a bad day. I worked the Band Parents' hotdog stand at the home games and helped you sell and deliver over 100 boxes of Girl Scout cookies, so you could win some stupid, stuffed lion. And don't forget all those times I moved you into and out of dorm rooms and apartments. Now I'm only asking you to treat me with a little dignity and respect!"

Sara gasped and threw her hand to her mouth. Tears rolled down her cheeks and her shoulders shook. "I'm so sorry," she blubbered and wiped her eyes. "You've always been there for me. Every time I had a problem, you were there. Any crisis, I could count on you to fix it." She paused to sniff and swallow. "Then suddenly, one day you were lying helpless in a hospital bed, and I thought you were dying. It's my time to take care of you now."

Alabama reached over and hugged her daughter. "I understand, Sara. But you have to remember what your father always said. 'Life is a terminal disease. When your time's up, it's up. You have to live life as though each day could be your last.' That's exactly what I want to do, Sara. I could live 20 more years or two more days. But I want the time I have left to be happy. Going to the Halloween Gala will make me happy. Moving into the Villas with Sunny will make me very happy. I guess my question for you is this: Do you want me to be happy or not?"

Chapter Twenty-Four

Alabama brought in the newspaper and placed it unopened on the living room table for Richard to read with his morning coffee. Her plan — her agenda for the week — was to be kind, thoughtful, and sweet beyond reproach. She wanted to be seen as a strong, healthy woman who had all of her faculties intact. If Geoffrey was right and her application to move into the Villas was approved this week, she wanted to be the picture of a woman who was capable and strong enough to take back her independence.

Usually, Alabama stayed in bed until nature called and she had to get up to relieve herself. But this morning, she was up an hour earlier than usual. Jake was coming, and she wanted to look nice for him. She pulled out a red, white, and blue pants suit, which had been one of Ray's favorites. He called it her patriotic outfit and always asked her to wear it to the annual July Fourth fireworks show on River Street. After Ray's death — and until her stroke — she continued to wear it on July Fourth in his honor.

Her patriotic outfit was somewhat loose due to weight loss after her stroke, but the elastic in the waist was tight enough that Alabama didn't have to worry about the pants falling down around her ankles. She combed her hair the best she could — it would never look as good as Sunny's — and applied a little blush and lipstick. When she pulled out her mascara brush, it was all dried up. Just as well, she thought. Too much makeup and she might look like a hussy.

Alabama planned to fill up Jake with scrambled eggs, buttermilk biscuits, and coffee. After she told him about her fun weekend at the Villas, she would discreetly talk to him about his own future plans. If she moved into the Villas, what would happen to Jake? She didn't want him sleeping in that cardboard box the rest of his life. He was so concerned about Clarence, why wasn't he concerned about himself? Alabama wanted desperately to help Jake, but first she needed to know how he became homeless. The question was—would he be willing to tell her?

Richard walked into the living room and paused. He glanced at Alabama and smiled. "You look really nice this morning. You have a doctor's appointment today or something?" He picked up his briefcase and the morning paper.

Alabama smiled back at her son-in-law. "No, after my weekend at the Villas, I decided it was important to dress for the day, comb my hair, and apply a good deodorant. You never know what the day will bring."

Richard chuckled. "You're so right about that, Alabama." He took a step toward the door, then stopped and turned back. "Did you and Sara get everything worked out between you two last night?"

"I hope so. I said my piece, and she said hers. Now we're both digesting what each other said." She cocked her head in his direction. "It'll all work out in the end, right?"

"I'm sure it will," Richard said with a nod. "Sara can be a reasonable person."

"I know she can, but like Sunny so succinctly explained, Sara is dealing with an emotionally charged teenage girl trying to loosen the apron strings and a crotchety, old woman demanding respect," Alabama said. "Plus, she's got a few hormonal issues herself. Triple stress, I call it."

Richard frowned. "You're right, Alabama. I haven't considered everything that Sara is dealing with. I need to do more to help her. That's something I have to work on." He reached out and opened the front door. "Thanks for pointing that out." He chewed on his lower lip. "And for the record, Alabama, I have your back."

"What do you mean?"

"I'm doing everything I can to convince Sara that you should move in with Sunny at the Villas."

Alabama stood and walked over to Richard. "I appreciate that, but don't push her. You know if she feels pushed to the wall, she'll just dig in her heels. She's always been stubborn that way."

"You're so right about that." He laughed and headed out the door. "Have a good day, Alabama!" A horn sounded out front. "Tell Alison Tina's here."

But before Alabama could say a word, Alison ran through the living room and out the front door. Two minutes later Doug appeared, struggling to carry what appeared to be a *papier mâché* volcano, painted with brown, black, gray, and red acrylics. Sara, dressed in her usual stylish navy-blue suit, followed behind him with her own briefcase and car keys. "Mother, I have to drive Doug to school on my way to work. There's no way he can carry that science project to school by himself. I have two house showings this morning, but I will be home for lunch around 1. Call if you need me."

Alabama opened her mouth to respond, but they were gone. The door shut soundly behind them. She could hear Sara telling Doug to be cautious all the way to the car. Two car doors slammed. The engine started. And they were gone. Alabama smiled to herself as the house became peaceful and quiet.

•   •   •

By the time Jake knocked on the kitchen door, the buttermilk biscuits were in the oven and the eggs were ready to be poured into the hot skillet. Alabama wiped her hands on her apron and opened the door. "Jake, good morning! You're right on time."

"Good morning, Balmy!"

When Jake walked through the door, Alabama caught a whiff of something citrusy. Was it from a morning shower at the shelter? His long hair was still damp, as if he'd shampooed it recently. And he had on clean clothes that weren't holey or worn around the edges. Something tingled deep down inside her. She liked Jake. What was it about him that appealed to her? He enjoyed her cooking, but there was something else about him. It had to be his free spirit, she decided.

"You're just in time, Jake. I'm ready to scramble the eggs, and the biscuits are due out any minute. Please have a seat."

Jake pulled out a kitchen chair and sat. "You're looking especially nice today, Balmy. Are you going somewhere?"

Alabama laughed as she stirred the eggs. "Funny, but Richard asked me that same question. Can't a woman put on decent clothes and comb her hair without everyone commenting on it?" Funny, she thought, that she'd just noticed the same thing about Jake. Alabama glanced at him.

Jake's smile faded. "Oops, sorry, Balmy."

"Nothing to be sorry about, Jake." She grabbed a potholder and pulled the biscuit-ladened cookie sheet out of the hot oven. Perfect, she thought, as she lifted each buttery, golden-brown biscuit onto a plate and covered them with a towel to keep them warm. "When Sunny arrived in town, she said I needed to stop looking and smelling like a bag lady. To be respected, she said I needed to dress like someone who warranted respect."

"Well, I certainly can't argue with Sunny on that. That's why I kept telling Clarence he had to shower and wear clean clothes if he wanted a job."

Alabama poured two cups of coffee and placed two plates of scrambled eggs on the table. "Here, Jake, now butter yourself several of those biscuits before they get cold."

Between bites, they talked about Clarence and his second chance at getting a better life and reconnecting with his sister. "I'm going to miss Clarence," Jake said, spreading peach preserves on his biscuit half. "But I feel good about him. He really wants to make this work."

Alabama swallowed her last bite of eggs and decided to jump right in. "What about you, Jake?"

"What do you mean?"

"Do you have a sister out there somewhere looking for you?" Alabama held her breath.

"What? No, absolutely not. Why would you ask that?" Jake frowned and pushed his plate back.

All right, Alabama, tread lightly, she told herself. "You never really talk about yourself, Jake. I know that you enjoyed working in theaters and that you were in the military at one point, but I don't know if you're from around here or how you ended up homeless. You don't seem like a drug addict or an alcoholic."

Jake rubbed the back of his neck and seemed a little bit flustered. "That's because I've never been either one."

Alabama, who had tensed up, relaxed at his response. "So, just a little down on your luck? Your company laid you off and at your age, you haven't been able to find another job?" She wasn't sure how old Jake was. Younger than her, she guessed. She remembered reading somewhere that anyone who lost a job after age 50 would have a hard time finding another one.

Slowly rising to his feet, Jake's cheeks turned pink. "Did you ever consider that maybe I enjoy being homeless? That maybe I retired from a day job that was killing me? That I love the freedom I have now to do as I please? That if I tire of living in Savannah, I can simply pack up my few belongings and move to another town?"

Alabama's jaw dropped. "No, Jake, I'm sorry. None of those things crossed my mind," Alabama said, standing up. "It's just that I can't imagine anyone who would enjoy living in a cardboard box or eating meals and showering at the homeless shelter. What kind of a life is that?"

Jake took a step closer to Alabama. She had never been this close to him before. That soapy, citrus smell wafted over her, again. Standing this close to him, she could clearly see the gray and white whiskers in his beard and the streaks of gray in his shoulder-length hair. Funny, she had not realized that his eyes were hazel like her daddy's had been. She wondered if his eyes changed to blue or green, too, depending on the color of his shirt?

He reached out his hand as though to touch her, but pulled back. "Balmy, there's so much I want to tell you, but I can't yet. You have to trust me." He paused and swallowed hard. "For the moment, I'll just say that what I'm doing now is more important to me than a ton of money and any corporate job. I love what I'm doing with my life." He paused, again, and looked directly into her eyes. "I have my independence, Balmy. It's my greatest hope that one day you'll have that, too."

Before Alabama could reply, Jake took her hand and gave it a gentle squeeze. His hand felt warm and smooth. Not rough and callused like she expected a homeless man to have. This hand did not belong to a manual laborer. Had he been laid off from a job as an accountant or a stockbroker or bank executive? Why couldn't he just admit that? There was no shame in that. On the news, she'd seen whole families living in cars because their low-wage jobs didn't provide enough money to rent a place. Jake was not the only homeless man in Savannah.

"Listen, Balmy, I need to leave now. You wouldn't believe how complicated my life is at the moment, but I promise you this — when I see you, again, I'll explain everything," he said, still holding her hand. "You are very important to me. Don't ever forget that. I'll be back in touch with you as soon as I can." He leaned over and kissed her cheek.

Alabama stood frozen in place, in shock. Unable to speak, she reached out with her hand to grab him, but he was already out the door. She played their conversation over and over in her mind. Then she gently rubbed the spot on her cheek where Jake's lips had touched.

Chapter Twenty-Five

When Jake didn't stop by the house Tuesday or Wednesday morning, Alabama reminded herself what Jake had said—he would tell her everything, when she saw him, again. His life was complicated. Still, by Thursday morning and no Jake knocking on the door, she was seriously worried. When the doorbell rang at 10 o'clock, she ran to the front door. That had to be Jake, she thought, but why was he at the front door instead of the kitchen?

With her adrenaline pumping, Alabama jerked open the door enthusiastically. But instead of Jake, a grinning Sunny Day greeted her with a smothering hug. She wiggled out of Sunny's grip. "What are you doing here?" she asked her friend.

"My goodness, but your panties are in a wad this morning. Is that any way to treat your best friend who has come bearing good news? Your application to move into the Villas has been approved, and I wanted to tell you in person." Sunny, dressed in orange slacks and a Halloween-themed sweater covered with bats and ghosts, grabbed Alabama's shoulders and gave her a gentle shake. "Why are you just standing there? Say something. For goodness sakes, Balmy! Jump up and down and scream for joy!"

Alabama gulped down air. "I—uh—thought you were Jake." She closed her eyes and took a deep breath.

Sunny pushed her way past Alabama, who followed her to the kitchen. Immediately, she spun around and faced Alabama. "You mean Jake and Clarence aren't already here scoffing down your buttermilk biscuits? I thought they came over for breakfast nearly every day?"

"Clarence won't be coming by any more." Alabama quickly explained how Clarence's sister had picked him up and how he had a place to live in a halfway house until he was able to live on his own.

"That was terribly nice of Jake to go to all that trouble to help Clarence," Sunny said. "Has Jake already eaten your biscuits and left?"

Alabama shrugged. "Haven't seen him since Monday morning." She was surprised at how sad she felt about not hearing from Jake.

"Why are you looking so hang dog about this?" Sunny asked, looking strangely at her friend. "Was he upset when you told him you were moving to the Villas to live with me?"

Alabama's shoulders fell. She turned and walked out of the kitchen.

"Balmy, you didn't tell him?" Sunny followed her into the living room.

Alabama shook her head. "No. He came over for breakfast on Monday, and I tried to pump him for information. Like how he ended up on the streets, and where he was from. But he shut me down and left."

Sunny pulled her friend over to the sofa and gently pushed her to sit, flopping down next to her. "Maybe that's for the best, since you're moving in with me. Did you tell him about Geoffrey taking you to the Halloween Gala?"

"No, no, no. Geoffrey's name never came up." Alabama crossed her legs and looked down at her feet. "He didn't like me asking personal questions."

"Uh-oh. How personal?"

"He assured me he was not and has never been a drug user or an alcoholic."

"Oh, Balmy! You offended him?" Sunny shook her head.

Alabama lifted her chin. "He seemed to take that okay. However, when I started asking questions about where he lived before coming to Savannah and how he became homeless . . . Well, let's just say he didn't want to talk about it. He said his life was complicated."

Sunny flicked the hanging silver strands on her earrings and was rewarded with a soft tinkle. "Hmm. I think I'm getting a picture. Guess he didn't like your attempt to pry information out of him."

"Not sure." Alabama sighed. "He said he would explain everything the next time he saw me. I just didn't realize it would be this long before he returned." She looked at Sunny and shook her head. "I really thought he kept coming here because he liked my company as much as I liked his."

"I'm surprised, too," Sunny admitted. "He really loved your buttermilk biscuits and coffee. I bet your cooking is better than any breakfast he could get at the homeless shelter."

Alabama sat up straight. "You drove here from the Villas?" she asked excitedly.

"I certainly didn't walk. I wanted to tell you in person that you can move in anytime. Today. Tomorrow. When Geoffrey brings you for the Halloween Gala. Whenever you think you can sneak away."

"I can't think about moving to the Villas now, Sunny. I'm too worried about Jake to focus my mind on that. Would you mind driving me to the park to check on him? Driving would be faster than walking." Alabama tried to look pathetically appealing.

Sunny's eyes widened. She sucked on her bottom lip as if considering Alabama's request. "Oh, all right. You can drop the hang-dog look." She stood and offered Alabama her hand.

• • •

As soon as Sunny parked the car, Alabama was out the door and hurrying to the bushes that hid where Jake slept. Sunny was right behind her. Alabama brushed aside the limbs and stared dumbfounded. Not only was Jake's refrigerator-size box gone, but the entire space had been swept clean of trash and belongings. No one would ever know that Jake had called this place home.

"He's gone," Alabama cried out, falling forward to her knees. "I scared him off, Sunny." She felt her eyes sting from her tears. "I shouldn't have said anything. I liked him, and I thought he liked me, too."

Sunny reached down and helped Alabama to her feet. "I'm sorry, Balmy. I didn't realize you cared about him this much."

Alabama wiped a tear from her cheek. The very cheek that Jake had kissed on Monday. "He told me he had something that I didn't have yet. He told me he had his independence."

Sunny put her arm around Alabama's waist and nudged her toward the car. "Maybe he found a job somewhere? Or maybe he thought he'd have a better chance of finding a job some place else?"

"But where would he have gone?" Sunny opened the passenger door, and Alabama slid onto the seat.

"Florida? Miami?" Sunny suggested. "With winter coming, it'd be much warmer and sunnier farther south."

Alabama mulled over that thought. Where would Jake go? She didn't think he would have left Savannah without letting her know. Where else? "I have an idea," she said, as Sunny got behind the wheel and pressed the power button to start the car. "Do you know where the Rose Dhu Mission is on Bull Street?"

Sunny carefully made a U-turn and drove slowly away from the park. "For some reason, that name sounds familiar."

"Eula Mae Davis," Alabama said, poking Sunny's memory.

"But of course. At dinner. She was talking about her daughter Georgia." Sunny banged the palm of her hand on the steering wheel. "I remember now. Georgia works at Rose Dhu College and married some rotten scoundrel who also works there."

"Which is why Eula Mae moved into the Villas. She didn't want to be a 'fifth wheel' living with the newlyweds."

"Very good," Alabama said, and laughed. "See? You aren't as senile as you think."

"But how is Rose Dhu College connected to Rose Dhu Mission?"

"Ah ha. At that point in Eula Mae's story, you were debating with Charlie Chan about Bollywood movies and if they were still popular."

"Yes, I vaguely remember that." Sunny nodded. "What is the connection?"

"In the social studies department, the college offers a year-long certification program where students learn about running a mission—providing housing, meals, training and support for men trying to turn their lives around," Alabama explained. "The college, with the financial support and backing of churches in the Savannah area, runs the mission, its programs, and the thrift store."

"And therefore, the mission is named after Rose Dhu College." Sunny turned onto Bull Street and slowed down, giving Alabama a chance to search for the building, which wasn't hard to spot. The complex—including a red-brick chapel with belfry, a two-story white-stucco residence hall, a large parking lot, and a fenced-in garden area—took up an entire city block. Electric-blue lettering over a double-door entrance screamed Rose Dhu Mission and Thrift Store.

Sunny pulled into an empty spot marked "Visitors" and parked.

The two friends sat silently and unmoving for a minute. Alabama was lost in thought. She was starting to wonder if this was such a good idea after all. What if Jake wasn't here? What if something had happened to him?

"Well, Balmy? Are we just going to sit here the rest of the day or what?"

Alabama sighed. "You're right. I need to go inside and see if Jake is here." She grabbed the door handle. "You can wait here."

Sunny opened her door. "Oh, no. I'm going with you as backup, girlfriend."

• • •

The lobby area reminded Alabama of a small motel with brown-painted concrete floors, four institutional chairs, an end table with a cheap lamp, and a front desk staffed by a young man. A blue-and-white name tag identified him as Dave, assistant to the director. Dave, who looked like a college student, had a smile that would put any wary visitor at ease.

"Good morning, ladies," Dave greeted them. "Welcome to Rose Dhu Mission. How can I help you today?"

Sunny opened her mouth, but Alabama elbowed her and whispered, "Let me do the talking. Follow my lead." Sunny closed her mouth and nodded. "Good morning, Dave. We're on the Women of the Church Board, and we wanted to visit the mission and see how our money supports the homeless."

"Not a problem." Dave propped up a "Ring Bell for Service" sign on the counter and stepped out from behind the chest-high oak desk. "But first of all, you should know that we try to avoid using the word 'homeless' here. We have 'residents' or 'friends' or 'neighbors in need.' How familiar are you with our ministry here?"

Alabama tried to remember what she'd heard about the mission from Jake and Clarence. They often praised the mission's work. "We know that you feed the hungry. That you provide beds, showers, clean clothes, and classes to help those in need to find jobs."

"That's right," Dave said. "Here at Rose Dhu Mission, we offer our mission guests food, showers, and clean clothes as a big step toward restoring dignity."

"We know that the mission is supported by Rose Dhu College," Sunny said. "Are you a student at the college?"

"Yes, I am. I've been in the program nine months now. The men I work with here in the mission have inspired me with their life stories," Dave said with enthusiasm. "Why don't I show you around our complex? Follow me, please."

First stop was a large room with bright-yellow concrete-block walls. If the mission was aiming for bright and cheerful, Alabama decided they'd accomplished their goal. An enormous television was mounted on one wall in front of several rows of green chairs and sofas—the inexpensive kind purchased for a college residence hall lobby. Four bearded men wearing faded, but clean jeans and flannel shirts sat watching CNN. Alabama noticed that two of the men wore red Atlanta Falcons baseball caps. She was disappointed that Jake was not one of the men.

On the opposite side of the room from the television, six wooden game tables were set up with four chairs. Four men were playing a card game at one of the tables. Jake was not one of them either.

Alabama was surprised that the dining room and kitchen were spotless. And empty, except for five older men assembling sandwiches, and two older women stirring a large pot of vegetable soup and making iced tea. "These volunteers are from St. Stephens,"

Dave explained. "Churches take turns sending workers to make lunch one day a week for one month. Volunteers who make dinner come from area churches, social organizations, restaurants, and Rose Dhu College."

"Who organizes that?" Sunny asked.

"Rose Dhu students in the certification program, of course. It's one of the many things we learn to do," Dave said.

Dave toured them through the Chapel—"here local pastors present uplifting sermons on Sunday evenings after dinner"; the Rose Dhu Thrift Store—"run by students and volunteers"; and the mission garden—"which provides fresh vegetables for meals, as well as work experience for the men staying in the residence hall," Dave explained.

Disappointed that she had not seen Jake anywhere at Rose Dhu, Alabama followed Dave back to the front desk. Along the way, she considered the possibility that if Jake had moved his belongings from the park to the mission, then he might be living in the residence hall.

"Dave, thank you for giving us the grand tour," Alabama began politely. "I recently met a man who said he often eats dinner here and showers. I didn't see him in any of the rooms we walked through. I was wondering if he was still here or if he had moved on?"

Dave shook his head. "I don't know. There are so many men who come through Rose Dhu for food, showers, and clean clothes. I really only get to know the ones who are here long enough to get rehabilitated and attend job training."

"Like Clarence," Sunny piped up.

"Clarence?" asked Dave and grinned. "Oh, yes, I remember him. He's one of our success stories. I heard his old employer offered him a job and he's now living in a halfway house. Is that the man you met?"

"Yes!" Alabama and Sunny chorused. "But he hung out with another man with a grayish beard and long shoulder-length hair," Alabama explained.

After listening to Alabama's description of Jake, Dave's eyes widened and he chuckled. "You're talking about Clarence's friend Jake, right?"

Alabama felt herself relax. "Yes, that's him. Have you seen him? Is he here?" If Jake were here, he had to be in a room upstairs.

Dave shook his head sadly. "No, not Jake." He put his hands in his pockets. "The last time I saw Jake was Monday night, when he stopped by to speak to the director. I'm pretty sure he won't be back."

"Why do you say that?" asked Alabama.

"I overheard him thanking the director for his assistance. Told him he appreciated all of his support and that he thought the mission was doing an excellent job serving the homeless community. After they shook hands, Jake handed the director a fat envelope. When Jake left, the director told me the envelope contained ten one-hundred-dollar bills."

"What?" Sunny gasped.

The young man laughed. "That was exactly my response. We don't have people dropping by and handing over a stack of cash."

"What was the money for?" Alabama asked. Was Jake selling drugs or something? Where could he have gotten that kind of cash?

"The director said it was Jake's way of thanking the mission for their help in whatever project he was working on." Dave looked down at his watch. "Sorry, but unless you would like to make a charitable donation, too, I need to run help with lunch. Bye."

"I think Jake was right," Alabama said, watching Dave walk briskly down the hallway.

"How's that?" Sunny asked, observing a throng of men ambling toward the dining room.

"He said his life was complicated." Now Alabama was left with more questions than ever. Where had Jake gone? How did he get the money he donated to the mission? And what sort of project could Jake be involved with that required the help of Rose Dhu Mission?

Chapter Twenty-Six

When Sunny stopped for lunch at Red Crustacean, Alabama rolled her eyes. Of all the family-owned seafood restaurants in Savannah that served fresh fish right off the boat, Sunny had to dine at a popular national franchise. However, since Sunny offered to pay for lunch, Alabama wasn't going to complain. She loved their sinful biscuits, clam chowder, and fried coconut shrimp.

Nibbling on a hot, buttery biscuit while waiting on her food to arrive, Alabama was lost in thought and worried about Jake. She washed her biscuit down with a swallow of iced tea. "You know, I'm not going to worry about Jake. He's a grown man. He can take care of himself. I don't care if I never see that man, again. So there!" She reached into the basket and grabbed another biscuit.

Sunny laughed softly and then louder. "Oh, Balmy, that is nothing but pure sour grapes, and I don't believe you."

"Well, believe me because it's true." She dropped the biscuit onto her bread plate.

Sunny threw a piece of biscuit at her friend. "If you don't care about him, then why did we go to the park and look in the bushes? If you never want to see him, again, why did we spend an hour touring Rose Dhu Mission hoping to spot him?"

The waitress set down a steaming bowl of clam chowder in front of Alabama and a bowl of shrimp bisque in front of Sunny. "Your food will be out in two minutes, ladies," she said and left.

"Bah humbug." Alabama muttered. Then she closed her eyes and sniffed the steam rising from the bowl. "That smells good," she said, blowing her breath on a spoonful of chowder before shoveling it into her mouth. "Ouch! It's hot!" She quickly gulped a swallow of tea to cool off her tongue.

"Here's what I think—" Sunny started to speak.

"If it's about Jake, this conversation is over," Alabama said.

Sunny wiped a bit of bisque off her lips. "That's fine with me." She paused. "I believe you said you wanted to get a cell phone?"

Alabama swallowed a mouthful of chowder. "Yes, but a smart phone. Maybe one of them Apple phones?"

Sunny bit her lower lip and raised an eyebrow. She chuckled. "I can see you know nothing about buying and maintaining a smart phone."

"What do you mean?" Alabama tapped her spoon on the side of her bowl.

"Do you realize you could pay $1,000 for a smart phone and then over $100 a month for a data plan?"

Alabama felt her heart jump inside her chest. That was an awful lot of money for someone on a tight budget. She'd only had a landline before her stroke and selling her house. How could such a little bitty piece of electronics cost so much? "That's crazy!"

"I know it is, Balmy. But before you have another stroke, let's finish our lunch. Afterwards, we'll go shopping. You need to look at all options before panicking."

Alabama nodded and finished her soup. If someone homeless like Jake could afford a cell phone, then surely there was a smart phone out there with her name on it.

• • • •

Getting an affordable data plan and smart phone turned out to be easier than Alabama thought it would be—thanks to the Retired Seniors Organization membership that Alabama had given Ray on his 50th birthday. He had complained about joining an organization for old people until he realized membership came with discounts on everything from eye glasses and drugs to hotels and restaurants. Even after Ray's death, Alabama renewed their membership, so she could read about aging celebrities in the magazine.

Alabama was happy to learn at the Consumer Wireless store that RSO members received discounts on their monthly data service. If

Sunny shared her Consumer Wireless account with Alabama, they could both get discounted monthly rates. All Alabama needed was a phone.

A young man with a freckled face and auburn hair parted down the middle stepped out from behind the counter. "Hello, I'm Max. How can I help you, ladies?" His toothy grin stretched from ear to ear. Alabama thought he looked like Alfred E. Neuman on the cover of the old *MAD* magazine.

"I want to buy a smart phone," Alabama said, looking at the array of cell phones stretching the length of the store's long counter. "I want an Apple phone."

"Balmy, I think you should look at something less expensive and easier to use." Sunny pointed a long, burgundy-lacquered nail at Max. "Let's look at those first."

His grin reduced to a smile, Max picked up a small phone. "Here's a nice, practical smart phone. It's a terrific value at only $50, and it has all the essential features."

Alabama turned the phone over in her hands.

Max pointed to the phone's screen. "Check out the vibrant display. It has front and rear cameras, too."

Alabama grunted. "How many gigabytes?" she asked. Doug had told her that was important if you planned to store photos or play games on your smart phone.

"It only comes in 32 gigabytes. Most of our older customers only use their phones for making calls or texting."

Alabama thrust the phone at Max. "I need more than that. 32 gigabytes is nothing. You may as well sell me two tin cans and a long piece of string."

Sunny looked up and down the counter. "I don't see any, Balmy. Guess they're all sold out."

Max's smile disappeared. He took a step back from Sunny and Alabama.

"Hold it right there, Max," Alabama said with a voice of authority. "I thought you wanted to assist me in purchasing the smart phone of my dreams?"

Sunny rolled her eyes.

Max turned to face Sunny. "Yes, ma'am. What exactly are you looking for?"

"Something inexpensive and easy for an old woman to operate," Sunny said.

Max glanced at Sunny. "We have several options."

Alabama stepped over into Max's personal space, between him and Sunny. "Young man, look at me."

Max shifted his attention to Alabama.

"Good, thank you. Now ignore the other old woman in the room. Look at me. Talk to me. I'm your customer. She's not going to fork over money to buy me a smart phone."

"Y-y-es, ma'am. What kind of smart phone are you thinking about?" He rubbed his fingers together nervously.

"I. Want. A. Red. Apple. Phone," Alabama said, carefully enunciating each word. Then she took a step back from him. She thought he needed some breathing room, since his freckles were looking a little bit pale. "I want the best bang for my buck, Max." She looked at Sunny, who was shaking her head. "Don't roll your eyes or shake your head at me, Sunny Day. What kind of smart phone do you own?"

"An iPhone 12 Mini." Sunny shrugged.

"Dang it, Sunny. You don't think I'm smart enough to operate an iPhone?"

Sunny took a deep breath and sighed loudly. "No, Balmy, it's not that. But I've had an iPhone for years. You've never had anything but a landline. It's like handing a Lamborghini over to someone who's only been driving a horse and buggy."

Alabama threw back her head and cackled. Sunny laughed out loud. Max stood there, his mouth hanging open.

Suddenly, the best friends were hugging each other. "Balmy, I'm sorry, if you thought I was being insensitive to your concerns."

"Sunny, I'm sorry if you thought I was being cantankerous," Alabama said.

"Let's face it, Balmy, we've been having disagreements since we were kids. Nothing has ever ruined our friendship." Sunny looked over at Max, who had finally closed his mouth, but was looking puzzled. "Okay, Max, let's get this show on the road. Sell my friend here a red iPhone so we can go home."

Alabama smiled at Max. "I've been reading about iPhones, Max. I don't want a $1,000-iPhone or a huge iPhone. I want a reasonably priced iPhone that will fit in my pocket. I want to be able to take nice photos, send texts, check my email, and play a few simple games. Show me what you have."

An hour later, Alabama handed over cash from her garage sale money for what she considered the perfect red iPhone SE with 128 gigabytes.

"I think you'll be happy with this one, ma'am," Max said. "It's the most powerful 4.7-inch iPhone ever. It gives incredible performance in apps, games, and photography for a price that fits your budget."

"I can call anywhere in the United States?"

"If you download the AnywhereApp, ma'am, you'll be able to call, text, and send images all over the world for free," Max explained, showing her how to get to the App Store and download apps.

As she started scrolling through the App Store offerings, Alabama began to squeal. "Look, Sunny! I can download a Scrabble game and bridge and mahjong."

"Of course, ma'am, before you can buy anything at the App Store, you will need to create an Apple account with your credit card," Max explained.

"Credit card?" Alabama grimaced. "I don't have a credit card."

Max looked incredulous.

Sunny grabbed Alabama's shoulders. "What do you mean you don't have a credit card?"

"I have savings and checking accounts at the Teachers Credit Union. I pay cash or write checks for everything." Alabama stared at Sunny, who covered her face in her hands. "What's wrong with that? Ray didn't like credit cards."

"How do you get money out of the ATM machine?"

"What do you think, Sunny? I go inside the bank and cash a check with the teller."

"The App Store does not take cash or checks," Max pointed out.

"Oh, Balmy, sweetie, if you're going to play with the big girls and wear big girl panties and buy a big girl's iPhone, then you have to have a big girl's credit card." Sunny hugged her best friend, grasped her hand, and led her toward the door. "Does your Teachers Credit Union offer a bank card?"

"Of course. They keep mailing me applications to apply for one, but I never felt owning a credit card was necessary," Alabama protested.

"Bye, ladies," Max called out. "Thanks for your business today."

Sunny opened the door and pushed Alabama out of the store. "Trust me when I say you need a credit card now."

Chapter Twenty-Seven

When Sara told Sunny there would be Italian meat loaf, mashed potatoes, asparagus, and make-your-own sundaes for dinner, Sunny graciously accepted the invitation to share the Webb family meal. That way, Alabama thought, Sunny would be present when Sara learned she'd been approved to move into the Villas.

"We heard about the big Halloween Gala at the Villas on Saturday," Richard said, spooning mashed potatoes onto his plate.

Doug elbowed Sunny. "Grandma's going to the party with some British guy. He's gonna pick her up here in his fancy Mercedes."

Alabama winced. "Thank you, Douglas Webb." She shrugged. "It's not like a real date. Geoffrey is merely providing transportation to the event."

"Of course, Dad will need to check him out just like he does anytime I go out with someone," Alison said, forking an asparagus spear and nibbling off the end.

"I'm sure Geoffrey Winston Churchill will be thoroughly grilled when he arrives," Sara agreed and smiled mischievously.

"Hmph." Alabama muttered, feeling like a teenager going on a first date. But it's NOT a date, she wanted to scream. He's my Uber driver.

Sunny raised an eyebrow and patted her lips with her napkin. "This meat loaf is delicious, Sara. It's so moist, not dry like a lot of meatloaves I've eaten. Do I see cheese and mushrooms stuffed in the middle?"

"Oh, yeah," Alison grumbled, carefully pulling slices of mushroom out of her meat loaf serving. "Mom, you know I can't stand mushrooms!"

"You can't call it Italian meat loaf, if it doesn't have mushrooms, cheese, and tomato sauce," Sara explained. "It has lots of Italian spices in it, too, Sunny."

"Yes, I can taste the basil and the oregano." Sunny licked her lips. "And the garlic and tomato sauce. Mmm. Delicious." Sunny took another bite.

"What brings you to Savannah today?" Richard asked. "Did you visit your brother?"

"No, not today. I drove here to tell Balmy the good news."

"What's her good news?" Richard asked. "Did she win the pumpkin-carving contest?"

"No, her Villas' application to live with me has been approved."

Alabama choked on a mouthful of mashed potatoes. She swallowed, coughed, and took a big swig of iced tea. All conversation at the table ceased.

Sara frowned and dropped her fork on her plate. "Mother, you didn't mention filling out an application. When did you do that?"

"At the end of my weekend at the Villas." I guess the cat is out of the bag now, Alabama thought. "It had been a really fun weekend, and I kept picturing how much I would enjoy living there."

"Yes, Mother, the Villas is a great retirement community, but I thought we had agreed that you only wanted to visit Sunny for the experience. I don't remember any discussion about you actually moving there." Sara sipped on her iced tea. "Besides, it's obviously way too expensive. I doubt if even Richard and I could afford to live there."

"That was my thinking, too. Living in the Villas was only a Cinderella dream until Sunny and I started looking at the numbers, like the money I have coming in monthly from Social Security and Teacher's Retirement. I quickly realized that I could afford to move in with Sunny. I didn't say anything, because I didn't know if my application would be approved."

"Well, congratulations, Alabama," Richard said with a smile. "I have to admit that I'd move there in a heartbeat. I really love the place. If you do decide to move to the Villas, I'll be glad to help you move your belongings. Just say the word."

"Richard!" Sara said loudly.

Doug scraped the last of the mashed potatoes off his plate and into his mouth. "I think it's great, Grandma. Living there would be like living at a vacation resort. Can I sleep over with you, Grandma? I'll bring my swimsuit and towel."

Alabama reached over and hugged her grandson. "Of course, Doug, come anytime you like."

"The living room sofa makes into a queen-size bed," Sunny said. "Also, any resident can rent a guest apartment for a family wanting to stay for a weekend."

"Really?" asked Richard. "I would love to spend some time in that model train room. The prime rib was fantastic, too."

Alabama noticed that Sara wasn't looking happy. In fact, Alabama thought her daughter was looking grim.

"I love the Villas because they serve delicious vegetarian dishes," piped in Alison.

"Alison," Sunny said, "your grandmother mentioned that you like to play games with your friends?"

"Yes, but no Monopoly or Scrabble or Clue or boring games like that," Alison said. "I like games like Ticket to Ride and Forbidden Island."

"Some of the residents at the Villas actually play those two games. But many residents love an ancient game once played with ivory or jade tiles. The game originally came from China, but today it's played all over the world. Can you guess which game that is?"

Alison blinked. "Are you talking about mahjong?"

"Yes, exactly. Yasuko said if you were interested, she would love to teach you how to play the game," Sunny said.

"I saw a mahjong competition on the Discovery Channel. The tiles are beautiful," Alison said with a smile. "Yes, I think I might enjoy learning to play mahjong." She turned to Alabama. "Grandma, I could visit you on the weekends."

As everyone seated around the table talked excitedly about the Villas, Alabama kept a watchful eye on Sara, who was sitting silently. When Sara slowly pushed back from the table and stood up, Alabama sucked in a deep breath and steadied herself.

"All of you make this sound like a done deal," Sara said. "Just because Grandma's application has been accepted doesn't mean she'll be packing her bags and moving to the Villas anytime soon."

Alabama slid her chair back and stood up, too, facing her daughter. "That's true, Sara. I have a lot to do and things to consider before I move in with Sunny."

"What?" Sara gasped.

"I won't have to worry much about furniture. The apartment is already furnished. My bedroom here can stay like it is, so I'll have a place to sleep when I come back for visits. I do want to buy a desk for my half of the office. Maybe a bookshelf. Something reasonably priced that can be easily assembled."

Doug raised his hand and bounced on his seat. "Ooh. Let me put it together for you, Grandma."

Richard raised his hand. "I'll help Doug. I'll bring the tools."

"Also, I need a laptop for my desk. I could probably use some help selecting one."

Sara gripped the table edge. "Mother, why do you need a laptop?"

"For email and searching the Internet, of course. If I'm going to move into a cool retirement community, I have to be computer savvy. Geoffrey says he teaches a computer class for residents who need help." She reached into her pocket and brought out her bright red iPhone. "I bought this today with part of my garage sale money."

Doug grabbed the smart phone out of Alabama's hands. "Oh, wow! It's an iPhone!" Doug's eyes widened. "You are the coolest Grandma ever!" Doug sat down and started scrolling through the phone.

Wiping her eyes, Sara walked slowly around the table to Alabama and gave her a hug. "Well, Mother, it looks like you've made up your mind. You are your own woman now. Who am I to stand in the way of your dreams?"

"Yes, dear Sara, moving into the Villas with Sunny will make me very happy."

Everyone immediately chorused loudly what they'd heard so many times before: "And you do want me to be happy, don't you?" Then the Webb house was suddenly filled with laughter.

Chapter Twenty-Eight

Doug, who had designated himself the lookout for Geoffrey's arrival Saturday morning, was the first to sound the alarm when the Mercedes pulled into the driveway. "Alert! Alert! This is not a drill! Old man leaving fancy black car and heading this way," he yelled. By the time Geoffrey reached the front porch, Doug had left his window perch and opened the front door.

Alabama, not wanting to appear too eager, peeked around the kitchen door and watched Richard set aside his morning paper to join Doug at the door.

"Are you the rich guy taking Grandma to the Halloween party?" Doug asked

"Guilty as charged, young man," said Geoffrey, bowing slightly.

Richard stepped forward and held out his hand. "Good morning, sir. I'm Richard Webb, Alabama's son-in-law, and this is her grandson, Doug."

Geoffrey grabbed Richard's hand and shook it. "A pleasure to meet you Richard. I'm Geoffrey Winston Churchill."

Sara joined her husband at the door. "Hello. I'm Sara Webb, Alabama's daughter." She shook his hand. "Please come in and have a seat. I'll let Mother know you're here."

Richard and Geoffrey sat on opposite ends of the sofa, while Sara disappeared into the kitchen. "Mother, why are you hiding in here," Sara asked.

"I'm not hiding," she said. "I'm giving Richard and Geoffrey opportunity to size up each other."

"Seriously, Mother?" Sara peeked around the kitchen door. "They seem to be doing okay. Are you ready to go out and speak to him? After all, he did spend an hour driving here to pick you up."

"Well, what do you think?" Alabama studied her daughter's face.

"Well, his British accent reminds me of that actor who played the first James Bond. What was his name?"

"Sara, Sean Connery was from Scotland, but yes, the accent is similar, but different."

"Oh. Well, I like his smile and thick white hair. Reminds me of that actor Cary Grant and those old movies we watched when I was growing up," Sara said. "He's a sharp dresser. That tweed jacket is very British." Sara paused. "He's quite a contrast from that homeless man you feed buttermilk biscuits."

No doubt about it, Alabama thought. Jake did not look or sound like either Sean Connery or Cary Grant. He reminded her of no actor at all. He just looked like Jake. Why was she thinking about Jake anyway? Forget Jake. She was going to spend an hour alone in a car with Geoffrey. She didn't know the man well. She wasn't even sure if she liked him all that much. This would be an opportunity to get to know him. But in the back of her mind, she was feeling sad because he wasn't Jake. Phooey on you, Balmy Knight, she told herself. Jake is gone. Good riddance. Geoffrey is here. Suck it up and move on.

• • •

Geoffrey managed to amuse and entertain the Webb family for about fifteen minutes before Alabama discreetly nudged him out the door and into the car. She was relieved there'd been no awkward or embarrassing moments or bad jokes. On a popularity scale of 1 to 10, she decided Geoffrey probably scored a big solid-hit 10 with the family.

"That wasn't so bad, was it?" Geoffrey asked, steering the car toward the entrance to I-95 South. "For a first time meeting the family?"

"I suppose not." Alabama put on her sunglasses and tried to relax in the passenger seat. She ran her hands over the soft, luxurious leather and wondered if Jake had ever owned a car? It certainly wouldn't be a Cadillac or any luxury car. What would he drive? An old, rusting truck, she thought. Definitely not automatic. The cloth upholstery would be well worn with holes here and there. Maybe a shotgun hanging in the back window. She sighed and cleared her throat. "You should know Geoffrey that I have not been in a car alone with a man since my Ray died four years ago."

"I find that hard to believe," Geoffrey said, setting the cruise control on 70 mph. "Is it because of your daughter being over-protective?"

"You picked up on that, did you?" Alabama considered that for a moment. Yes, over-protective was a good word for Sara. "Yes, that's my Sara. You see, not long after Ray's death, I suffered a debilitating stroke. The doctors said I could no longer live alone."

"How bloody awful! Did you move to a care home?"

"Care home?" Alabama was not familiar with the term.

"Here I think you call it a nursing home or a convalescent center," Geoffrey said.

"Heaven forbid, no. My Sara didn't even consider that. She insisted I move in with them." Alabama counted herself lucky that she didn't end up in a nursing home.

Geoffrey glanced briefly at Alabama. "Weren't you a lucky duck to have a family willing to take care of you? My mum spent the last eight years of her life in a care home. She refused to cross the pond to live with me. She told me the only way she'd move to America was if she didn't realize what was happening. My sister at the time was living in a cramped, three-room flat with two little girls to raise. The care home was the only solution."

"I'm sorry, Geoffrey. That must have been a terrible decision for you and your sister." Alabama bit her lower lip. "It could have been worse, you know?"

"I certainly don't see how that could be bloody possible." Geoffrey's hands tightened on the steering wheel.

"Suppose she hadn't been able to afford moving to a care home?" What if she'd ended up homeless, Alabama thought. What if she'd ended up living in a cardboard box in the park?

Geoffrey shook his head. "No, not my mum. The National Health Service paid for her to live in a comfortable care home near my sister in Rustington."

"Where you were born and grew up?"

"Yes, that's jolly good that you remembered that." He flashed her a quick smile.

"Whatever possessed you to leave your family and friends and move to the States?"

"Probably the same reason you left your home in Georgia and moved to New York City," he answered. "I finished school and thought the end of the rainbow — my personal pot of gold — was over here in the 'land of opportunity.' I was looking for adventure and excitement."

"That's exactly what Sunny and I felt about moving to New York City and becoming Broadway stars," Alabama said. "As soon as we graduated from high school, we took our graduation money and bought one-way train tickets. How happy we were when we got off the train at Union Station." And how scared we were, Alabama remembered.

"My best friend Miles and I saved our money from working the line with British Motor Company," Geoffrey said. "We worked 48 grueling hours a week until we saved up enough money to take a ship to New York. I remember the morning we sailed past the Statue of Liberty."

Alabama nodded. "Funny, but the first weekend we were in New York, we went down to the waterfront to see the Statue of Liberty and look for any ocean liners that had arrived from Europe."

"Did you see any ocean liners docked there?"

"The *Queen Mary*. What ship did you and Miles come over on?"

"U.S.S. *America*." He glanced at her. "We already had a place to live when we arrived."

"Now who was the 'lucky duck'?" she asked with a laugh.

"Righto. We were indeed 'lucky ducks.' Very, very lucky." Geoffrey turned on his signal and passed an 18-wheeler. "Miles had an aunt and uncle who'd immigrated to America during the war. Their son married and moved to California, leaving them with an empty bedroom in their Lower Eastside flat. They were happy to rent it to us. Rather cheaply, I must say."

"Sunny and I roomed together at the Y. We worked hourly day jobs to pay for our room and food, while we did cattle-call auditions and waited on a break. Were you able to find jobs right away?"

Geoffrey laughed his deep-bass laugh. "No, not right away and not in the New York area."

"No?"

"No, but because of our work with the British Motor Company and dynamite letters of recommendation from our line bosses, we were able to get interviewed and hired by the Ford Motor Company in Hapeville, Georgia."

"Aha," Alabama said. "That's how you ended up in Georgia?"

"Righto!" Geoffrey said. "I worked there for over 30 years. Took classes at a nearby college in the evening, earned my business degree, and worked my way up the ladder into management. After saving my money and investing carefully in the stock market, I bought a luxury car dealership—the Churchill Automotive Center. Then I bought me another one and another and another. It turned out to be a very lucrative business for me."

"That's quite impressive, Geoffrey," Alabama said. "You are definitely an immigrant success story. You arrived in America with nothing, you worked hard, and you became very successful. Do you have family living in Georgia who took over the business after you retired?" Alabama noticed that Geoffrey's hands tightened on the steering wheel.

After a few seconds of silence, Geoffrey took a deep breath and let it out slowly. "Sadly, Balmy, my biggest regret is that I never married or had children. I have no one to blame but myself."

"Oh?" Alabama said, mulling over what he'd said. "Why's that? You never met the right woman?" she finally asked.

He chuckled. "That was part of it, but primarily it was because I was driven to be a success. I was married to my job. My job was my life. I had no life outside of my work." He paused. "This may sound a bit daft to you . . ."

"Daft?"

"Silly?"

"I seriously doubt if anything you did would sound any sillier than what Sunny and I did."

He laughed, again. "I don't know about that. Anyway, to sell luxury cars to well-heeled Americans, I discovered you had to be charming and cultured with a magnetic personality. I signed up for acting and voice classes, took up golf, refined my British accent, learned about fine wines, and joined the country club."

"You sound like the perfect bachelor. I can't believe you never had a relationship with a woman."

Geoffrey sighed. "How did the conversation move from my successful business career to my relationships with women?"

"I'm sorry, if that's too personal for you to answer. Since you are so popular with the women who live in the Villas, I find it difficult to believe that you've never married, unless . . ." The sentence faded out as it left her lips.

"If you're wondering if I'm homosexual, the answer is no. To satisfy your curiosity, Balmy, I have been in numerous relationships with women over the years. But to be blunt, my job always had a higher priority, the women always wanted more than I was willing to offer, and they quickly moved on to better prospects. Is that a satisfactory explanation for you?"

"Yes, Geoffrey, and thank you for satisfying my curiosity." She paused and thought over what he had said. "Answer one more question for me, please."

"Yes?"

"Since you're retired and living in the Villas—surrounded by women who find you charming and absolutely adore you—how do you feel about women now? Do you think you could possibly be in a long-term relationship with a woman now?"

Geoffrey exited I-95 at the Golden Isles Parkway sign and stopped when the traffic light turned red. He turned to face Alabama. "I didn't think that was possible, Balmy—NOT until I fell *arse over tit* for you."

Alabama felt her face turning warm at his words "*arse over tit*." Was that vulgar? It certainly sounded like it. "Geoffrey, what does that phrase mean in England? In my day, words like that would get your mouth washed out with soap."

Geoffrey's body began to shake. Then he opened his mouth and guffawed.

His reaction sent Alabama reeling. "What's so funny?"

He wiped tears from his eyes. "I'm sorry, Balmy. Sometimes I forget that Brits and Yanks don't speak the same language. '*Arse over tit*' is a slang term. I believe over here you say 'head over heels,' right?"

Alabama giggled softly, relieved to hear Geoffrey's explanation. "Alright, I get that, but what I don't understand is what's so special about me? I'm not an aging beauty. If you'd seen me pushing my walker down the street a few months ago, you'd have thought I was a homeless bag lady. So, I don't get why you are head over heels — or *arse over tit* — with me?"

"There. That's just it. What you just said, Balmy. You just don't get it." He paused, as though to gather his thoughts. "You're an independent free-spirited woman. You never met a stranger, you make me laugh, and you're feisty. Not afraid to call a spade a spade. But most important of all, you don't throw yourself at me. I'm an Englishman who enjoys pursuing women. I love the thrill of the chase."

That was a eureka moment for Alabama. She mulled over everything Geoffrey had said. That explained a lot about him and why he'd never married.

Geoffrey brought the Cadillac to a stop at the entrance to the Villas. He opened the passenger door and helped Alabama out of the car. "Thank you for the transportation here," she said. "I enjoyed getting to know you better."

"I enjoyed getting to know you better, too, Balmy." He handed over her small overnight bag. "I hope I was able to charm and impress you. I look forward to seeing you at the Halloween Gala tonight."

Then unexpectedly, he leaned over and quickly kissed her cheek in the same spot kissed by Jake. Alabama touched her cheek and watched Geoffrey drive away. Her stomach fluttered and she felt conflicted.

Chapter Twenty-Nine

"Those were his exact words, Balmy? *Arse over tit*?" Sunny giggled. "Seriously? That reminds me of that song in *Chorus Line* about 'ass and tits.'"

Alabama nodded. She and Sunny were sitting on the balcony eating BLTs and kettle chips for lunch, while watching a party boat cruise under the Sidney Lanier Bridge. She swallowed a mouthful of Cheerwine and wiped her mouth on her napkin. "I googled it, and it's definitely British slang for head over heels."

"Are you saying he's head over heels in love with you, Balmy?"

"So, he says. I'm not so sure. He tried to explain why he liked me, but we've only just met. Did you know he's never been married?"

Sunny grunted. "A confirmed bachelor?"

"He said he was married to his job. That he wanted to be a success. But now that he's retired, he has time for a long-term relationship with a woman."

"What?!" Sunny slapped her hand over her mouth to stifle a laugh. "He said that?"

"He implied that. Goodness gracious, Sunny, I barely know the man." Alabama frowned. "For all we know, he could be Jack the Ripper."

"No, he's too young to have been him."

"Alright, then, any serial killer." Alabama finished the last drop of her drink. "Probably the most enlightening and startling revelation to come out of his comments was how much he loves pursuing women. But he doesn't like for women to chase after him. That is apparently a big turn off for him. He made it sound like a fun game for him." She stood and picked up her empty plate and soda can. "Enough about

Geoffrey, let's talk about costumes. You told me you were taking care of everything."

"Follow me. You'll love my idea."

From her closet, Sunny pulled out two khaki-colored skirts and shirts, black belts and neck ties, and military caps.

"What in the world?" Alabama asked, picking up one of the military caps and putting it on her head. She went into Sunny's bathroom and looked at herself in the mirror. "You want us to show up tonight dressed as World War II WACs?"

"No, as the Andrews Sisters."

"What? Why them?" Alabama placed her hands on her hips.

"Because the costumes were simple to pull together, because you always loved singing and dancing to the 'Boogie Woogie Bugle Boy' at the night club, and because we still remember the lyrics and the dance steps."

"True, the tune is still popular today. And yes, it's possible that I might remember the steps. But I don't remember the Andrews Sisters serving in the military." Alabama hung one of the ties around her neck.

"No, but they did wear similar outfits when they performed at military bases all over the world during World War II."

"Okay, I do remember seeing them perform in a USO documentary, but there were three of them and only two of us." She grabbed a shirt out of Sunny's hands and examined it. "Where on earth did you get this stuff?"

"From Eula Mae."

"What? Where did she get it? It doesn't look like a Halloween costume you could buy off the rack in Walmart," Alabama said.

Sunny sat on the corner of her bed. "You remember that her daughter Georgia works at Rose Dhu College?"

Alabama nodded, carefully arranging one skirt and shirt with belt and neck tie on top of the bed.

"Well, last year, their drama department produced the musical *South Pacific*. They had a number of military uniforms left over from the production. Eula Mae asked her daughter if we could borrow three of them, and Georgia said we could."

"Oh, that's why the quality looks so good. The costume director probably ordered them from a military surplus store." Alabama paused and stared at Sunny. "Why do we need three?"

"Three Andrews Sisters?"

"I'm getting a bad vibe here, Sunny. Are you saying Eula Mae is going to be the third sister?"

Sunny smiled a hokey-looking smile and shrugged her shoulders. "She did find the uniforms for us, after all, and she asked to be one of the Andrews Sisters. How could I say no to her?"

Alabama buried her face in her hands and peered through her fingers at Sunny. "Can she sing?"

"She says she does."

"Were you planning to sing if they asked us to?"

"We don't have to worry about that, Balmy," Sunny answered. "I've already signed us up to perform in the talent show."

"Let me see if I understand you correctly." Alabama sat on the other corner of the bed. "We're going to be the Andrews Sisters, wearing military uniforms. And without asking me, you signed us up to sing and dance on stage in front of real people?" She closed her eyes. Her shoulders convulsed. "Now you tell me that the third person in this group may or may not sing or dance? Why pick 'Boogie Woogie Bugle Boy'?"

Sunny smiled. "Eula Mae said it's her favorite Andrews Sisters song, too."

Alabama jumped to her feet and leaned over Sunny. "Okay, how sure are you that she can dance, sing the words or even carry a tune?"

Sunny stood up. "I've been rehearsing it with her. She sounds okay." Sunny put her arm around Alabama. "Stop fretting, Balmy! Performing in front of this group is like performing in front of family. Even if we forget the words or sing off-key or trip and fall on our butts, they will cheer, applaud, and love us."

Alabama's jaw dropped. "Why do you think that?"

"Because we're all old geezers, Balmy. Anyone living at the Villas brave enough to get up on stage to entertain and make a fool of themselves is royally appreciated for their efforts."

"I see," Alabama said. "We would be the equivalent of the 4-year-old singing 'Twinkle, Twinkle Little Star' at the family Christmas party?" Sunny nodded and giggled. "We'll be performing in front of folks who've had an extended happy hour, and they'll be happily amused no matter what we do on that stage?" Alabama asked.

"Exactly."

On the one hand, Alabama felt relieved to hear this. Performing in front of a bunch of inebriated, happy-to-still-be-breathing seniors could be fun. Strutting her stuff on a stage for the first time since she and Ray left New York City excited her. But on the other hand, she had always prided herself in doing her best and reveling in the applause and enthusiasm afterwards. Even though the residents of the Villas at Kensington Grove were mostly strangers to her now, soon she'd be moving here to become one of them. But if she performed on that stage, she wanted to be recognized as that former Broadway singer-dancer who still "had it" — not some sad, old "has-been."

• • •

After lunch, Sunny and Alabama met Eula Mae in the Garden Room, a medium-size, multi-purpose room with floor-to-ceiling windows overlooking a small garden that in the spring popped in color from a variety of flowers. The room was mostly used for exercise classes, visiting lecturers, and small parties. This afternoon, the faux-Andrews Sisters were using it for a practice run.

"Good afternoon, Eula Mae," Alabama greeted the older woman warmly. "Sunny told me that when you were a student at the University of Georgia back in the Sixties, you studied dance."

"Honey child, back in the old days — before I became old, arthritic, and stiff in the joints — I danced with wild abandon every chance I got," Eula Mae said. "Heavens to Betsey, I remember the day Martha Graham came to campus and taught my modern dance class. I thought I was in high cotton."

"Martha Graham?" Sunny squealed.

"You danced with THE Martha Graham?" Alabama said, impressed that she was in the same room with someone who had. The legendary Martha Graham and her dance company were renowned in New York City. "I'm humbled to know you."

Eula Mae gave Alabama a gentle shove backwards. "Ah, pshaw, it was nothing," she said. "The gym was packed with bright-eyed, bushy-tailed girls, all fit to be tied to see the great Martha Graham. I could barely see her from my spot in back, but I was plumb tickled just to be there. It was a glorious day that I will never forget. Now let's get this show on the road."

Sunny turned the sound up on her cell phone and pressed to start the music. Immediately, the first notes of "Boogie Woogie Bugle Boy" wafted through the room. The three women huddled together and swayed to the music as the lyrics rolled off their lips.

Alabama was relieved that Sunny had toned down and simplified the choreography. Even with only a few shuffles, step-slides, hip-wiggling strutting, and hand waving, she was somewhat winded by the time the music ended. She sat down next to Eula Mae, who was also breathing hard, and thanked Sunny for a bottle of water.

"Goodness gracious," Eula Mae said, pausing to take a swig of water. "I'm plumb tuckered out. I'm sho'nuff not a spring chicken anymore."

"None of us are," Sunny said. "No matter what happens tonight though, remember we're performing in front of folks who're our age and older. If we're willing and able to get up on that stage, make fools of ourselves, and have a good time, then they'll love us for it."

Eula Mae laughed. "Bless your pea-picking heart for pointing that out to us."

"We can do this, ladies!" Alabama said. "Because we rock!"

Chapter Thirty

What Alabama noticed first, as she followed Sunny and Eula Mae into the ballroom, were dozens of hand-carved, lighted jack-o'-lanterns lining black-cloth-covered tables along one side of the room. Small placards displayed names of the pumpkin-carvers. The three women admired and laughed at the creations—even their own contributions.

Some of the pumpkins bore award ribbons: Best of Show, First Place, Second Place, Third Place, and half a dozen Honorable Mentions. Alabama was disappointed, but not surprised, that her tombstone pumpkin had not received a ribbon. Special awards included Funniest—a ferocious-looking, big-toothy-mouth pumpkin eating a smaller, scared pumpkin; Scariest—pumpkin carved with the words "HAPPY HOUR CANCELLED;" Most Creative—pumpkin in pain with gaping mouth vomiting out pumpkin innards and seeds; and Best Effort, which went to Eula Mae Davis, who had used a black Sharpie pen to draw a traditional jack-o'-lantern face on her pumpkin.

Alabama laughed at Eula Mae's creation. "Why didn't you carve your pumpkin like everyone else?" She expected her to say that she didn't want to mess up her hands or something, but that wasn't what Eula Mae said.

"Bless that pumpkin's heart, Mother Nature made it a thing of beauty. Dang it all if I was gonna cut into it and scramble its innocent brains."

"Uh-huh." Dumbfounded, Alabama nodded at Eula Mae. Then she was distracted when Yasuko and Charlie walked into the ballroom dressed as Gomez and Morticia Addams. Obviously rented from a costume shop, Alabama thought. Where else could Charlie have found a black-and-white striped suit? Or Yasuko, the black, body-clinging, floor-length gown? She laughed and waved. "Hello, Yasuko! Charlie!" She turned to Sunny. "Come on, let's see if we can all sit together."

Round tables for eight filled the ballroom. Alabama, Sunny, Yasuko, Charlie, and Eula Mae picked a table, second row center in front of the stage. They were soon joined by Geoffrey, wearing a navy three-piece, pin-stripe suit, complete with bowtie, top hat and a fat cigar hanging out of his mouth. Clearly, he was Winston Churchill. Geoffrey was followed by Carolina and Ron, who were sporting Sonny and Cher outfits from the 1960s — striped bell-bottoms; colorful, tie-dyed shirts; tie belts; and hip-length orange vests. Both wore long straight-hair wigs, with Carolina's black faux-hair hanging down to her waist.

The three Andrews Sisters sat together. Sunny maneuvered herself between Alabama and Eula Mae. By the time the two couples sat down, the only empty seat left was the one next to Alabama. Whether this was intentionally arranged to work out this way, Alabama did not know, but Geoffrey was happy to sit next to her.

Alabama smiled at Geoffrey, but quickly looked away to get a view of the traditional Halloween decorations displayed around the ballroom — witches and ghosts, zombies and mummies, scarecrows and monsters. Each table was covered with a black tablecloth and decorated with a Halloween-themed centerpiece. Alabama was thinking how much time and effort members of the Halloween Gala decorating committee had devoted to this, when Geoffrey leaned over and nudged her.

"Balmy, look. The menu is quite *corking*," he said, pointing to a black notecard on which the menu was printed in white ghostly ink.

The Villas at Kensington Grove
Halloween Gala Dinner
Creamy Pumpkin Soup with Bite-Sized Eyeballs
Graveyard Salad with Monster Wraps and Bloodshot Deviled Eggs
Chicken Pot Pie with Crawly Hands
Spiderweb Chocolate Ganache Cake with Vanilla Bean Ice Cream
Purple Potion Punch, Tea, Coffee

"What do you think, luv?" Geoffrey asked, casually placing his hand on her hand.

"I think someone tried hard to be clever and amusing." Alabama moved her hand aside. "Do you think the soup will be served from a witch's caldron?" she asked.

Ron and Carolina laughed out loud. "I can't wait to see these Bite-Sized Eyeballs," Ron said.

"I remember as a young boy being blindfolded at a Halloween party and fed eyeballs and worms, which turned out to be peeled grapes and spaghetti," Charlie said. "It's crazy what your brain will tell you when you're blind to the truth."

"That is so true," said Yasuko. "Anybody remember the ExtraTERRORestrial Alien Encounter attraction in Disney's Tomorrowland?"

"Hell, yes," Ron said. "Wasn't that the one where they strapped you down in your seat so you couldn't move?"

"Yes," Alabama said, remembering going there with Ray and Sara. "They had imprisoned an alien in a glass case."

"That's right," Yasuko said. "At the right moment, the lights went out, the glass case shattered, and you could hear the footsteps of the alien coming up behind you."

"Then you could feel his warm breath on the back of your neck. I remember getting goose bumps on my arms, my hair stood on end, and everyone was screaming, but no one was able to run out." Alabama remembered it all. Including the nightmares that Sara had for three nights afterwards.

"Lordy, Lordy, Lordy," said Eula Mae. "I would have keeled over with a major coronary."

• • •

After dinner, Mistress of Ceremonies Grace Billings greeted everyone and welcomed them to the Halloween Gala at the Villas. She thanked the members of the planning committee and announced the winners of the pumpkin-carving contest. "And now, the judges of the costume competition have announced the winners of the holiday weekend trip for two to the Biltmore Estate." She opened up the envelope. And the winners are Lilly and Archie Sigman."

The applause went up around the ballroom as Lilly and Archie made their way to the stage in their prize-winning Tinker Bell and Peter Pan costumes. Alabama could see that Lilly had spent a lot of time and effort making their costumes. No Walmart special costumes here. She thought the detail was remarkable. Lilly was able to make her sparkly green wings flap, as she sprinkled fairy dust every step of the way. Archie had an authentic-looking quiver bag full of arrows slung over his shoulder. He carried a real bow in his hand and a hunter's knife was stuck in his belt. After a few photos were taken of the winners, they accepted their prize envelope and returned to their table.

"And now, for your after-dinner entertainment, we'll present six acts highlighting the skills and talents of certain residents at the Villas. Let me assure you that no one was blackmailed or unduly pressured into volunteering to perform tonight. At this time, could all participants in tonight's show please make their way backstage to the Green Room. The first act will begin in ten minutes. Now is your time to stretch your legs or have another cup of coffee."

The three Andrews Sisters and Geoffrey pushed back from the table and stood up. "Are you stretching your legs, Geoffrey?" Alabama asked, following Sunny and Eula Mae through the ballroom and toward the stage door.

Geoffrey grinned and winked. "I'll have you know I'm part of the show tonight. Ta da!"

"You are?" Alabama was stunned. "You sing?"

"Hardly, good lady. There are other things one can do to entertain." He pushed open the door marked Green Room and ushered the faux-Andrews Sisters in, along with the other performers.

Alabama sat down on one of two sofas in the room with Sunny and Eula Mae. Geoffrey chose to stand instead of sit. Nervous energy, she thought, looking around the room. Alabama had seen her share of Green Rooms in her lifetime. This one contained seating for about a dozen performers. A kitchenette area lined one wall of the room, offering bottles of water and canned soft drinks and a basket of snacks. She couldn't imagine who could be hungry after what they had eaten. One door marked Toilet, already had several women lined up in front of it. A TV monitor hung from one wall and appeared to be live-streaming the ballroom and the stage.

After a few minutes, the door opened and a man with a bald head and a white mustache popped his head in. "Geoffrey, you're up first. You ready?"

Geoffrey tipped his hat and trudged out the door.

"Break a leg, Geoff," Sunny shouted after him.

All eyes in the Green Room turned to the monitor to watch Grace, the MC, walk to the microphone. "If everyone will please be seated, we're ready to start." Within seconds everyone sat down and silence spread throughout the ballroom. The overhead lights dimmed. "Put your hands together to welcome our first entertainer this evening, our own magician—Geoffrey Winston Churchill."

Applause, whistles, and foot-stomping sounded from the enthusiastic audience. Geoffrey strutted out onto the stage, grinning and exuding confidence. "Good evening, my friends!" Cheers and more applause.

Geoffrey took off his top hat and placed it rim up on a small square table next to him. Then he reached inside his coat and pulled out a black wand. Raising both arms over the hat, he shrugged and rolled his shoulders. The audience seemed to lean forward in expectation.

"Such a ham," Alabama whispered.

"Shh," somebody behind her shushed.

Geoffrey tapped the rim with his wand, while reaching into the hat with his left hand and pulling out a bouquet of flowers. "For you, gracious lady," he said, tossing the bouquet to Grace, whose face turned a little pink.

Card and vanishing-coin tricks followed the flowers. He even pulled a bunch of colorful scarves out of his coat pocket and stuffed them into his closed hand. When he opened his hand, it was empty. It was all tricks Alabama had seen many times before. She wondered how Geoffrey would end his act. Would his final trick shock the audience? Would he make someone in the audience disappear?

"Dear Grace says I have time for one last trick." Geoffrey ended his act as he had started. He tapped his wand on the brim, reached into the hat, and pulled out something black. As he opened his hand, it spread wings and flew off across the ballroom. "It's a bat," someone yelled. Women began screaming. Then suddenly the bat stopped flying and dropped on top of Agatha Pinholster's head. Agatha yelped and swatted the creature tangled in her hair. Her husband Horace gamely removed the so-called bat, examined it, and guffawed. "It's a toy!" He held it high over his head, ran down to the stage, and returned it to Geoffrey.

The audience went wild. They cheered and applauded until Geoffrey bowed five times, put on his top hat, and walked off the stage. It took Grace a minute to calm everyone and get them to sit back down. "Please, everyone," she begged. "We have five more acts and it's edging toward some folks' bedtime." Laughter erupted across the ballroom.

The next four acts went fast. Frank Gingles, dressed like a clown, whistled several tunes, until he ran out of breath and had to be helped off-stage. Harry Deadwyler, looking very much like an aging lumberjack, played two songs on his banjo, while his wife Shirley sang the lyrics to "Over the Rainbow" and "Tea for Two." Prudence McAfee, dressed in a Scottish-plaid tartan skirt, played "God Bless America" on the bagpipes. And Hildegard Brown, wearing a red pants suit and red, floppy sun hat, put her Boston Terrier Ferdinand through his repertoire of tricks that included shaking hands, rolling over, sitting, playing dead, and answering simple "yes" questions that sounded like the same bark over and over.

"I guess they saved the best for last," Sunny mumbled as the three of them waited in the wings for Hildegard to catch Ferdinand and carry him off stage.

"Sho'nuff," Eula Mae agreed. "But if we're lucky, most everyone will be half asleep or three sheets to the wind and won't remember what they saw or heard."

Finally, Grace announced that for the final act, the Andrews Sisters—Eula Mae Davis, Sunny Day, and Balmy Knight—would sing and dance to "Boogie Woogie Bugle Boy."

Gritting her teeth and squeezing Sunny and Eula Mae's hands tightly, Alabama stood in front of the audience and waited for the music to start. She took a deep, deep breath and felt the excitement and that adrenaline rush. She had forgotten how much she loved that feeling. Then suddenly Alabama was caught up in the song, the lyrics, and moving to the music. When the final words — *boogie woogie bugle boy of Company B* — left her lips, she was jarred back to reality by thunderous applause. She joined hands with Sunny and Eula Mae, and bowed. Everyone was still clapping and cheering as they walked offstage. As the Andrews Sisters exited, Alabama found herself thinking about Jake and wishing he had been there to watch their performance.

Chapter Thirty-One

"You know, Sunny, the Golden Isles Spring Music Fest season looks good," Alabama said, closing the season information brochure and reaching for her *caffé latte*. "This is a much better prize than a basket of fruit and chocolate."

"I know, can you believe this line-up of local performing artists?" Sunny asked, sitting across the kitchen table from Alabama. "That popular Jekyll Island guitarist Edwardo Gonzales, who won *Georgia's Got Talent;* Butch Sherman's Family Washboard Band from Brunswick; Miss Sugaruth's All-American Coastal Twirlers from St. Simons; the Pea-Picking Banjo Boys from St. Mary's; bagpiper Tim Campbell, from Darien; and singer-guitarist Betty Lou Williams from Sea Island. Plus, food trucks representing the best restaurants in Coastal Georgia."

"It's something to look forward to," Alabama said. "Do you think Geoffrey was upset that he didn't win? I mean, if we hadn't performed, he surely would've won."

"Sure, he would've been happier if he'd won, but that's life. If he'd really wanted to win, then he should have sawed somebody in half or made himself disappear." Sunny paused. "Speaking of Geoffrey, Balmy, is it true you rebuffed an invite to his apartment last night for congratulatory wine and cheese?" Sunny took a bite of her breakfast bagel, well slathered with cream cheese, and waited for an answer.

Alabama shrugged and sipped her coffee. "I was tired, okay?"

"Yes, I noticed how quickly you showered and hopped into bed. You barely spoke two words before you turned out your light." Sunny licked a smidgeon of cream cheese off her finger and waited.

Alabama sighed. She knew Sunny wasn't going to let up until she heard all the details. "Fine. If you want the truth, I didn't want to be alone with Geoffrey."

Sunny let out a cackle. "What? Why?"

"I'm still trying to figure him out," she said, squirming in her seat. "To be honest, Sunny, the man makes me feel uncomfortable."

"Because he likes you and admits it?"

Alabama chewed her lower lip and considered her response. "I haven't known him very long, Sunny. Something feels a little off."

"You know, Balmy, he's very popular among most of the female residents here?"

"I know that." Alabama pushed her empty plate to the side and picked up her coffee cup. "I know he's good-looking, has a great personality, no beer belly, isn't bald, hasn't lost his brains or his teeth, and isn't bedridden." She took a swig of coffee and grimaced. "Phooey. It's cold. Now I have to heat it up." She stood and walked over to the microwave.

"But he's *arse over tit* for you. Don't forget that."

Alabama gave her coffee a minute and 30 seconds and pressed START. "I know that, Sunny. But he's getting all touchy-feely too fast for me. I'm not a chunk of ice with no feelings, it's just . . ." She paused. "Well, I keep thinking about Ray."

Sunny walked over to Alabama and gave her a hug. "Maybe you're also thinking about Jake?"

The microwave dinged and Alabama removed her cup. "Yes, I confess, I do think about Jake. I enjoyed our friendship, and I'm worried that something has happened to him. I don't understand why he just disappeared."

Both women headed into the living room and sat on the sofa. "Maybe he thought you were getting feelings for him and he couldn't reciprocate?"

"That is preposterous, Sunny. I . . ." Alabama stopped when she noticed the big smirky grin on Sunny's face. "You are such a tease!" With Sunny's howls of laughter exploding, Alabama tried to tune her out. She pulled out the Lifestyle section from the Savannah Sunday paper and gasped. There on the section cover was a photo of Jake, Clarence, and Clarice, and a feature story by Jacob Weatherby, the same writer who had written an article about the Villas.

Rose Dhu Mission supports Savannah homeless

[EDITOR'S NOTE: *Investigative reporter Jacob Weatherby spent nine months living as a homeless man on the streets of Savannah. He interviewed dozens of men and women living in tents, cardboard boxes, cars packed with meager belongings, and shelters across the city. He visited numerous missions and shelters that provide food, clothing, showers, beds, and assistance programs. Here is his story and photos taken throughout his journey.*]

Clarence Williams dropped out of high school at age 16 and went straight to work on the *Lady Margaret*, a shrimp boat working out of Brunswick. Just like his daddy and his uncles before him.

Good at his job hauling in the shrimp nets, Clarence was able to rent a small apartment in Darien and begin saving money to purchase his own shrimp boat one day. His life was going well until one day during a rain storm, he slipped and fell pulling in the shrimp nets. He hurt his back, had to have surgery, and ended up hooked on painkillers.

Because of his addiction, Clarence lost his job. Unable to make rent, he was evicted from his apartment. He was left with no job, no place to live, addicted to drugs, and too embarrassed to ask his family for help. His life took a turn when Brunswick physician Louis Rightmyer found Clarence dying in a crack house from a drug overdose. The doctor saved Clarence's life with a shot of **Naloxone**. Because Rightmyer's own son

Zachery had died of an overdose a few months earlier, the doctor went the extra mile to help Clarence. He did not want another young man to die like his son had.

Dr. Rightmyer found a place for Clarence in a rehab center in Savannah and drove him there himself. But once Clarence was drug-free, he was released from the rehab center. But with no job and no place to live, he was back on the streets, again.

Alabama wadded up the paper. "Unbelievable!" she yelled, shaking it angrily.

Sunny, who was reading the front page of the paper, looked up on hearing Alabama's outburst. "What's wrong, Balmy?"

"Sweet, homeless Jake is a dang reporter!" Alabama threw the wadded paper toward Sunny. "Look at the article on the Lifestyle cover," she fumed.

Sunny smoothed out the section and started reading the story.

"Can you believe he's been researching for nine months to write this story?" Alabama fussed. "I can't believe I felt sorry for this man. I invited him into my home and cooked for him. I fretted and worried about him. And this is the thanks I get?" She collapsed on the sofa. Jake had deceived her, and it hurt. She thought they were friends, but he apparently didn't trust her enough to tell her the truth.

Sunny continued to read, not looking up to address Alabama. She turned to an inside page where the story continued. "He's an excellent writer, Balmy. Look at these photos he took at Rose Dhu Mission."

Alabama reluctantly leaned over to see where Sunny was pointing. Good photos of men, women, and children going through the food line, she thought. Other photos of men watching television in the activity room and working in the Thrift Store. One large photo showed a long row of tents housing the homeless. "So?"

"I can see that you're upset, Balmy, but look at this from his end. He had to go undercover to do research for his story. Like an undercover FBI agent. He was doing his job, and he didn't want to blow his cover."

Alabama sniffed. "Doesn't matter. I'll never see that man, again, and I'm fine with that." At that moment, tinkly bells could be heard playing from Alabama's purse. "What's that?" she asked.

"If I had to guess, I'd say your new iPhone is ringing," Sunny said with a laugh.

"What?" Alabama rummaged around in her purse until her hand came out holding her new red smart phone. As her phone continued tinkling, she started giggling. "My very first call," she spluttered excitedly. "I wonder who it is?"

"Well, answer it."

Alabama finally slid the button. "Hello?"

A deep-bass British voice sounded on the other end. "Good morning, Balmy! Did I wake you?"

"No."

"Jolly good. You sound flustered. Everything spot on?"

Alabama glanced at Sunny. "Geoffrey, is that you?"

"Correct."

"How did you get my new number?" she asked.

"I coerced Sunny into providing it for me. We need to coordinate our departure for Savannah. You promised your daughter you would return to Savannah in time for Sunday lunch, remember?"

Alabama sat down and rubbed her forehead, trying to remember that part of the conversation when they left Sara standing at the door. "Yes, Geoffrey, you're right."

"Brilliant! It's about 10 o'clock now. Shall I meet you by the entrance in say 30 minutes?"

"Yes, Geoffrey, thank you. See you then." Alabama pushed the disconnect button. "Good thing I'm dressed and packed." She picked up her coffee mug and dropped it next to the sink.

Sunny placed the two mugs in the dishwasher. She turned to face Alabama and gave her a big hug. "You look absolutely flustered," Sunny said, gripping Alabama's shoulders. She neatly folded up the Sunday Lifestyle section and handed it to her friend. "Take this with you. Read the article slowly. Pretend you don't know Jacob Weatherby. Think positive thoughts."

"I'm thinking how annoyed I am with that phony homeless person." Alabama headed to her room. "Let me get my stuff."

Sunny followed her. "I hope you'll be back soon for good. Do you know when that might be?"

"I need to work things out with Sara and Richard. Maybe in two weeks or less." She smiled at Sunny. "Now that I have my own phone, I can call and let you know when to expect me."

• • •

Geoffrey drove his Mercedes out of the Villas parking lot at exactly 10:30 a.m. At Sunny's insistence, Alabama had started a list of Geoffrey's good and bad points. Promptness was definitely a good point. Other positive points included great head of hair, attractive, deep-bass British accent, body in good shape, charming, affluent, and a safe driver. Bad points? She found it difficult to find the words.

"What's that newspaper you're carrying?" he asked.

"Oh, just an article I wanted to show Sara and Richard about homeless people in Savannah." She shoved the folded newspaper section between her seat and the door and forced herself to relax. She had an hour to find out more about Geoffrey. Unlike Jake, this overly confident Brit didn't have a problem talking about himself.

Chapter Thirty-Two

To Alabama's relief, the conversation between her and Geoffrey on the ride back to Savannah was quite sanguine. The topics ranged from the Halloween Gala and winners of the pumpkin-carving contest, best costumes, and best talent to why British food was so boring, compared to the food of other countries.

When Geoffrey pulled into the Webb driveway, they were greeted by Sara and Richard. Alabama was relieved when Geoffrey turned down Sara's invitation to stay for lunch. He never left the sidewalk, handing Alabama's overnight bag to Richard. "Thank you, Sara, but I'm meeting two brothers in Savannah for lunch. They are interested in opening a Churchill Automotive Dealership in Savannah to sell luxury cars, like Bugattis and Barchettas, which sell for millions of dollars, and the relatively inexpensive Bentley Flying Spur Speed, costing a mere quarter of a million."

Richard gulped. "I can't imagine paying that kind of money for a car."

"I can't imagine us even being able to afford buying a cheap little Bentley," Sara said. "That's ludicrous."

Geoffrey laughed. "That's precisely what I intend to tell the gentlemen I'm meeting with today. They would have to open that kind of dealership in Dubai or Monaco. Not enough sheiks or princes buying luxury cars in Savannah to even pay the overhead on that sort of dealership. A Maserati/Ferrari dealership might be doable, but they'll need to do diligent research before they start investing."

"Thank you for driving Mother to the Villas and returning her safely," Sara called out.

"My pleasure. Cheerio, Sara. Richard." He turned to Alabama and held her hands in his for a brief moment. "And *ta-ta* to you, gracious lady. Thank you for attending the Halloween Gala with me. I look forward to seeing you very soon." In seconds, Geoffrey was in his Mercedes and backing it out of the driveway.

Alabama, Sara, and Richard waved goodbye as Geoffrey drove off. Sara put her arm around Alabama and gave her a hug. Then they followed Richard up the front steps and into the house.

Doug and Alison, who were setting the table for the family Sunday lunch, stopped what they were doing to give Alabama big, welcome-home hugs. "We missed you Grandma," Doug said. "We're having a yummy seafood fest to show you just how much we missed you."

"How sweet of you. I was only gone overnight. But lunch smells delicious. What're we eating?"

"Fried fish, fried shrimp, and fried oysters," Alison said. "With roasted potatoes and green beans."

Doug grabbed Alabama's arm and shook it excitedly. "And chocolate lava cake with a scoop of vanilla bean ice cream."

Over their seafood fest, Alabama gave a full report on the Halloween Gala with details on the pumpkin-carving contest, the winning costumes, and what it felt like to perform on stage, again.

"I'm sorry I missed your prize-winning performance, Mother," said Sara, sounding very disappointed.

"Yeah, I would've loved to see that, too," Richard said. "You really sang and danced to the 'Boogie Woogie Bugle Boy'?"

"If you go to the Villas at Kensington Grove website, the director posted photos from the event. The best photo is the one of me, Sunny, and Eula Mae accepting our prize. We were so exhausted from our performance we look like we're ready to keel over."

"What was your prize Grandma? A fruit basket?" Doug asked.

"Hardly," Alabama said. "We received tickets to the Golden Isles Spring Music Fest, and we get to ride there and back in a limo!"

"Wow, Grandma! What a way to go!" Alison said, giving her grandmother a high five. "You rock!"

"Oh, before I forget," Sara said, "you received a phone call today from a reporter at the Savannah paper. I believe he said his name was Jacob Weatherby."

Chapter Thirty-Three

When Alabama heard the name Jacob Weatherby, she felt faint and sick to her stomach. She immediately sat down with her head in her hands and breathed deeply. A phone call from Jake was the last thing she wanted.

Sara rushed to Alabama's side. "Mother, what's wrong? Are you okay?"

"She's not having another stroke, is she?" Richard asked.

"Grandma!" chorused Alison and Doug.

Alabama held up a hand to calm everyone down. "I'm fine. Hearing that name . . . Knowing that he called here . . ." She lifted up her head. "I'm sorry. I wasn't expecting this. It's such a shock."

"Are you saying you know this reporter?" asked Sara.

Nodding her head, Alabama tried to make sense of what she was thinking and what she should tell her family. "You haven't read the Sunday paper, I'm guessing?"

"No," Sara answered.

"Only the front page," Richard said.

"The comics," Doug offered.

"Don't look at me," Alison said. "I never read the paper. Nothing in there worth my time."

"Bring me the Lifestyle section. There's an article on the front that you need to see."

Doug dashed to the end table and picked up the Lifestyle section, checking out page one while he took it to his grandmother. He stopped in his tracks and blurted, "Grandma, it's Jake!"

"What?" Sara asked, grabbing the paper out of Doug's hands. "Jake, the homeless guy? Was he arrested for something?"

"I'm not surprised. He did steal my sleeping bag," Richard remembered.

As Sara spread the section on the table, everyone except Alabama huddled around Sara to read the article about Jake. Sara pointed to the long-haired, bearded man in the photo. "That's him, that's Jake. And the man standing next to him is the other homeless man. What's his name?"

"That's Clarence," said an excited Doug. "And the woman standing next to Clarence is his sister, Clarice. Grandma took that picture the day Clarice took Clarence home."

Sara turned to Alabama. "Is that true, Mother?"

Alabama sighed and dragged herself over to her daughter. "Yes, Jake wanted to get Clarence off the street, so he tracked down and found the sister. Clarence is now living in a halfway house and is gainfully employed."

"Then Jake should get a job and get himself off the streets, too," Richard said.

"Jake already has a job. And a home."

Sara looked puzzled. "I don't understand. I thought he was living in a cardboard box in the park?"

Alabama nudged Doug aside and tapped on the photo of Jacob Weatherby. "This is Jake. He wrote this feature story about the homeless in Savannah. He only pretended to be homeless in order to do research for his story."

Sara's eyes widened. "So, the entire time you were feeding him and I was worried that he was going to rob us blind or worse . . ."

"He was writing about homeless people." Alison howled with laughter. "I love it! He scammed us!"

Yes, indeed, thought Alabama. And now he was taking back his real life as Jacob Weatherby and reaching out to her. Why? Did he want to apologize for deceiving her? Did he want to come over for coffee and buttermilk biscuits, and a game of Scrabble? It didn't matter. She didn't care what Jacob Weatherby had to say to her. She was moving on with a new life at the Villas, and it most definitely didn't include him.

"Mother, are you telling me you didn't know Jake was a newspaper reporter?" Sara asked.

"Correct."

Sara smiled. "Alison's right. This is funny. I can't believe he fooled you, Mother." Sara reached out and gave Alabama a big hug. Then she pulled out her smart phone, pressed a few buttons and Alabama's new iPhone pinged on the side table.

Alabama turned her head toward her phone. "What was that?"

"That was me sharing Jacob Weatherby's contact information with you, so you can return his call." Sara smirked. "Mother, it looks like you have two men very much smitten with you now."

Alabama frowned. "Doesn't matter. I have no intention of calling that man back. He should've told me right off the bat he was only pretending to be homeless."

Richard chuckled. "Did you ever consider that he didn't because he enjoyed your buttermilk biscuits and your company too much? He was probably afraid if you knew the truth, you wouldn't have anything further to do with him."

Could that be true, she wondered? "I don't care why he didn't tell me. I only know I don't ever want to see or talk to or talk about that man, again."

Chapter Thirty-Four

With input from Sara and Richard, the family agreed to move Alabama to the Villas in less than two weeks. She insisted it would be a day of celebration, as she began a new chapter in her life. A chapter full of new friends, fun, and activities. Maybe even excitement and adventure, if Carolina, Yasuko, and Eula Mae decided to take the cruise awarded to them last year. The *Emerald Dream* officers had awarded them a free cruise for their help with the stowaway, smugglers, and kidnappers on board the ship. Carolina said if Alabama and Sunny were interested in going along, they could get them a cabin at a deep discount. Alabama told Sunny she'd be interested, as long as she had ear patches to prevent seasickness.

The time flew by. Sunny called every few days with a list of more things she would need. Geoffrey called, too, to make sure she was still coming. Jake called after a week of waiting on her to return his call. "Sara, I don't want to talk to him," Alabama told her daughter.

"But, Mother, he says it's urgent. He sounds sad. What should I tell him?"

Alabama took a deep breath and let it out slowly. She considered taking the call, but decided that would only upset her. She was afraid in a moment of weakness, she might still have feelings for him. She decided it was best not to take his call. "Please tell him that I'm moving, and I'm too busy to talk." She paused for thought. "And don't you dare 'share' my new phone number with him."

Sara sighed what Alabama knew was her daughter's okay-but-you're-making-a-big-mistake sigh. "I'll tell him, Mother, but you may regret your decision to cut him out of your life."

"How can I cut Jacob Weatherby out of my life when he was never in it?"

Sara rolled her eyes. "Fine. It's your decision."

• • •

Finally, the big day arrived. At the end of breakfast, Doug slipped a wrapped gift out of his lap and handed it to Alabama. "Here, Grandma. This is a parting gift from all of us to you. A gift that will keep on giving. A gift to show you how much we love you. And we have expectations that it will get used a lot."

Surprised, Alabama quickly unwrapped the box. She looked at the thin white box with the Apple logo in the center of the lid. She covered her mouth with her hand. "Is it . . .?" She removed the lid. "Goodness gracious, my own iPad." A tear rolled down her cheek. She wiped it away. "Thank you! All of you! This means so much to me."

"Now I can FaceTime you every day," Doug said.

"We know you'll be busy at the Villas, Mother, but we hope being able to do FaceTime with you often will help us stay connected as a family," Sara said.

"Yes, the miracle of social networking," Alabama said. "Alison has signed me up for Facebook, but I may be too busy to do much with that."

"Grandma already has six friends," Alison said proudly. "I bet by the end of the year she'll have 600."

• • •

Alabama watched as Richard shut the hatch on Sara's SUV. The back end was completely packed with two suitcases and four boxes of stuff that Sunny said she would need. She turned to Richard. "Aren't you glad I'm leaving lots of my belongings here with you?"

"What's still in your room, Mother?" Sara asked.

"Books, puzzles, games, photo albums. Stuff I probably won't need right away, but I can always get them later. It's just that Sunny says we have limited storage space at the Villas," Alabama explained. "She says residents who live in smaller units have been known to store boxes of their stuff in a second bathtub or even the dishwasher. Fortunately, Sunny bought the largest apartment available."

"Yes," agreed Richard. "I've seen retirement apartments not much bigger than a dorm room. I would get claustrophobic living in one that size. But I wouldn't have any problem living in the Villas." He looked off to the side. "Imagine the life. No yard to keep up. Someone else to take care of plumbing or electrical issues."

"Yes," piped in Sara. "And don't forget a housekeeper to clean weekly and change the sheets. No preparing daily meals, unless you wanted to. Being able to leave town without worrying about stopping mail or burglars. Lots of social life and plenty of activities and field trips."

"And a big model railroad to play with and a giant swimming pool," Doug said.

"I personally would move there just for the gourmet vegetarian dishes," admitted Alison.

Alabama laughed. "It sounds like you're all envious of my new life in the Villas."

"It does sound that way, doesn't it?" Richard said. "Okay, if we're going to make it to the Villas in time for me to sink my teeth into a prime rib lunch, everybody better hop in the car now."

• • •

Sunny was waiting at the lobby entrance with Geoffrey and two luggage carts. Alabama was certain that Richard was happy to have any help that an octogenarian like Geoffrey could offer. The men shook hands and began loading Alabama's stuff onto the carts — one suitcase and three boxes per cart.

"Why are you grimacing, Sunny?" Alabama asked. "Is this too much stuff?"

"We will be glad to take anything back to the house, if necessary," Sara offered.

"I don't think it'll be a problem, but we'll see."

"Okay, ladies, I'm going to park the car," Richard said. "With Geoffrey and Doug assisting, do you think you can make it to the fifth floor?"

Doug held up his thumb. "We got this Dad," he said, as Alison stepped up to help him push the cart.

Sara grabbed the front pole and pulled. "I'll steer."

Geoffrey bowed and swung out his right hand. "Ladies? Sunny, did you want to steer while Balmy and I give this buggy a heave-ho?"

The group pushed and guided the carts through the lobby and into a large elevator. Since the elevators were made large enough to accommodate an ambulance or funeral home stretcher, Alabama was not surprised that both carts and six people fit with room to spare.

By the time Richard showed up, both carts had been unloaded in Alabama's room. Alison and Doug wasted no time in gluing themselves to the floor-to-ceiling windows in the living room. "Look, Alison, here comes a pontoon boat," Doug excitedly pointed down to the river. "If we wave, do you think they'll wave back?"

Alison snorted. "Don't be stupid. No one on a boat can see us up here on the fifth floor."

"How about if we went out on the balcony and leaned over the rail and shouted?"

"No, Doug, not even if we were outside waving a red blanket over the rail."

"What are you two yakking about?" asked Sara.

Alison rolled her eyes and pointed at her brother. "I'm just pointing out to Doug the error of his ways."

Alabama smiled. She would certainly miss the daily banter and squabbling between Doug and Alison. She would miss hugging Doug, but soon he would be too old for that. There's a lot she would miss, but she was looking forward to her future life at the Villas.

"Hey, is it lunch time yet?" asked Richard. "I'm ready for my prime-rib lunch at Le Bistro. Who's joining me? Geoffrey?"

"Sorry, mate, not this time. I have a date to play poker with some friends," he said. "While you're enjoying your prime rib, think of me swigging down a beer and raking in the winning chips." Geoffrey reached for Alabama's hand. "As for you, gorgeous lady, I'll see you tonight. Welcome back to the Villas." He gave her a wink. "*Ta ta*, everyone." Then he was out the door before Richard could thank him for his help.

On their way to Le Bistro, they dropped off the two luggage carts at the security desk. The hostess at Le Bistro seated them at the same table in the corner. Richard ordered the prime rib, medium rare; Doug and Alabama decided to give the egg salad croissant a try; Sara ordered bouillabaisse; and Alison chose the vegetable quiche. For dessert, everyone in the group, except Sunny and Alabama, ordered the *profiteroles* — a French choux pastry ball filled with ice cream and covered in chocolate sauce. Sunny and Alabama went for the chocolate mousse.

Richard, looking happily sated, stifled a yawn as they exited Le Bistro. "You look like you could stretch out on a chaise lounge on our balcony and take a nap in the afternoon sun," Alabama suggested.

"I wish I had time to do that. I look forward to doing it when I retire." Richard paused and counted on his fingers. "In about 20 years." He made a face, causing Alabama to laugh. Richard faced his mother-in-law. "Seriously, Alabama, are you going to be okay here? If this doesn't work out, you just call me and I'll come get you. Your room is not going anywhere."

Alabama was touched by his words. Once again, she felt guilty for all the times she pushed his buttons and tried to get his goat. "Look around you, Richard. Doesn't this seem like heaven on earth to you?"

Richard glanced around the huge lobby area graced with potted plants and flowers, and up at the stunning crystal dome where sunlight filtered down to the greenery. "You're right. It's definitely the perfect place to spend the rest of your golden years." He gave her a hug. "Enjoy every minute, Alabama."

Sara stepped up beside Alabama. "I guess we're off, Mother. Remember, we're only a phone call away, if you need anything. And don't forget, I get a minimum of two FaceTime calls every week." She hugged her mother. "Alison, Doug, come tell your grandmother bye. Dad's getting the car."

"Don't worry about Balmy, Sara," Sunny said. "I'll keep her out of trouble. If she does get into trouble, I'll call you to bail her out of jail."

As the group headed toward the lobby entrance, Sara stopped. "Before I forget, Thanksgiving is in two weeks. We're expecting you two to join us for the traditional Webb Thanksgiving dinner."

"You know I wouldn't miss it," Alabama said.

"Me, neither," Sunny agreed. "I can't remember the last time I went to a family Thanksgiving dinner. Let us know what we can bring. We do have a big kitchen, so we can cook most anything."

The group hurried through the automatic doors to find Richard waiting in the SUV. He tooted his horn and waved.

As soon as the SUV was gone, Sunny and Alabama grabbed each other and jumped up and down and squealed like two teenage girls dropped off at the mall with $200 to spend.

Chapter Thirty-Five

Geoffrey did not join the group for dinner. Alabama noticed his absence and was surprised, since he always seemed to show up wherever she was. "Where's Geoffrey tonight?"

"Maybe his poker game is still going?" That was Ron's guess.

"Or perhaps he had a losing streak today, drank too much beer, and passed out in his room," suggested Charlie.

Alabama nodded. In a way, she was relieved he wasn't there. His constant attention and adoration did wear her out somewhat. "He did help move me in today," she said. "We invited him to join us for lunch in Le Bistro, but he said he had a poker game with friends. But he did say he would see me tonight."

Eula Mae snorted. "Lordy, Lordy, Lordy. Everyone at this table knows what happened. Stop pussy-footing around. Balmy may as well know the truth about that strutting-king rooster." Eula Mae reached out and squeezed Alabama's hand. "Bless old Geoffrey's heart, he played poker, all right. Strip poker with Penelope Pendragon. Problem was Phil's golf game got rained out, and he went home to his wife before the poker game was over."

Alabama heard herself gasp. She felt like she had been sucker-punched. She didn't have to look around the table to know that every eye was on her. A server slid a plate of Dover sole, boiled potatoes, and steamed asparagus in front of her. A wave of nausea swept over her. Alabama's first instinct was to run out of the dining room. Then she took a deep breath to calm herself. Alabama Knight, she told herself, get a grip. These folks are your new friends. They are concerned about you. You really didn't care for Geoffrey, remember?

Sunny leaned over and whispered in her ear, "Are you okay?"

"I'm good," Alabama whispered back. "I didn't like the man anyway."

"Sour grapes," Sunny said.

Alabama giggled and smiled. Then she lifted her chin and looked directly at Charlie. "Are you and Yasuko still ordering wine tonight to celebrate my official move into the Villas?"

"Yes, yes, we've ordered two bottles of Barefoot Cellars Riesling white wine, since everyone seems to be eating fish."

"Two bottles should do it, as long as I get several glassfuls," Alabama replied. "I want this to be a night to remember." Later, she swore she heard everyone at the table sigh with relief.

"What did you do this afternoon, Balmy?" Carolina asked.

Alabama sipped her wine. "I unpacked and put away my stuff."

"Lots and lots of stuff," Sunny teased her.

"That's a big problem when moving into a retirement community like this. You have to downsize to fit," Ron said. "When I married Carolina and moved in here, she'd already filled up the entire apartment with her stuff."

Carolina elbowed her new husband. "Stop it! I gave you your own drawer, didn't I?"

Everyone laughed.

"I downsized to move in with my daughter several years ago," explained Alabama. "Even then, everything I couldn't part with filled up my daughter's two-car garage. Before I decided to move in here, I had a garage sale. Now my daughter and son-in-law can park both cars in their garage."

"It was terrible for me when I moved from Florida to live with my daughter in Georgia, too," Eula Mae said. "Couldn't give my stuff away. Those Millennials and the younger generations don't want old people's stuff. I hired an auctioneer to sell it, but still ended up with Goodwill hauling most of it away."

Ron lifted his wine glass. "A toast to new friends. Here's to everyone downsizing and moving to the Villas. The most perfect place to live out our golden years."

Alabama rose to her feet, glass in hand. "Cheers, everyone, for welcoming me to the Villas with open arms. You've made me feel like

I've known you forever. And a special thanks to Sunny for inviting me to share her perfect apartment."

• • •

In the days leading up to Thanksgiving, Alabama was very busy adjusting to her new life at the Villas. There were plenty of FaceTime calls to and from the Webb house. More from Doug than anyone else. But, as Alabama had expected, as soon as Doug knew his Grandma was only one finger push away, he called less and less.

Geoffrey seemed to keep a low profile after his poker game went awry. Alabama was happy about that. Eula Mae said she passed him in the lobby the day after the poker game. "He tried to cover up his face," she gleefully told everyone at dinner, "but I could see he definitely had a large bruise under his right eye."

The morning before Thanksgiving, Sara called Alabama on FaceTime. "Mother, good morning! Are you and Sunny still coming tomorrow?"

Alabama studied her daughter's excited face on the iPad screen. "Of course, we are. Sunny and I are making pies today to bring tomorrow. Chocolate and pumpkin, right? You did say Alison is making a pecan pie, right?"

"Yes. That will give us three pies for dessert. I'm calling to see if you invited Geoffrey? Is he coming?"

Alabama heard muffled laughter from Sunny behind her. "Sara, I can tell you right now, Geoffrey will not be joining us."

Sara's smile of excitement turned into a big grin. "Thank goodness for that," she said. "By the way, the family has decided to dress up for Thanksgiving. Even Richard is dressing nice. Can you believe that? Okay. Gotta go. See you tomorrow." Then Sara disconnected before Alabama could ask any questions.

• • •

With their two pies in tow, plus a bottle of Alabama's favorite holiday wine, Cupcake Moscato d'Asti, Sunny and Alabama pulled into the

Webb driveway promptly at 11 a.m. Alabama did not recognize the red Jeep Wrangler parked in the driveway. Perhaps Alison's friend Tina had gotten a new car for an early Christmas present, she thought. Maybe one day, Alabama hoped, she would be able to drive to the Webb house in her own new car.

Alabama opened the car door and carefully eased herself out of the car. She didn't want to tilt the chocolate pie and risk getting whipped cream on her new outfit from Chico's—forest green pants and jacket with a white knit top. Sunny had loaned her a beautiful gold-coin necklace with matching earrings and helped comb her wiry hair into a snug bun. Then Sunny encouraged her to apply a little mascara and some blush to her cheeks. Nobody can say I look like a bag lady today, she told herself.

Of course, Sunny was wearing a high-end Hollywood outfit with sleek, black leggings, and a white, mid-thigh, V-neck tunic. A solitaire tear-drop emerald on a gold chain hung around her neck with smaller tear-drop emeralds for earrings. Her long nails were lacquered black and white with gold-glitter highlights. Alabama thought she looked like she'd stepped off the pages of a fashion magazine.

Doug opened the front door and almost knocked Alabama and her pie over with his enthusiastic hug. "Oh, Grandma, you came," he said, and gave her a second hug. "Mom made me wear my dress-up clothes," he announced softly.

Richard, sporting a knitted vest and white dress shirt with a blue bowtie, hugged both Alabama and Sunny. "Happy Thanksgiving!" he said, rescuing the two pies and handing them to Doug. "Give these pies to your mother." He noticed the bottle of wine in Alabama's hands and took it. "I'll take care of that."

Alison, who was dressed in an ankle-length black skirt and top, pushed by Richard to greet her grandmother and Sunny. She tossed her black hair and gave them a hug. "Good to see you, Grandma. Sunny." She lowered her voice. "Warning. Spoiler alert. Beware." Then she nodded and moved back to her seat on the sofa.

Alabama thought that was totally weird, but then Alison often did and said weird things. Alabama continued in the direction of the pies, only to be waylaid by Sara rushing breathlessly out of the kitchen.

"Mother! Right on time, of course." Sara turned to Doug. "Young man, why are you standing there with the pies? Please take them to the kitchen. Richard, the wine needs to go in the fridge." She reached for Alabama's arm. "Mother, we have a surprise guest."

"You have been forewarned," Alison whispered.

"Alison, please," Sara called out. "Mother . . ."

A man dressed in a suit and tie stepped out of the kitchen. "Hello, Balmy." He walked toward Alabama and held out his hand. "Allow me to introduce myself. I'm Jacob Weatherby, a reporter for the *Savannah Daily News*."

Feeling numb and in shock—like this was happening to someone else—Alabama watched her hand reach out toward a clean-shaven, short-haired Jacob Weatherby and clasped his warm hand.

The man calling himself Jacob Weatherby smiled warmly and shook her hand. "I've been looking forward to introducing myself to you for a long time. I've heard so much about you, I feel like I already know you quite well."

Alabama pulled her hand from his grasp and stepped back. "Sara, what is this? What's this man doing here?"

Sara opened her mouth to speak, but the man called Jacob, waved her away. "I believe you met a close friend of mine. A nice, homeless fellow called Jake? And his friend Clarence? Jake told me how kind you were to him. How you invited him into your home and fed him the best buttermilk biscuits he'd ever tasted. How you took pity on him and gave him an old sleeping bag to keep him warm when the evenings became chilly. How you befriended him, in spite of him being a homeless person living in a cardboard box in the park."

Alabama pressed the back of her hand to her mouth and felt her eyes sting with tears. "Stay away from me. You deceived me, Jake."

Jacob took a step toward Alabama. "No, that's not true. Jake was an honest-to-goodness homeless man that you helped. I'm not Jake. I'm Jacob Weatherby, a newspaper reporter. I couldn't have written my story without Jake's help and yours."

Sunny stepped up behind Alabama and squeezed her shoulders.

"I don't understand, Mr. Weatherby," Alabama said. "How could I, an old, frail woman, possibly have helped you write your story?"

"By showing the world that there are people who care about the homeless like Jake and Clarence. That there are homeless shelters and missions and people who feel passionate about helping in any small way they can." He took another step closer. "Then people like me can spread the word and encourage others to step forward and help, too. Savannah is working hard to help the homeless, to feed them, to find them homes, and to help them become working citizens." Another step brought him a few inches from Alabama. "I accepted your daughter's kind invitation for her family's Thanksgiving dinner. I accepted because I personally wanted to meet you and thank you for your kindness and generosity. And to see if there is any chance that we might be able to be friends."

Alabama gulped. She searched Jacob Weatherby's face for any trace of Jake and found it in Jacob's eyes. This was the man she'd secretly fed and entertained in her kitchen. The man who helped her get through her garage sale and fought off the monster who tried to steal her grandson's bike. The man who found Clarence's sister and helped turn around his life. The man who carefully documented what it was like to be homeless in Savannah and who the people were who stood on the front line to help them.

"Yes," she said, softly. "Yes, Jacob Weatherby, it would be my pleasure to get to know you and maybe become your friend." Then suddenly, she was in his arms and not caring about her family and Sunny who were watching and cheering them on.

Doug went over to Alabama and hugged her and Sunny from behind. Then he spoke firmly, "Grandma, if we're through with all this mushy stuff, then I'm ready to eat some turkey."

Jacob Weatherby tousled Doug's hair. "Doug, I'm with you. Let's get moving." With his arm around Alabama, Jacob walked her to the table and seated her. "This is going to be my best Thanksgiving ever." He reached down and squeezed her shoulder.

Alabama looked up into his face and smiled. Then she placed her hand on top of his and squeezed. "You know, Mr. Weatherby, I think this might also be my best Thanksgiving ever."

Author's Note

Sour Grapes and Balmy Knight is based on months of researching retirement communities in Georgia, Florida, California, and Virginia. I visited and toured each retirement community, ate in their dining halls, and stayed overnight. I interviewed residents and asked why they moved to a retirement community, what they liked best and least about living in one, how many years they'd lived in one, and if they had any funny stories they would like to share.

Based on my research, I created the perfect place for seniors to spend their golden years. My advisory board of readers named it the Villas at Kensington Grove. Influenced by a popular retirement community in Athens, Georgia, I located the Villas in a high-rise on the Georgia coast. The Villas' lobby is similar to a beautiful, spacious one I saw in Glendale, California. The large, airy apartments are like those I saw in McLean, Virginia.

Stories about life in the Villas evolved from humorous stories told by residents I interviewed. The fictional characters who live in the Villas were created from physical traits, quirks, and characteristics of the real residents I met.

Through my research, I learned that even though the majority of residents are in their 80s and 90s, an increasing number of residents are in their 60s and 70s. These residents are physically active and stay busy volunteering, taking classes, attending seminars, playing bridge and mahjong, and participating in other events organized by activity directors.

After eating at least one meal at every retirement community I visited, I found that food in the dining halls does not consist of mac and cheese and lime jello. In nearly every dining hall where I ate, I was ushered to a table with cloth napkins, silverware, and elegant glasses, and handed a menu with entrees that could rival upscale restaurants.

The incidents and funny stories scattered throughout *Sour Grapes and Balmy Knight* are based on stories I heard from real-life residents who reside in the retirement communities I visited. And if one day I decide to sell my home and move to a retirement community, I want to become a resident of the Villas at Kensington Grove—the absolute perfect place to live out one's golden years.

About the Author

Photo by Avry Pritchett

Muriel Ellis Pritchett writes fun fiction about feisty, older women, who have been wronged, but pull themselves out of the muck smelling like a rose. An award-winning author, Muriel lives in Georgia. She started writing books for older women after retiring from a career in journalism, and her doctor told her she needed a hobby. When not cruising around the world with her computer guru husband, Muriel enjoys drawing with graphite or ink, and painting with watercolor. She and her husband — both Disney-holics — love to visit Disney parks. *Sour Grapes & Balmy Knight* is Muriel's fifth novel.

Note from the Author

Word-of-mouth is crucial for any author to succeed. If you enjoyed *Sour Grapes & Balmy Knight*, please leave a review online—anywhere you are able. Even if it's just a sentence or two. It would make all the difference and would be very much appreciated.

Thanks!
Muriel Ellis Pritchett

We hope you enjoyed reading this title from:

BLACK ROSE
writing™

www.blackrosewriting.com

Subscribe to our mailing list – *The Rosevine* – and receive **FREE** books, daily deals, and stay current with news about upcoming releases and our hottest authors.
Scan the QR code below to sign up.

Already a subscriber? Please accept a sincere thank you for being a fan of Black Rose Writing authors.

View other Black Rose Writing titles at
www.blackrosewriting.com/books and use promo code
PRINT to receive a **20% discount** when purchasing.